In the Shadow of Death

IN THE SHADOW OF DEATH:

A Chautauqua Murder Mystery

By

Deb Pines 7/5/13

TO MISSY,

 FROM A

CHAUTAUQUA

FELLOW

LOVER.

Deb Pines

In the Shadow of Death: A Chautauqua Murder Mystery is a work of fiction. Names, characters, places and incidents are the products of the author's imagination or are used fictitiously. Any resemblance to actual events, locales or persons, living or dead, is entirely coincidental.

While the setting is Chautauqua, NY, the address 12 Park Avenue does not exist.

Cover Design by Paul Riney

Book design by Walton Mendelson, www.12on14.com

ISBN 978-1490357614

To my mom,
Irene Pines

Introduction

In the Shadow of Death wasn't just set in 1997. It was written in 1997. Before cell phones were everywhere. Before newspapers went digital. Before some Chautauqua landmarks in this murder mystery moved and others disappeared.

Nearly twenty years later, while tweaking the book for publication, I decided to leave the time frame and setting intact. It was easier. But I also found myself enjoying being transported to a quieter time in one of my favorite places in the world: Chautauqua, New York.

Just a little more background.

Chautauqua, New York, is NOT Chappaqua, New York, the New York City suburb (famous for being the adopted home of Bill and Hillary Clinton) that I find it's most mistaken for.

Chautauqua, New York, is in the middle of nowhere on Lake Chautauqua, in the far western corner of New York State. While 400 miles north and west of New York City, it is only 60 miles east of Ohio.

Founded in 1874 as a tent retreat for Methodist Sunday school teachers, the Chautauqua Institution has evolved into a summer community with a nine-week season of lectures, concerts, church services and other activities.

It inspired hundreds of spin-off "daughter Chautauquas" in rural areas mainly out west. And it inspired me—a former newspaper reporter/award-winning *New York Post* headline writer/Chautauquan by marriage—to set an Agatha Christie-like whodunit in this idyllic paradise.

I hope you enjoy the ride. And I welcome all feedback, good and bad, and gotcha corrections to my e-mail, chautauquamystery@gmail.com.

All the best,
Deb

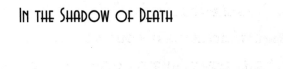

IN THE SHADOW OF DEATH

CHAPTER ONE

THE PERFECT CRIME?

The figure watching the Chautauqua cottage from behind the fat sugar maple at the corner of Park and Fletcher smiled.

Perfect was right.

The plan *was* perfect.

But a crime?

Hardly.

More like justice finally being served.

That night, August 2nd, 1997, was on the cool side. Probably in the fifties. What many Chautauquans would call great sleeping weather.

But sleep was out of the question. Or even leaving. The figure was too excited.

The next day was the big day. The culmination of all

the planning. Things were going so well, some might celebrate already. But that wouldn't be smart.

It was one in the morning. The last sign of anyone else up was thirty minutes earlier when a big green Chevy rumbled down Park and made a sharp turn at the lake.

An hour before that, the new Mrs. Hansen had closed up. She turned off the last flickering innings on the TV downstairs. She stepped onto the porch, threw a tarp over the courtship swing and white wicker furniture.

She turned off the bright globe over the house number, 12, and "Circa 1882" plaque. Back inside, she made her way upstairs, dimming lights. In the kitchen. On the second floor. In the bathroom.

When she turned off the last bedroom light, the three-story clapboard house felt transported.

Back to pre-electricity days.

Back to how the place looked in a sepia-toned archival display, now up at the library. A caption speculated 12 Park's first tenant—a Pittsburgh minister and Temperance leader—was something of a loner.

Building this far south, he'd have had little company. Away from the Pier Building where people arrived by steamer with trunkloads of belongings. Away from the open-air torch-lit platform the founders used for daily lectures and church services.

To this day, Chautauqua's south end was still quieter. A fifteen-minute walk to the main gate. Ten minutes to the bell tower and its deafening-up-close quarterly chimes.

The Hansens had neighbors in the small brown bungalow behind them on South. They owned and rented out six units in the blue-and-white house next door.

Listening, the figure stayed put.

It was quiet.

Quiet and dark.

When the moon made a belated appearance, emerging from behind filmy clouds, the figure shivered.

It was a strange orange hue, the color of a crossing guard's vest. But that wasn't the spooky part. It was how surface splotching made the moon look like an eye.

An orange eye.

Watching the watcher.

Nonsense, the figure, mouthed without saying aloud.

Nonsense, nonsense, nonsense.

The repetition felt good. So good, the figure tried another phrase: *utter nonsense.*

Utter nonsense, utter nonsense, utter nonsense.

Then *ridiculous.*

Ridiculous, ridiculous, ridiculous.

Fear of the moon was as ridiculous as fear of Brad Hansen's intellect.

Brad Hansen was smart. No question. He'd bought his Chautauqua houses for next to nothing before property values here went crazy. He'd built his business, a carpet empire, in Erie, Pennsylvania, from nothing, too.

But that didn't mean, in his presence, others should feel somehow, diminished. Or overmatched.

The figure had come up with a perfect, or near-perfect, crime.

A thing of genius.

When you poison a guy who thinks all sick people are pathetic whiners, you don't hear complaints.

Alarms aren't sounded by someone who claims never to have missed a day of work in his life. Who thinks viruses and cancer are signs of personal weakness. Who believes he, not General Eisenhower, led the Allies to victory in the last real war.

From henceforth, the figure just had to stay the course. Be careful but not too careful. And stick to the plan that wasn't guesswork, but the product of serious research.

Especially in terms of the poison. There were many options, each with its own pros and cons.

Cleopatra's choice, for instance, wouldn't have been

right here. The library books said the Egyptian queen wanted something that would kill instantly and cause minimal suffering for herself and her attendants. So she chose to be bitten by a venomous asp.

Here suffering didn't matter.

The job just had to be finished today without raising suspicions.

Chapter Two

Six hours later, Mimi Goldman, one of the Hansens' tenants in the house next door, checked the Hansens' porch light.

It was on, signaling that breakfast was ready.

So Mimi yelled for her always-hungry fifteen-year-old son Jake. Together, they hurried over, only stopping on the Hansens' porch to grab *The Chautauquan Daily*, the newspaper where Mimi had been sports editor since June.

They let themselves in the Hansens' side screen door. While Mimi headed for the coffee machine, Jake headed for the breakfast spread—eggs, bacon, hash browns, French toast, fruit salad and various pastries—beyond where their landlady, Francine Hansen, sat lost in thought.

"Oh, whoa," Francine said, when the screen door slammed. "I didn't hear you come in."

"Want me to pour you a coffee, too, while I'm at it?" Mimi asked.

"Good idea."

Mimi brought over two steaming mugs. She set one in front of Francine, a curvy dark-featured former teacher who, that morning—dressed in a small red kimono, red high-heeled slippers and big dark sunglasses—looked more like a former Italian screen star.

"Where is everybody?" Mimi asked. "I never thought we'd be the first ones up."

"You're not. The other tenants have come and gone. I'm just waiting for His Majesty."

Francine gazed upwards.

Brad Hansen, the tyrant she married three months ago, was stomping around above them. And probably, Mimi thought, dreaming up new commands for Francine and the rest of the world he treated like personal staff.

Francine, maybe consoled by the two-karat rock on her finger and sporty red BMW parked outside, seemed more bemused than annoyed.

"How early did people leave?" Mimi asked.

Francine, distracted again, didn't answer.

"Francine?" Mimi asked. "Are you okay?"

"Oh, yeah. Sorry. I'll feel better after a shower. What'd you say?"

"I asked how early people left for the race. I didn't know when Jake and I should get down there."

"Not everyone's at the race. But, since they knew breakfast was early, they came and left."

One by one, Francine ticked off the other tenants' whereabouts.

Francine's brother-in-law, Millard Hansen—a retired school custodian and avid gardener everyone called "Mole" for all the time he spent digging—was, of course, in his garden.

"The yard looks like a construction site," Mimi said. "What's he up to?"

"He says he's moving the hostas away from his precious roses. Something about them not working in the shade. He said he couldn't stand to look at them another minute."

Francine said Betsy Gates, a twenty-something nurse and new mom from Buffalo, who just moved in below Mimi and Jake, was out walking her screaming baby.

Betsy's next-door neighbor, the imperial Mrs. Greenwood, was off antiquing with a friend.

"But not before stopping by with her complaint-du-jour," Francine said.

"Which was?"

"She wondered if I had any better towels for her. The ones in her bathroom, she said, are worn around the edges. I gave her a few from our own bathroom. And I reminded her we're just running a summerhouse here. Not a five-star resort."

"I'll bet that went over well," Mimi said. "How about the Warren sisters? I thought I heard them puttering around next door."

"They said they're going to the race," Francine said. "I think they went home to gather their chairs and whatnot. Apparently, they have a regular spot where they like to sit and watch the runners pass, at the top of South."

Mimi wasn't surprised.

Chautauqua was a place obsessed with ritual and tradition. It was founded in 1874 in the middle of nowhere—in far Western New York State—as a tent retreat for Methodist Sunday school teachers. It evolved into a gated summer community with a nine-week season of lectures, concerts, church services and other activities. But it did much the same way—or got grief from many of the same families that returned, generation after generation.

The race, a 2.75-mile run/walk, was only twenty-three years old. But once it caught on, it was repeated. With few changes. On the same Saturday before the first

Tuesday in August when Chautauqua celebrates its birthday, known as Old First Night.

"What about Doc?" Mimi asked.

"Left maybe an hour ago."

"You're kidding. It's only seven-fifteen. And the race isn't until nine."

Doc Segovian, a widower and retired Buffalo doctor, worked with Mimi as *The Daily*'s main photographer.

"And you and Brad?" Mimi asked, as she got up for a coffee refill and a donut. "Aren't you guys in the race?"

"Mom, why don't you leave her alone?"

Jake, after scarfing down bacon, eggs and an English muffin, was ready to jump in. "Not everyone wants to be interrogated first thing in the morning."

"Not everyone wants to be scolded by their smart-ass kid either," Mimi said.

Jake shrugged.

"My mom solved a couple of murders last year at her old job," he told Francine. "And now she thinks she's Sherlock Holmes. Questioning people nonstop. Imagining mystery and intrigue everywhere."

Francine smiled.

"I heard about your mom's heroics. Pretty cool. And I don't mind giving her the rundown. Brad and I are signed up to walk in the race. And, normally, that wouldn't be a problem."

For walkers, the "race" wasn't a speed contest. Winners are the participants who finish closest in their age category to finish times they predicted.

"What's the matter?" Mimi asked.

"You've probably seen that Brad hasn't been himself all week?"

Mimi nodded.

"I've been trying to get him to see a doctor. But he's so stubborn, he keeps refusing. This morning, he's been up there battling stomach cramps. When I repeated that he should go to a doctor, he exploded. He said doctors and hospitals are what kill people. And I shouldn't be in such a blankety-blank rush to get rid of him and get his money."

Francine shook her head.

"There's no point arguing with him when he's like this," she said. "So I'm crazy with worry."

"What do you think you'll do?"

"I think we should sit out the race. But you know Brad's mantra?"

"What?" Mimi asked.

"Never say die."

Chapter Three

When Mimi and Jake reached the race's start/finish line by the Sports Club, the redbrick Miller Bell Tower at the north end of the lake was chiming eight-fifteen. And launching into a gonging rendition of "Chariots of Fire."

It was forty-five minutes before the race. But several hundred people were already there. Jake, signed up to run, joined a group stretching on the grass by the Athenaeum, the historic wooden hotel where every rocking chair on a grand wrap-around front porch was already taken.

Others pinned numbers to their race T-shirts. Posed for photos. Socialized with friends. Or did sprints past bushes, trees and benches decorated with blue and yellow ribbons.

The race's oldest participant, an 89-year-old Florida man Mimi had written about for a race preview last week, waved to her from a bench.

Mimi parked her bike. Then she took a moment to indulge in one of the great pleasures of her job: staring at the lake.

An eighteen-mile shimmering stretch between Mayville and Jamestown, New York, about a mile wide in most parts, the lake was magnificent.

And it looked different whenever Mimi checked. Depending on the time of day, her angle and mood.

That morning, it was gray and still. The line between sky and lake was blurred as if someone had placed a gray acetate over the scene. Later, the gray might lift to reveal a bright green lake, electric blue sky and vividly colored boats and houses on the other side.

"About time you showed up. I was starting to think you'd miss the whole shebang."

When Mimi wheeled around, she saw Doc Segovian.

And thought: Japanese tourist.

That's what he resembled being small. With shiny black hair and dark eyes. Neatly dressed in pressed khakis, a button-down shirt and glasses. With multiple cameras around his neck.

"I don't see how showing up forty-five minutes before the race is late," Mimi said.

"Thirty-five minutes?"

"Forty-five," Mimi repeated louder. "Forty-five."

"Suit yourself," Doc said. "I don't like to rush."

Of course not.

Doc, though youthful in many respects, had the body clock of someone his age. One that told him an hour early was punctual. And that punctuality—like patriotism, frugality and good penmanship—were forgotten virtues.

"My plan is to roam the course, shooting *color*," meaning cute kid pictures, Doc explained. "Cheryl"—*The Daily*'s other photographer, Cheryl Stevenson—"will get the winners as they cross the finish line."

Doc said if he got what he needed quickly, he wasn't even going to stick around for the end of the race.

"I've got to get back to the office to do my Old First Night retrospective. I've found some great old shots in the archives. And I've got some of my own from the forties and fifties."

"Do I need to wait by the finish line?"

"Not unless you want to. The Sports Club people will get you a printout of the times after the race. You can interview people at the awards ceremony. Or tomorrow. It's all for Monday's paper anyway."

The Daily, a six-day-a-week paper, didn't come out on Sundays.

"But is that what the sports editors did in the past?"

"Some did, some didn't. If you want, you can get a sense of the leaders by rushing to the one-mile mark by the fire station for the splits, then hurrying back. Up to you."

Liking that strategy, Mimi walked with her bike to the start/finish line as a woman atop a ladder called for the crowd's attention.

"Ladies and gentlemen?" the woman said through a bullhorn. "Ladies and gentlemen?"

As the crowd quieted, Mimi drew near.

"We're going to get started on time, in two minutes," the woman said. "But before we do, I'd like all walkers to move to the back, BEHIND the runners. Please. And then I'd like all elite runners to move up to the very front. Elite runners only."

There was some reshuffling of positions. Walkers— some with dogs and baby strollers—moved back. Several skinny young men and women—some track stars at nearby high schools and colleges—moved up.

"At the end of the race," the woman on the ladder said, "women stay right. Men, left. The chute is longer this year so keep going to the end. This is not the end," she said, pointing to the ladder. "Keep going so we can get accurate results."

When the woman thanked participants and wished everyone good luck, a hush fell over the crowd.

Like the hush in a courtroom when a jury returns with its verdict. Or when the lights dim at a show.

Conversations stopped.

Heads turned.

"Runners ready," the lady said.

Bang.

The starter pistol's crack was followed by a stampede of pounding feet.

The elite runners shot out faster than Mimi had expected. In seconds, they were beyond her. And past the Athenaeum. The lakefront cottages. Heinz Beach. And the YAC—Youth Athletic Club—hangout for teens.

As they sprinted up "Heartbreak Hill," the tongue-in-cheek nickname runners gave the moderately steep hill past the Chautauqua Boys' and Girls' Club day camp, Mimi could barely see them. And she realized no way she'd catch them at the splits.

So she decided to do what she *really* wanted to do—staying put and cheering on Jake.

He had lined up with his buddies, B.J. and Bob Ryan, seventeen-year-old twins from Jamestown, near the cutoff between runners and walkers.

One glance and Mimi found the three of them.

Her mom-radar was usually sharp.

But, in this crowd, Jake's curly black hair stood out in the sea of blondes—WASPy Chautauquans and townies from this heavily Scandinavian corner of far Western New York.

Once the bunched-together crowd behind the front-runners could actually run, and not just walk, Mimi also recognized Jake's loping stride. And his gangly build. Similar to her own as a kid that earned her the nickname *langeh loksh* (Yiddish for skinny noodle).

"Go, Jake, go," Mimi yelled, dropping all pretense of journalistic objectivity. "Goooo."

As Jake ran past, he ignored her.

But both of his buddies waved.

"Hi, Mrs. Goldman," called the more outgoing one who had longer hair and pirate-style earrings.

Mimi, enjoying the warmth of the sun on her shoulders, put on her mirrored shades. She watched more runners and walkers pass along the blacktopped lakefront route. She waved to the few she knew.

She glanced from road to lake. At the bobbing sailboats. And at a family of mallards gliding past the worn wooden docks.

She thought about the daunting job ahead: typing

up the names, ages and finish times of the race's 426 runners and 182 walkers. And spelling all of those names right.

Her mind drifted lazily until a shrieking siren reclaimed her attention. Old journalistic instincts kicking in, Mimi jumped on her bike and pedaled furiously toward the sound.

Nearly upon it, she saw an ambulance parking on the grass near the base of Heartbreak Hill. She ditched her bike.

Hanging back, she followed two EMTs to where a Chautauqua cop was directing racers around someone on the ground.

"This way," the cop said. "This way. Keep moving, please. We have a sick person. Don't stop. Don't stop. This way, racers. Please keep moving."

As the EMTs did their thing, Mimi focused on their patient.

A man.

That's the first thought that registered.

Then: A man, eyes closed, legs splayed, maybe unconscious.

Then, holy crap: A man Mimi recognized.

It was her landlord Brad Hansen, clung to by his frantic wife Francine.

"Mr. Hansen?" the older of the two EMTs asked,

loudly. "Mr. Hansen? Can you hear me? Please nod or say yes if you can?"

After a brief silence, Francine lost it.

"Answer the man, dammit," she yelled. "Answer him. Oh please, God, please. SAY SOMETHING!"

Chapter Four

Brad Hansen's daughter, Mary Hansen, a thirty-year-old violinist with the Chautauqua Symphony Orchestra, didn't usually shower at five at night. But after hearing the news about her dad at the race, all she wanted to do was retreat.

She was sick of the phony condolences she was getting on the street. From neighbors. From strangers. From the other musicians in the 77-member resident orchestra who seemed thrilled to have some link, no matter how tenuous, to what passed for big news in this hick place.

Mary couldn't concentrate enough to pick up her violin, to fool around, work on her scales or practice the hard parts of Bach's Concerto No. 1 in A Minor that they were playing Wednesday.

So at five o'clock, she stepped into the shower of the basement efficiency she was renting for an obscene sum behind the bookstore on Roberts. She pulled the sticky curtain shut. And she turned the water on as high and as hot as she could bear.

Her aim was escape. To empty her head of all thoughts. Good and bad. And to focus on the mundane: soaping up and rinsing off.

The job was no challenge. But Mary put her all into doing it right. Same as she remembered doing in high school when her youth orchestra, touring Japan, visited a public bath. Feeling judged by the old Japanese ladies, Mary remembered scrubbing and re-scrubbing every inch of herself before stepping into the communal bath.

Done with her body, Mary was moving on to shampooing her hair, when she heard the phone ring. Or she thought she did.

She strained to be sure. And, shit, it was the phone. In a hurry, she rinsed out the shampoo. She toweled off. And ran.

But, by the time she reached her phone, on a wobbly table next to her music stand, violin case and unmade Murphy bed, it was silent.

The answering machine said she had three messages. The same number she'd already listened to.

"Arghh."

Now what?

Mary considered her options. She could get dressed and go out. She could get dressed and stay in. Or she could return to the shower.

She chose the third.

Back in the shower, she stood under the spray for maybe five minutes. Then it was back to business. She grabbed her hair conditioner.

Methodically, she worked the lavender-scented goo through her hair that was turning the same carroty-orange color of her mom's.

The label said keep the stuff in her hair for five minutes. Mary planned to until, yowza, she heard the phone again. This time, she didn't hesitate. She grabbed her towel and, dripping wet, ran for it, picking up the receiver as her answering machine clicked on.

She heard herself playing a snippet of Mozart's Violin Concerto No. 3, then her own voice.

"I'm not here," she said. "Record your own masterpiece at the beep."

As Mary started drying off, she heard her younger brother's tentative voice.

"Mare?" he asked. "Mare? Are you there?"

When she didn't move, he continued.

"It's, uh, Brad, returning your call."

When she couldn't stand more hemming and hawing, she picked up.

"Where the hell have you been?" Mary asked. "I've been trying to reach you all day."

"Out and about," Brad Hansen Jr. said, defensively. "The usual Mr. Mom stuff for a Saturday. Dry cleaner. Grocery store. Kids' birthday parties. But I just got the news. I can hardly believe it. Is it true?"

Mary, who had set down the phone to finish drying, had moved on to wrapping the towel, turban-style, around her head.

"Are you there?" Brad pressed. "It's true, Mare, isn't it?"

"Yes," she said. "Yes, it is. Bradley A. Hansen Sr., is really dead at the age of sixty-seven. But, before we get into the details, Brad, you know you need a better alibi. 'The usual Mr. Mom stuff, dry cleaner, grocery store, kids' parties' won't cut it with the police. You've seen enough 'Law & Order', haven't you?"

"Not funny, Mare. Really," Brad huffed. "C'mon. You know the police aren't going to call. They didn't call you, did they?"

"No."

"Well, they won't," Brad said.

"What makes you so sure?"

"I got the official word. Natural causes. A fatal heart attack."

"News sure travels. Where did you hear it? All the way in New York City?"

"Uncle Millard, the Mole. He called. He must have figured you'd already know, being on the grounds and all."

"He didn't even try me."

"Maybe he thought you'd just hang up on him like you usually do. The short version I got is that Dad had been complaining of stomach and chest pains all week. But he soldiered on and thought the exercise of walking in the race would do him good."

"Wrong," Mary said.

They grew silent for a minute.

"Think it's weird he died on August second?" Mary asked.

"You mean because it's Mom's birthday?"

"Exactly."

"A little weird," Brad said. "But the whole thing's weird. I thought Dad would outlast us all."

As Brad reminisced, Mary's mind wandered. To how, even after she'd tried to cut her dad out of her life, he still cast a tremendous shadow.

She'd be running for a subway near her apartment in downtown Manhattan and, gasping, stop in her tracks, when she saw a stranger with her dad's gait. She'd feel a stab of something—nostalgia? hatred?—when she overheard what sounded like his voice or one of his pet phrases.

Like "School of Hard Knocks."

Her dad loved telling anyone who'd listen how much he'd take the "School of Hard Knocks" over any "egghead college" any day. For good measure, he'd often add his certainty that, "Too many books can ruin a person's mind."

Exhibit A to Bradley Hansen Sr. was the college-educated owner of the tiny Dalton, Georgia, mill he'd tricked into giving him a two-year exclusive on the first nylon carpets.

Exhibits B and C were his own college-educated kids who were too stupid to join the forty-store carpet empire he'd built and named for himself, "Big Brad Carpets."

It wasn't clear if their dad was more appalled by Mary's decision to become a musician or Brad Jr.'s to quit the law and become a full-time house-husband.

"Mare, are you with me?"

"Oh, yeah. I was just thinking about how he used to blame mom for not teaching us how to live in the real world. Remember?"

They both spoke at once.

"Made them into a couple of goddamned Irish dreamers," they said, before laughing together.

When Mary grew silent, she wiped away an unexpected tear.

"I think I should come for the funeral," Brad said. "I'll have to make arrangements for the girls. Then I'll stay in a hotel so I don't impose."

He rambled on and on until Mary got the distinct feeling he was stalling, afraid to say what he really wanted.

"Uh, Mare," he said, finally.

"Yeah?"

"Do you, well, feel the least bit sorry?"

"No."

After a brief pause, he spoke softly.

"Me, neither."

CHAPTER FIVE

ON THE OTHER SIDE OF CHAUTAUQUA, Betsy Gates was surprised to find her least favorite of the other tenants, Violet Greenwood, walking up the Hansens' front porch steps as she was.

Betsy finally had gotten her nine-month-old, Max, to finish his bottle and go down for a late nap. So she was eager to use her downtime to check on Francine.

"Is she back yet?" Betsy asked. "I didn't see her car. But I wasn't sure if she might have gotten a ride or parked somewhere else."

"Who?" Mrs. Greenwood asked.

"Francine."

"I certainly hope so. The more I go through my things in my kitchen, the more I can't understand how she possibly could have advertised, 'Fully stocked kitchen.' There are only two small knives. And neither is suitable for chopping. There's a bottle opener. But no corkscrew. And there are only two dish towels to speak of."

Betsy, appalled, just stared. And, though a minister's granddaughter and a nurse, she allowed herself an uncharitable thought.

What the hell was this woman doing here?

Betsy was okay with Chautauqua's push to welcome more outsiders. Like the few new Catholics and Jews. Even the black people, especially the churchy ones.

But Mrs. Greenwood?

A chain-smoking complainer? Who dressed like trailer trash (white pantsuit that day with a rhinestone-studded vest)? And piled on the makeup? And looked more like the old ladies at the slots in Atlantic City than the old church ladies at Chautauqua?

No, thanks.

"What are you staring at?" Mrs. Greenwood yelled. "Did you get more than two?"

"Two what?"

"Dish towels. Dish towels. That's what I'm talking about."

"No, I'm sorry," Betsy said. "I didn't mean to stare. It's just that. Well, you must have been away all day and you —"

"Yes, I left early for antiquing. Practically at dawn. And I'm exhausted. My feet are killing me. It's hard work if you do it right. I found two lovely dry sinks in Jamestown. But who needs two? They each have a basin, a pitcher and a place for a towel on the side. I couldn't make up my mind between the oak and the walnut. The oak was lovely but the marble top had a chip. The dealer is holding both for me. He wanted a deposit, a sizeable deposit, but I told him in no uncertain terms that—"

"I hate to interrupt," Betsy said. "Mrs. Greenwood, I—"

"Then don't interrupt, young lady. It's a bad habit."

Mrs. Greenwood, overcome by a coughing fit, hacked long and hard until her face turned purple and tears came to her eyes.

"Are you okay?" Betsy asked. "Do you need me to get you some water?"

"I'm fine," she said, when the coughing finally stopped. "Damn cigarettes."

"It's important that I tell that you that, well, you can't go in there now with your complaints. You just can't."

"And why in God's name not? I paid good money for my apartment and, if it isn't what was advertised then I want a refund. Or I want something close to a fully stocked kitchen."

When Mrs. Greenwood pulled open the Hansens' screen door, Betsy grabbed her hand.

"You can't go in now," Betsy repeated. "Because Mr. Hansen died today. Suddenly. This morning. At the race. Francine followed him to the hospital. But it was too late. I hear he was dead when they got there. Of a fatal heart attack. It's so awful. The poor woman must be in shock."

Mrs. Greenwood, turning pale, let the screen door slam.

"Mr. Hansen? Brad Hansen?" she repeated.

"Yes," Betsy said.

"Dead?"

"That's right."

"Of a heart attack?"

"Yes."

"In the race?"

"Yes."

"That can't be. It's just can't be."

When Mrs. Greenwood stumbled, as if she might collapse, Betsy reached an arm around her.

"You're sure I can't get you something?" Betsy asked. "Water? Coffee?"

Mrs. Greenwood, staring blankly, didn't answer.

Then, remembering where she was, she shook off Betsy's arm and backed away.

"I'm fine, young lady. Thanks. I was just surprised by your report. That's all. Surprised. Not always a pleasant thing when you get to be my age."

Chapter Six

It was hours later, nine-thirty at night, when Francine Hansen finally did make it back to Chautauqua.

The people at WCA Hospital—what everyone called the Women's Christian Association Hospital in Jamestown—were extremely solicitous. They offered to find two drivers to take her and her car home.

But when Francine finished with the EMTs, doctors and funeral home people, she was able—with the help of a catnap and vending-machine coffee—to rally.

The thirty-minute trip back took her forty. Still, she managed to keep her emotions in check—the whole way from Jamestown, onto 86, then 394. She waved at the teenager at the South Gate and made it another block to the corner of Haven and South.

A glimpse of the Hall of Philosophy, the roofless

Greek Temple-like structure where she and Brad Hansen had exchanged vows just three months ago, though, was too much.

Francine pulled over and, weeping uncontrollably, she remembered their wedding day.

It was a glorious day, sunny but not hot. She felt great in the coral-colored silk Chanel suit Brad had bought for her and her mother's pearls.

Brad looked great, too, like the war hero he was. Tall and fit in a black tux and red cummerbund. His face was rosy from cocktails at the cottage. But he was a perfect gentleman when they posed for pictures and toasted again with Champagne.

"Good riddance to the past," she'd told herself as they clinked glasses. "Starting over."

When a horse-drawn Cinderella-type carriage arrived after the ceremony, it seemed too good to be true.

"Twice around the perimeter," Brad told the driver. "Nice and slow."

He gave Francine a naughty wink and, inside, she discovered why.

As the carriage drove off, Brad was all over her, groping and grabbing. When he ordered her in a raspy voice to remove her panties, Francine was surprised more by her own feelings than his.

She wanted Brad as much as he wanted her.

But the sounds outside—the snap of the driver's reins, the horses' clippety-clopping steps, shouts of "A wedding. A wedding"— felt too close. And she dreaded more comparisons to the saintly first Mrs. Brad Hansen.

Impatient, Brad roughly yanked down her underwear himself. He mounted her and thrust repeatedly as she held the thin red curtains closed with a trembling hand.

In the end, Francine had to bite her own fist to keep from crying out. Brad grunted, shuddered, rolled off and had to be woken for their wedding dinner.

Parked outside the Hall of Philosophy, Francine tried to blink away the X-rated memory. Now wasn't the time to sort out her feelings for the man.

Now was the time to endure. To get through a few hours. Then a few more hours. Then a few more after that. To stitch together periods of sanity that gradually—she knew more than most people—become a life.

When she parked on the gravel in front of 12 Park, she dashed onto the porch, chilly in the race clothes she'd worn to the hospital. She turned on the porch light. She was heading inside, straight for the liquor cabinet, when voices made her stop.

"Francine? Is that you dear? Are you home?"

Dammit.

It was the Warren sisters, the busybody retired

spinster teachers, waiting in Francine's own darkened kitchen.

Francine didn't move. Foolishly, she hoped ignoring the sisters would make them go away.

"Francine?"

Damn.

Approaching, Francine flipped on hall sconces that illuminated a gallery of Hansen family photos: Brad and Mole, as boys on bikes; Brad looking jaunty in his World War II Army uniform; Brad's kids, Mary and Brad Jr., looking, Francine hated to say, unattractive at every milestone—birthdays, graduations, Christmases.

Too bad, the kids got their mom's fleshy builds, carrot-red hair and features—and not Brad's chiseled dark looks.

"Hope we didn't startle you," said Evangeline who, at eighty-three, was the older and bossier sister. "We're so very sorry about Mr. Hansen. Terribly sorry. We came by to be sure you're okay and got something to eat."

And to nose around, Francine was sure.

"Eating's probably the last thing on your mind," Evangeline continued. "But, in times like this, it's practically a duty. You have to keep up your strength."

Francine, after a deep breath, prayed for tact.

"Thanks for your kindness," she said. "But I hope, well, you understand I'm not really up for company now. And you took me by surprise. What were you doing sitting in the dark?"

"No point wasting electricity, I always say."

Francine tuned out as the sisters, both white-haired with bright blue eyes and small silver glasses, bickered over whether they should just leave the food or stay.

"Let's go," Philomena said. "We're in the way here."

"In a minute," Evangeline said, shuffling toward the stove with her silver-tipped cane. "Hold your horses."

Without any encouragement, Evangeline ladled noodles and beef from a pot into a bowl and set the steaming bowl before Francine.

"Slumgullion," she proclaimed. "Our mother's specialty. Warms you from the inside out."

Francine wasn't hungry. But she made herself take a few bites while answering Evangeline's questions.

Yes, she said, Brad was "*only* sixty-seven."

Yes, Mole had contacted Brad's children. And, yes, Mole was starting on the funeral arrangements.

"Glad he's shouldering some of this," Evangeline said. "Mole's a tough one to know. Doesn't talk much or go to church. But I've always suspected that, deep down, he's a decent fellow. Certainly, great with his roses. And dahlias. Won prizes in his day. A man who, I'm sure, would have turned out differently if he'd found a wife."

"He did," Philomena said. "Only she got away."

"Idle gossip," Evangeline snapped. "Enough."

Eventually, after more bickering and interrogating, the sisters, finally rose. They walked to the door but still didn't leave.

"Is there a friend or relative we could call for you to spend the night?" Evangeline asked.

"No, I'm fine."

"Would you like one of us to stay?"

"No, thank you," Francine said. "That's very kind. But it's been a long day for you as it is."

"At our age, we don't do much sleeping anyway. We could —"

"No thank you," Francine repeated, more forcefully. "Really. That's unnecessary."

"How about if we stop by in the morning?" Evangeline pressed. "On our way to church?"

"Fine," Francine agreed through gritted teeth. "That would be very kind of you."

After they agreed on a time, nine o'clock, the sisters, finally, finally left.

Francine locked the door and headed for the living-room breakfront/liquor cabinet. Carefully, she reached inside. From behind a delicate gilt-edged antique tea set, she extracted a bottle of Brad's single-malt whiskey and a shot glass.

Francine unscrewed the top, poured herself a shot, downed it, and sighed.

Now *that* felt good.

Way better than the slumgullion.

After a second shot, Francine had a crazy impulse to make a phone call.

She waited for the impulse to pass.

When it did, she poured herself a third shot and drank it in gratitude.

CHAPTER SEVEN

AFTER A FITFUL SLEEP that had her checking the clock at three, four and five, Mimi Goldman, at six, decided to surrender—and just get up and go to *The Daily*.

She left a note for Jake, grabbed a banana and decided to loop wide and take the scenic lakeside route.

It added five minutes to her amazing-after-life-in-the-big-city ten-minute commute. In exchange, she got another look at the lake.

It was calm again. But it had more color, blue-green, than race morning that, unbelievably, was just the day before. There were frothy patches. Where a solitary man swam laps at Heinz Beach. And where a golden Labrador retriever paddled near the bell tower.

At this hour, Chautauqua was quiet, but not deserted. Mimi passed seven other people, all dressed for church, walking, too. When everyone waved and smiled, Mimi made herself wave and smile back.

No easy feat.

By nature, by upbringing and by dint of yesterday's grim events, Mimi was wary.

But she pasted on a fake-friendly smile as she continued to the bell tower, then up Miller, past a row of adorable gingerbready Victorian cottages and on to Bestor Plaza, Chautauqua's town square.

There, Mimi dug *The Daily* keys out of her purse. She let herself into the office. Turned on lights. And headed for the paper's well-equipped coffee station. Once she brewed a pot and poured herself a cup, she felt a million times better.

For a moment, she just sipped her coffee and looked around.

Like every newspaper where she'd ever worked— starting with *The Madison Moment* (at Brooklyn's James Madison High School) and *The Kingsman* (at Brooklyn College)—the place was a firetrap.

Old newspapers, mail, announcements and notes sat on nearly every desk arranged in three crowded rows. In addition to paper, each desk also held a computer. And a phone. And a label for its occupant's off-beat beat.

At *The New York Post*, where Mimi rose from copy

kid to covering courts and cops, reporters covered typical things for a typical audience.

The *Chautauquan Daily* audience wasn't typical. The newspaper that only came out during Chautauqua's nine-week summer season didn't just serve the year-round population of 400. Or the 8,000 seasonal residents.

It served an itinerant group, as large as 100,000. People who came and went for parts of the Chautauqua Institution's program that claimed the high-minded purpose of nourishing "mind, body and soul."

Reporters at *The Daily*, thus, had high-minded beats like religion and morning lectures, theater, opera and women's club.

"Sports" said the label on Mimi's desk and on her computer that Jake, thankfully, had customized with a few "save" keys so she'd never have to type out the words *Chautauqua* or *Old First Night Run/Walk*.

Mimi had expected to see Doc, already here, and have a chance to talk out her suspicions before anyone else showed up.

Since he wasn't in, she switched gears and decided to get a jump on her race story.

The powers-that-be wanted it to be a straight sports story with no reference to Brad Hansen's fatal collapse.

So Mimi reread the race stories from previous years. Using them as a model, she began typing:

Setting a new race record, Joel Washington led a pack of 426 runners and 182 walkers in the twenty-third annual Old First Night Run / Walk Saturday with a time of 13:40.

Karen Michaels was the fastest woman with a time of 18:19 in the 2.75-mile race commemorating Chautauqua's birthday and sponsored by Vacation Properties.

Mimi typed a few more paragraphs. When she got up to refill her coffee cup, she heard someone fiddling with a key in the front door lock. When the fiddling stopped, Mimi thought she recognized Doc's footsteps.

She saw him as he rounded the corner. But Doc, hard of hearing and not expecting anyone, didn't see her until they nearly collided.

"Oh, my Lord," he said. "You scared the hell out of me. Mimi Goldman, what are you doing here at this hour?"

Mimi hesitated.

"I couldn't sleep," she said. "And I thought I might catch you here because I have something I want to run by you. See what you think. But why don't you have a cup of coffee first?"

"Okay, be mysterious," Doc said, grabbing the coffee pot. "How fresh is this?"

"I just made it a half hour ago."

Doc, apparently satisfied, filled his mug and, when Mimi extended her mug, he filled hers, too. He opened the fridge, sniffed at the milk carton and added milk to both.

After Mimi also stirred in some sugar, she returned to her desk.

Doc walked off to do what he usually did first thing. He posted his schedule—for assignments and darkroom time—on the office bulletin board so he could always be located, if needed, for any last-minute photographs.

When Doc plopped down next to Mimi in the religion editor's desk, he looked exhausted.

"Are you okay?" Mimi asked.

"I've been better. Brad's death rattled me more than I expected. It's not, as you well know, that I was any great fan. The man was tough to like. It's just that, at my age, each death hits you a little harder. And I'm wondering if there was more I could have done for Brad."

"Didn't he refuse to let you check him out?"

"He did. But I could have insisted more forcefully."

They drank their coffee in silence.

"Okay, now your turn," Doc said. "What did you want to ask me?"

Mimi took a long swallow.

"Please don't laugh," she said. "But I'm wondering if you found Brad's death strange?"

"In what way strange?"

"Suspicious? Unusual?"

Without answering, Doc just stared.

"What if I said I'm suspecting Brad Hansen might not have died of a heart attack?" Mimi asked. "That maybe he was a victim of foul play?"

"I'd ask for the basis of your suspicions."

Mimi, grateful Doc didn't just dismiss off the bat, took a deep breath.

"You know how I used to work for *The New York Post*?"

Doc nodded.

"Well, Brad's death reminded me of a weird crime we covered when I was there. This woman, Judy Santiago, killed a son and two husbands before anyone even realized they hadn't died of natural causes. When Judy took out a big life insurance policy on a third husband and he nearly died, too, the cops, finally, got suspicious. They had all three earlier bodies dug up. And they found arsenic in all of them."

"I think I remember the case."

"We called her The Black Widow."

"Of course."

"Anyway," Mimi continued, "I don't think I was just imagining it. But I think Brad Hansen had some of the same symptoms I remembered from that case. A yellowish tinge to his skin. And painful stomach aches, especially yesterday."

Mimi paused, waiting for Doc to say more.

But he just kept nodding and sipping his coffee.

"So you don't think I'm crazy?"

"No," Doc said. "I don't. A lot of what you just said makes sense. Scary sense. And makes me want to dig out my old medical texts to do some reading on poisons. And maybe take a close look at any recent photos I can find of Brad Hansen. And maybe even make a call or two."

"I didn't mean to dump all the work on you."

"Don't worry about that," Doc said. "I have a few ideas for you, too."

"Like?"

"If possible, why don't you see if you can get me a hairbrush that Brad Hansen used recently? Put it in airtight baggie and I'll explain my reasons later."

"And?"

"Why don't you use your great local law-enforcement

contacts to see if anyone's already tested Brad for poisons? And if they haven't, why don't you propose they do?"

CHAPTER EIGHT

MIMI WASN'T SURE she still had any great local law-enforcement contacts.

In her early days at *The Mayville Record*, where she worked for a college friend and fellow Brooklyn lifer, she'd made a few. But near the end, many seemed miffed—by her figuring out who had killed two of her colleagues before they did.

The Chautauqua County Sheriff, Josiah Cunningham, would still return her call. But that didn't mean much.

A notorious press hound, Sheriff Cunningham made a point of being on good terms and a first-name basis with everyone with a press pass. He used to invite every local reporter to his blowout Christmas parties—and just the guys to an annual "hog nuts" birthday bash that featured barbecued hog testicles.

When he was up for re-election, Sheriff Cunningham sent Mimi and every reporter with kids, a "Junior Sheriff's Kit" that included: a round cloth patch with the Chautauqua County insignia, a bicycle safety coloring book and two "Re-elect Sheriff Cunningham" bumper stickers.

When Doc excused himself to visit his darkroom, Mimi returned to her desk. She found the sheriff's number in her old address book, started dialing it, then stopped.

Who was she kidding?

The sheriff, even if he was in on a Sunday, which was highly unlikely, was too far removed from the day-to-day to be much help.

So Mimi hung up. She took a deep breath. And, instead, she dialed the Sheriff's Department's Investigations division number she still knew by heart.

"Investigations," said an unfamiliar man's voice.

"Is Sergeant Mackenzie in?" Mimi asked. "Or can I leave a message for him?"

When there was no immediate response, Mimi exhaled, unaware, she'd been holding her breath.

"If he's not in until tomorrow, that's okay," Mimi added. "He can call me tomorrow. This isn't—"

"He's in," the man interrupted. "He's in. Just gimme a sec and I'll page him."

Mimi, though she'd asked for Mack, felt like hanging up.

Not expecting Mack to be in, she thought she'd get more time to prepare for talking to the best-looking guy she'd ever dated.

Blond, blue-eyed and buff, Mack looked more like a TV cop than a real cop.

"Not husband material," Mimi's Grandma Fanny would have sniffed, mainly due to religious differences. But Mimi wasn't looking for a husband. At least not yet. She just wished she'd gotten to date Mack longer.

Their timing was terrible.

Shortly after they met last June, Mack's 12-year-old son Kevin was struck and nearly killed by a hit-and-run driver. Mack dropped everything. He lived at Kevin's bedside and tried to grant his every wish. Even one asking Mack to reconcile with his estranged wife-slash-Kevin's mom Tina.

After the reconciliation, Mimi called Mack a few times to ask about Kevin. But when Mark and Tina "re-married" in a private ceremony with new rings and vows in October, Mimi stopped calling.

Waiting for Mack to pick up, Mimi could hear the first organ chords from the church service that was starting at Chautauqua's main gathering spot:

its 4,000-seat wooden-roofed, open-sided Amphi-theater.

Then she heard the phone receiver rattling around at the other end.

"Sergeant Mackenzie."

"Mack, uh, hello. It's Mimi. Mimi Goldman."

"I know who it is. God, it's great to hear your voice. How are you?"

"Same here. I mean, uh, it's great to hear your voice, too."

Crap.

In some respects, Mimi showed her thirty-eight years. Crow's feet. Gray strands. Less lift to her boobs.

But, relationship-wise, she still had the poise of a tongue-tied teen.

Where was the justice in that?

"I've been thinking about calling," Mack said. "A few times. But I've been, well, trying to make this work. This remarriage thing and all and I . . ."

"How's Kevin?"

"Better than ever. It's unbelievable how resilient kids are. The doctors are calling him a miracle of modern medicine. He's already back pitching. Starting tonight, in fact, against the Jamestown Jaguars. How are you?"

"Fine. It's beautiful here. But harder than I expected to fill the sports pages. I'm finally getting the hang of it.

You run long lists of participants. In golf tournaments. Fishing competitions. Tennis matches. Whatever. People love to see their name in the paper."

"And Jake?"

"He's fine, too. But growing up so fast, it scares me. He goes to camp during the day. Then he's off at night with a crowd of older boys doing who knows what. I feel a little cut out."

"That's life. Leaving the roost, finding his way sound like good things. To me, anyway, since I'm not the mom."

"Hey, Mack, what are you doing working on a Sunday? I thought you were using weekends for law school homework and studying?"

There was an awkward pause.

"Mack?"

"I dropped out," he said. "Or maybe I should say I'm taking an indefinite leave. I thought you might have heard."

"I thought you were dong well and enjoying it. Heading for Law Review, weren't you?"

He sighed.

"I was doing okay. But it was taking too much time and money. You wouldn't believe what the law books cost. We're battling the insurance company over some of Kevin's medical bills. And, well, now that the department's making more overtime available weekends, Tina thinks law school's not something we can currently afford."

"What do *you* think?"

As soon as Mimi asked, she wished she hadn't.

"I'm sorry, Mack," she said, softly. "Please ignore that. It's none of my damn business. I never know when to shut up and . . ."

Mack chuckled.

"If you did, people would wonder what's wrong with you—if you were sick or something. As the lawyers say, *for the record*, I agree that law school would be too much for us now."

Mimi was sorry to hear Mack talk that way. He loved his first-semester courses. And he was proud that a cop, who hadn't cracked a schoolbook in ten years could keep up with his younger classmates.

She tried to switch the conversation to safer, neutral ground.

"I'm calling for a professional favor," she said. "That I'm hoping won't be tough."

Mack chuckled again.

"I'll help if I can. What do you need?"

In general terms, she described the death of her landlord Brad Hansen at yesterday's Old First Night Run.

"The hospital, I guess, said he died of natural causes

from a heart attack. But I'm wondering if the police were involved in any way? If they investigated the death? Ordered an autopsy? Or did any kinds of tests to rule out other possible causes of death like maybe poisons or drugs?"

"I can get you everything that's on the public record," Mack said. "Death certificate. Police reports. I can talk with the EMTs at the scene. But, from the little I've heard, the deceased was an elderly man who died of a heart attack at the race. I don't think anyone had reason to suspect anything else."

"Thanks," Mimi said. "The records and EMTs' observations would be great. You could pass them on to me. Or, if I'm not in, to or my colleague at *The Daily* Doc Segovian. We'll take it from there."

"Take what?" Mack said. "What's this about? Why are you interested?"

"Let's just say *The Daily* wanted me to do some preliminary investigating into the death."

When Mack cracked up, Mimi's face burned.

"You're trying to tell me this is some kind of a *Chautauquan Daily* assignment?" Mack asked.

"Yeah."

"C'mon, Mimi. I've lived here all of my life. A death, a suspicious death, whatever, is not anything *The Daily* would ever touch. It covers good news. And culture.

Lectures. Concerts. Church services. I don't remember them writing a single story about death or crime."

Mimi, lacking a decent retort, said nothing.

"What are you up to?" Mack pressed.

When Mimi still didn't answer, he laughed again.

"Okay, okay. I get it. You don't want to tell me. Well, I'll find what I can about the death and pass it on to you or your friend Doc. And maybe you'll fill me in then?"

"Maybe."

"One more thing?" Mack asked.

"What?"

"Please be careful."

Chapter Nine

Mack's warning seemed laughable when, after typing up race results and grabbing a quick dinner with Jake, Mimi resumed investigating in the guise of paying a condolence call on Francine Sunday night.

As a reporter for *The New York Post*, Mimi had been in some scary spots.

Assigned once to cover a protest of racist cops in Bed-Stuy, Brooklyn, Mimi, the only white person for miles, was surrounded by an angry mob. She only escaped when two EMS guys waded into the crowd, dragged her into their ambulance and sped off.

Another assignment to interview a Hell's Angel accused of a rival's torture-murder, ended in Mimi getting chased, at gunpoint, from the man's apartment, by two drunken gang members.

In contrast, the crowd Mimi faced at the Hansens' house consisted mainly of little old ladies, also paying their respects, while drinking nothing stronger than decaf coffee.

"I'll take those."

Betsy Gates intercepted Mimi wandering with a plateful of chocolate chip cookies.

"Just over here," Betsy said leading her to a folding table with a very organized spread of food: hors d'oeuvres with hors d'oeuvres, salads with salads, casseroles with casseroles, desserts with desserts.

"Looks yummy," she said, sliding Mimi's cookies between a rhubarb pie and fruit compote. "And it's great of you to stop by. I'm sure Francine will be glad to see you."

Betsy—trim, blond and excessively smiley—reminded Mimi of a small-town weather forecaster. Maybe for a 24-hour station, given her nonstop cheery patter.

"How'd you get stuck with the hosting duties?"

"I don't mind at all," Betsy said. "Least I can do. I just feel so terrible about the whole thing. Also my husband Don's up for the weekend, watching the baby. So I was able to get out." When someone else approached, Betsy excused herself. Mimi grabbed a decaf and headed for the living room.

From the entrance, she was surprised by the size of the crowd. Francine was a newcomer. And the guests, including the Warren sisters, were Sunday night regulars at the Sacred Song Service at the Amphitheater.

It took a moment for Mimi to locate Francine.

She was in the middle of things, dressed in a tasteful black suit. But, overnight, she looked older. And frailer. And, uncharacteristically, wild-haired with smeary makeup.

When Mimi approached, the other women backed off to give them privacy.

"Francine?"

Francine, narrowing her eyes, didn't seem to recognize Mimi either.

"Francine?"

"Oh, Mimi," she finally said. "Glad you could come. I'm practically blind without my glasses."

Mimi delivered the condolence speech she'd been practicing in her head about how sorry she and Jake were about Brad Hansen's death.

"It's so hard to believe," Mimi said.

"For me, too. It doesn't seem real." Francine's big, long-lashed brown eyes filled with tears. "Brad seemed so big and strong and healthy when we met. A big strong stubborn ox. He was . . ."

Francine stopped, apparently confused about what she was going to say next.

"I'm sorry," she said. "I'm not myself. I still feel like a newlywed. I do. Friday I got a wedding present from my sister in California, a cut-glass Tiffany bowl. Then the next day . . ."

When Francine choked up, Mimi nodded sympathetically.

Then she tried to switch gears and ask some of the business questions she'd brought with her.

"I remember you'd mentioned Brad's stomach cramps before the race yesterday. Had Brad been ill for a while?"

"I think it was for about a week. But, with him, you never knew. He had a high threshold for pain. And even if he was suffering, Brad wouldn't complain. Or see a doctor. I think he considered it unmanly."

"Did you suggest he go to the doctor?"

"More than *suggest*," Francine said. "I begged the man. I begged Brad to be examined. You saw that yourself."

Mimi saw no such thing. But this wasn't gotcha police time.

"Before the race, I even made an appointment for him with a doctor in Jamestown," Francine continued.

"But he refused to go. Or to even let Doc check him out."

"Did you think Brad was suffering from some kind of food poisoning or something?"

Francine scrunched up her face, confused.

"What do you mean?" she asked. "Didn't you hear it was a heart attack?"

"I did. But I just wondered if he might have been especially uncomfortable because of something he ate?"

Mimi knew her comeback was lame. But Francine, thankfully, didn't call her on it.

"No," Francine said, thoughtfully. "No. Brad never said anything about eating something funny."

"What did he eat before the race?"

"Not much. Maybe a bite of toast. Some tea."

"Any medications?"

"He might have had some Tums. Or vitamins. Or energy pills. I'm not sure. Why in the world would you care about all this?"

Hmm.

Mimi, again at a loss for words, just tried to backpedal gracefully.

"I don't know what started me down this path. I was just wondering," she said. "Sorry to bother you about it."

"It's just so hard to believe. I can't seem to. . . I'm not thinking clearly myself. Crazy thoughts fly in my head and I end up saying them aloud, too. It's too much to bear."

Francine choked back tears.

And, Mimi thought, if this was a performance, it was a masterful one. Francine's grief seemed sincere.

Grief for a man whom Doc had aptly described as hard to like.

Mimi's last memory of Brad Hansen was typical.

He came downstairs for breakfast the day before the race, Friday, as Francine sipped coffee with a blueberry muffin.

Mimi and Betsy Gates were there.

But that didn't stop Brad from angrily snatching the muffin from Francine's hand, as if she was a child.

Grabbing her butt, Brad explained to Mimi, "Somebody's gotta watch Francine's figure if she won't."

When Francine tried to laugh it off, Brad got ugly.

"She might think it's funny," Brad said. "But I'd hate to think I've fallen for some bait and switch. Marry a hot piece of ass. And, in no time, she's a goddamned heifer."

When Mimi rejoined the conversation, she noticed that Francine was struggling to keep her eyes open.

"Do you want to go upstairs and take a nap? You look exhausted."

"Not yet," Francine said. "Soon. Betsy, Betsy Gates, said she'll help me upstairs when I'm ready."

"She seems like she's really stepped up and done a lot for you."

"Total angel," Francine said. "She's a registered nurse. Seems happy to lend a hand. And always has a cheery attitude."

"Maybe this isn't nice to say," Mimi said. "But I might like her more if she was a little less cheery."

"I know what you mean," Francine said, chuckling. "But I can't complain. She's taken charge of the guests. And the food. And me, even. She got a doctor to give me something to ease the pain. It's making me a little dopey but far less blue."

"Maybe Betsy's on the same stuff."

"Maybe," Francine smiled.

"If you think of anything else you need, please ask me or Jake. Maybe we could run some errands for you? Get you some groceries?"

"That would be nice."

"I'll call tomorrow before we go."

"I expect to be home all day except around noon. That's when I'm meeting the funeral director in Mayville and probably running across the street to get my hair done."

Note to self, Mimi thought: Noon might be a good time to snoop around for Brad's hairbrush.

If she were a more patient sort.

"I'll call tomorrow about the groceries," Mimi told Francine. "Now, I've gotta get home and check on Jake. After a quick restroom stop upstairs."

Chapter Ten

As many times as Mimi had been in the Hansens' house, she'd never been upstairs.

So she moved tentatively, finding the stairs, then grabbing the burled oak banister and heading up. Along the way, she admired the many wall photos including: old-timey shots of two boys, probably Brad Hansen and his brother Mole, and more recent shots of Brad and his red-haired first wife and their red-haired kids.

Beyond the photos were framed posters from previous Old First Night races and a framed newspaper clipping about the opening of a "Big Brad's Carpets" in Lakewood, New York.

At the second floor, Mimi expected to be alone. Instead, she saw three old ladies on a hall bathroom line.

Mimi nodded hello and continued down the hall to

the master bedroom at the end. Hand on the bedroom doorknob, she felt the old ladies' stares. Her plan was to ignore them and say nothing. But, always way too conscious of what other people think, she couldn't.

"There's another bathroom in here, isn't there?" she called. "I've REALLY gotta go."

The explanation, of course, didn't help. The women kept staring. And scowling. And, wordlessly, conveying a view that rules like "Wait Your Turn," are damn near sacred.

Mimi, trying to keep her mission front and center, opened the bedroom door. She stepped into an L-shaped room so well-appointed it could have been in a magazine.

The "Country Cottages" edition.

On the walls were a series of pretty watercolor paintings of Chautauqua scenes. On the windows were ivory shades and sheer curtains.

In the middle was a four-poster canopy bed with a patchwork quilt and eight pillows, big and small.

The bed was kind of a divider. To its right, was obviously Francine's territory. Her dresser had a framed wedding photo of her and Brad, smiling at the Hall of Philosophy that would also be the site of Brad's funeral.

Next to the photo were a jewelry box, cut-glass perfume bottles and a loose strand of pearls.

On the other side of the room was a more masculine-looking six-drawer dresser. On top were papers and a peanut-butter jar loaded with coins.

That had to be Brad's dresser. But if his hairbrush was close, it wasn't obvious.

Mimi was going to go through the drawers then search a master bathroom she figured was around the bend, in the vertical part of the "L" she couldn't see.

"Young lady? Can I ask what you're doing in here?"

Mimi, who had both hands on a dresser-drawer pull, dropped them to her sides.

"I'm, uh, looking for a bathroom. I was told that . . ."

Mimi's interrogator, a woman so large she looked like a man in drag, was making a shushing gesture.

"This room is off-limits," she stage-whispered. "Reverend Johnson needs some privacy while he's on the phone."

She glanced toward where Reverend Johnson, presumably around the bend, was on the phone.

When Mimi didn't move, the woman added, "The guest bathroom's down the hall."

Not wanting to give up and go home, Mimi joined the very same bathroom line she'd snubbed.

The two ladies left on the line said nothing. But their

expressions, again, conveyed a unanimous thought: "Served you right."

By the time Mimi reached the front, two new old ladies had joined the line behind Mimi. So she couldn't take forever.

She entered the bathroom that had a small shower, toilet and sink with a mirrored medicine cabinet above the sink and more storage space below.

There was, of course, no hairbrush out. Flanking the sink faucets were a liquid soap dispenser and a soap dish with a pink clamshell-shaped bar of soap.

When Mimi opened the medicine cabinet, again, there was no obvious hairbrush.

Making herself be methodical, she eyed all four shelves. And she found the usual cold remedies and his-and-hers toiletries.

For Brad, there was a straight-edged razor, shaving cream, styptic pencil, nail clippers and after-shave. For Francine, there were tweezers, nail polish remover and Tampax. There were also unisex band-aids and Tylenol.

Aware of the line outside the bathroom, Mimi knelt down and opened the cabinet under the sink. There, she found extra toilet paper rolls, sponges, a foot-itch powder and what looked like a man's black leather travel toilet kit.

Eagerly, Mimi unzipped the kit. Inside, she found

more razors, a mini shaving cream, a toothbrush and—hallelujah—a hairbrush with a few gray strands in the bristles.

Imitating TV forensic guys, Mimi stayed clear of the bristles. She grabbed the hairbrush by the handle and dropped it into a zip-lock baggie she had in her purse. She re-zipped the toilet kit and returned it to the cabinet.

Then, to complete her ruse, she flushed the toilet, washed her hands and stepped outside.

Pretty pleased with herself, Mimi raced down the stairs toward the front door. But, a few steps from the door, she was intercepted by Evangeline Warren.

Chapter Eleven

"Where's the fire? Where are you rushing off to?"

Evangeline, who had her right arm on her silver-tipped cane, hooked her left arm through Mimi's and leaned close.

"Nowhere really," Mimi said. "I was just going home to, well, check on my son."

"The quick getaway made me wonder if you were here on some kind of an assignment?"

"Oh, no," Mimi laughed. "No. No. No."

Before Mimi added a fourth "No," protesting too much, she stopped herself.

"Just a social visit," Mimi said. "I wanted to see how Francine was doing. And I brought her some cookies. Chocolate-chip cookies I baked. Although there doesn't seem to be any shortage of food."

"If you have a moment, I'd love to hear how you and your son are enjoying your time in Chautauqua so far? Unless you have to rush off?"

Mimi felt torn.

Her urge to flee was visceral.

To get away from Evangeline's clutches. Her musty old-lady smell. And her overwhelming negativity.

Mimi's Grandma Fanny had two words for the type: *Farbissineh ponim* (sour puss).

But Mimi's mind told her to stay put.

And learn what she could from this busybody.

"Do you mind if I get myself some more decaf?" Mimi asked Evangeline.

"Not at all. I'll wait for you over here."

When Mimi returned, Betsy Gates was helping Evangeline into a folding chair she'd dragged over and Evangeline was thanking her profusely.

"What a godsend that girl is," Evangeline said when Betsy left.

"Is she an old friend of the Hansens? Or a relative?"

"No," Evangeline said. "As far as I know, she's no relation. Just a good Christian."

If Evangeline meant that as a dig at a non-Christian,

Mimi ignored it and sipped some decaf before returning to Evangeline's original question.

"Back to how Jake and I like Chautauqua?"

"Yes," Evangeline said. "Had you heard of it before you came here?"

"Not really. The name rang faint bells. Maybe from learning about the Chautauqua movement, in terms of adult education, in school. But some of my friends misled me, confusing it with Chappaqua, a suburb of New York City."

"What do you and Jake think now that you're here?"

"Mr. Hansen's death has shaken us both some," Mimi said. "But before that, I'd say we were both falling in love with the place."

"Most people do," Evangeline said.

"Jake, especially, is enjoying the freedom here that you don't get in a big city. He can come and go himself and he's made some good friends. I love the pace. And I can't get over how beautiful Chautauqua is."

"Glad you like it."

"Would you mind if I asked you a few things, too?"

"Go right ahead."

"Have you known the Hansens for long?"

"Brad Hansen I've known for maybe forty years. Philomena and I started renting from him in, oh, the early sixties."

"That's when we started coming for just a few weeks, the way we had come here as children. Our father, a Methodist minister in Shaler, near Pittsburgh, used to come to Chautauqua every August to get ideas for his sermons. Gradually, Philomena and I came for longer and longer. Four years ago, we decided to move here permanently."

"Would you call yourselves friends of the Hansens?"

"Not really. With Brad Hansen everything was strictly business. We enjoyed his first wife, Margaret. A lovely person who was also very gifted artistically. She restored this whole house practically herself. Following her own vision. She did a lot of the planning and decorating. Only hired out technical jobs, like plumbing and electrical work, she couldn't do herself."

With Evangeline on a roll, Mimi just sipped her coffee and tried to stay out of her way.

"The new wife?" Evangeline continued. "She's a pretty girl we're just warming to. She certainly caught Brad's eye fast."

"Do you know how they met?"

"I don't. I hear she's from Indianapolis, a former teacher. But she doesn't talk much about it. I believe she was selling real estate since she moved here."

"Nice of all of these people to show up tonight,"

Mimi said. "Do you think Brad's brother or his children will make an appearance?"

"I wouldn't hold my breath."

"Why is that?"

"You're certainly as nosy as they say," Evangeline said.

Mimi, face coloring, tried to laugh it off.

"Sorry," she said. "Occupational hazard, probably. Hard to turn off the interrogating switch when you're a reporter."

"And part-time investigator?"

When Mimi didn't answer, Evangeline continued.

"We all read about your crime-solving adventure last year."

"Tonight, I'm just being nosy on my own behalf."

When Evangline made a snorting laugh, Mimi ignored her and plowed ahead.

"So why won't Brad's children show up?"

"Brad and his children were estranged since their mother died in March. And Millard, the brother, Mole, wasn't speaking to Brad either."

"Do you know why?"

"You've probably noticed, Mole doesn't speak much to anyone. He has a stutter that made him 4-F in the war and uncomfortable around people. Over the years, the brothers also had their differences."

"Is he retired?"

"Yes, Mole was a custodian for the Chautauqua County schools and also did a lot of the schools' landscaping. He's an excellent gardener. Won prizes for his roses and dahlias."

"And Brad Hansen's children?"

"The oldest is a girl, Mary. A career girl who never married."

"What's her career?"

"Music. She's a violinist in the Chautauqua Symphony."

"So she's here now? For the summer?"

"Absolutely. She's renting an apartment, I hear, on Roberts Street, behind the bookstore. The rest of the year, she lives in New York City. Teaches music. Performs some at Broadway shows and the like."

"And the son?"

"Never made much of himself," Evangeline said. "He went to law school but, from what I hear, never practiced law. He also lives in New York City with a very ambitious wife and two lovely children."

Mimi kept sipping her coffee and nodding to try to encourage Evangeline to keep talking.

"As far as personalities, the Hansen children couldn't be more different. Night and day. The boy's a softy who never raises his voice. I'm afraid people walk all over him. Always have. Like his mom. The girl got the mother's looks. The red hair and green eyes. But, I'm sorry to say, her father's disposition."

"Do you know if any of them had fought with Brad Hansen recently?"

"I don't."

"Did they go to Brad and Francine's wedding?"

"No."

"Can I ask you what you thought of Brad Hansen Sr.?"

Evangeline smiled.

"What?"

"You can ask whatever you like. You don't need my permission."

"Okay, fair enough. Then I'll just go for it. What did you think of Brad Hansen Sr.?"

"Decent enough," she said. "Not a churchgoer. But he was always a fine provider for his wife and children."

When Evangeline finished, she flashed Mimi a challenging look. As if to say, "You know that's not what I *really* think. But waddya gonna do about it?"

Mimi did nothing.

She let Evangeline's assessment sit out there, unquestioned. As she considered her next move, Evangeline, clearly losing patience, leaned her weight on her cane. And, with a tremendous amount of effort, rose to her feet.

"Well, young lady, we've certainly covered a lot of

ground. I'm starting to run out of steam. I might not look eighty-seven years old. But I certainly feel it. And I think Philomena and I need to get home and attend to our babies."

Mimi raised an eyebrow.

"Our cats," Evangeline explained. "We spoil them like babies."

Mimi, rising to her feet, too, thanked Evangeline for her time.

"I wonder if, before you go, you'd humor me and answer one more thing?" Mimi asked.

"Like Columbo?" Evangeline said smiling. "With the one more thing?"

"Something like that."

"Philomena and I loved that show. That and 'Murder She Wrote.' And 'Perry Mason,' of course. And 'Dragnet'. What's your one more thing?"

"I was wondering if you knew who stands to inherit Brad Hansen's estate? Especially the Chautauqua houses?"

"That I wouldn't know."

"Any idea who would?"

Evangeline hesitated.

"Probably Brad's personal lawyer, Everett Thompson, who has an office in Jamestown."

Chapter Twelve

Everett Thompson was easy to find in the Jamestown phone book. He was in the general lawyer listings. And in a boxed ad next to the listings calling himself a "caring, compassionate lawyer."

Mimi tried calling Thompson before she went to bed on Sunday, then again when she woke up Monday morning. When she only got a machine both times, she didn't leave a message.

She rushed to *The Daily*, planning to try Thompson again before the weekly nine-thirty Monday staff meeting. When she got the machine again at nine-ten, this time she took a deep breath.

"This is Mimi, uh, Mimi Grace," she said at the beep. "I'm calling from the Chautauqua Institution. I have, uh, a real-estate question I think you might be able to help me with. Please call back at your convenience."

As Mimi recited her real phone number, she cringed.

Leaving her real number probably wasn't the smartest move. Or using an alias so close to her own name. Or speaking in a tentative-slash-guilty tone of voice.

But what the hey?

By now, she knew she was a terrible liar. And an average investigator.

Practice might help.

In the meantime, she'd try to follow Jake's advice: "Fake it 'til you make it."

Feign the confidence you want—until it's yours.

"Boys and girls? Boys and girls?"

The Daily's main editor, Joe Wentworth, liked to start the weekly meeting at nine-thirty on the dot. So at nine-twenty, he began rallying the troops.

Taking the hint, Mimi and most of the staff took their seats as Doc showed up, posted his schedule on the bulletin board and sat, too.

When their eyes met, Mimi tried to read some news in Doc's expression, but couldn't. If he had something to say, it would have to wait until their coffee date after the meeting.

"I wanted to start the meeting with a reminder,"

Wentworth said. "Something's been creeping into the copy that shouldn't."

He paused.

"The use of *today* or *tomorrow* in Saturday and weekend stories. EVERYONE," he said. "PLEASE. Be more aware of the time element in your stories. If an event is not tomorrow, don't say tomorrow. Okay, boys and girls?"

Wentworth, a longtime Chautauquan in his sixties, taught journalism at the University of Maryland during the off-season. So he sometimes treated *The Daily* staff—that ranged in age from 17 to 77 (Doc's age) —like his students.

He dressed like a teacher, too, at a fancy prep school, not a public college.

No matter the weather or time of day, Wentworth wore khakis, a white button-down shirt, Oxford loafers and a bow tie.

The staff nodded.

After a few more reminders, Wentworth went around the room asking reporters what they expected to be covering that week.

When it was Mimi's turn, she said that, after printing all of the Old First Night runners' times in Monday's paper, she'd have the walkers' times for Tuesday. Plus a feature story about the 17-year-old and 19-year-old brothers who finished first and fifth in the race.

"Sounds good," Wentworth said. "What about for later in the week?"

"I've got some calls out," Mimi said. "So does Mike, our fabulous intern. So we'll probably write about yachting, volleyball and/or tennis early in the week and softball later."

Other reporters described concerts, operas and guest speakers. But Mimi's ears perked up at the turn of Jerry North, the morning-lectures editor.

"What's the theme this week?" Wentworth asked since each Chautauqua week had a theme for the main 10:45 a.m. daily Amphitheater lecture—like the Middle East, the Civil War, Making Peace in a Nuclear World and Women's Issues—that, over the years, had been delivered by huge names in politics, business, religion and the arts.

"Looks pretty interesting," North said. "The title is 'The Mystery of Good and Evil.' Speakers will address how the concepts are covered in literature, history, religion. Whether evil really exists?"

Good question, Mimi thought.

Did Brad Hansen die of natural cases? Or was he murdered by someone evil?

When Wentworth finished polling the staff, he wrapped up with a report on pending letters to the editor.

"Good news," he said. "We have enough letters to carry us through Thursday."

Around the room, there were smiles and sighs of relief from the staff who didn't want to try to scare up more letters from friends and family.

"Many deal with the latest Chautauqua controversy," he said. "Needlework during amphitheater programs."

"A lot of people are weighing in on whether it's too noisy and distracting. But my favorite quotes Eleanor Roosevelt's view on the matter. I have it right here."

Wentworth pulled the letter from his breast pocket, put on reading glasses and read aloud.

"Eleanor supposedly invited one Chautauqua audience to knit during one of her talks and here's what our letter writer says Eleanor told them, 'I do it myself because I can pay close attention when my hands are better occupied.' "

When the meeting broke up, Doc stood by Mimi's desk.

"Want more coffee?" he asked.

"Always."

Chapter Thirteen

Their destination, the Refectory, was next door. A cafeteria-style restaurant and ice cream shop, it made up the east leg of the rectangular Bestor Plaza along with the long brick building that housed *The Daily* upstairs and the bookstore and post office below.

The west leg included a student dorm and the Saint Elmo, a former hotel that, to the dismay of longtime Chautauquans, had been converted into luxury condos. The south leg had the library and archives. The north had the Colonnade building with Chautauqua administrative offices, an ATM, several shops, public restrooms and *The Daily*'s darkroom.

At virtually all hours, Bestor Plaza was busy. That morning, clusters of older people sat on tree-shaded benches reading mail and newspapers. A groundskeeper watered giant flower boxes.

Two boys chased each other on the rim of a central fountain with a four-sided sculpture depicting Chautauqua's ideals: Music, Art, Religion and Knowledge. A girl splashed her hand through water spewing from the mouth of a cement fish into the fountain.

"How's it going?" Mimi asked after they served themselves coffee and waited to pay at the cash register.

"What was that?"

"How's it going?" Mimi repeated louder.

"The Old First Night photo retrospective is taking longer than I expected."

"Because you're enjoying it too much and don't want it to end?"

"Maybe. I am having fun walking down Memory Lane, reviewing the history."

"Need help?"

"Maybe when I get down to some finalists. I can't tell if I'm partial to the ones from 1945 because I was here. And it was one of the most memorable moments of my life."

"What happened?"

"They announced the end of the war from the Old First Night stage."

Doc's face glowed with the memory.

"It was Ralph McAllister, program director, I think. He got on stage and said he had the greatest announcement that could be made to Chautauqua or the whole world: The war is over. The crowd barely let him finish his sentence. Everyone went wild and started singing 'The Star-Spangled Banner.' I was back from the service. I had my first serious camera. And I couldn't stop taking pictures. I have hundreds, including some pretty great ones."

"Well, if they're the best, you should use a lot of them."

"I'll probably use a few. The problem is that any photo that never ran in *The Daily* means more work. I've been calling around trying to get help identifying people for captions."

"You can't leave some people unidentified?"

"I could, but I'd rather not."

Seeking privacy, Mimi and Doc took their coffees to a rickety round table under an umbrella on a porch behind the Refectory.

Only one other table was filled, with a bickering young couple. When Mimi was sure the teens were absorbed in their own drama, she pulled out the baggie with the hairbrush.

"Mission accomplished," she said, handing it over to Doc. "At least I hope so."

"You think it's Brad's brush?"

"I do. It came from a manly-looking toilet kit with a razor at the Hansens'. And it also has gray hair in the bristles. Francine's hair is colored, not gray."

"Where'd you find it?"

"In an upstairs hall bathroom."

"Think Brad used it recently?"

"That I can't say. The kit looked like something he'd take on a trip and not use every day. I couldn't get into the Hansens' main bathroom. It was off limits."

When Doc, put the baggie in a fanny pack he wore around his waist, Mimi asked: "What are you going to do with it?"

"Since the police aren't going to do any of their own tests, I . . ."

"How do you know that?"

"Your old beau, Sergeant Mackenzie—"

"He's NOT my old beau," Mimi interrupted.

Doc smiled.

"Anyway, your old friend called. I was in the office early this morning, so I took the call and didn't get back soon enough to tell you about it before the meeting."

"And?"

"Your friend sounded very nice and apologetic. But,

basically, he said, 'No dice.' His superiors found no reason to test Brad Hansen for poisons. The hospital said the man died of a heart attack. Without more specific grounds for suspicion, or a request from the family, they plan to release the body for burial Wednesday."

"So our questions aren't enough to trigger tests?"

"I guess not."

"And they had no suspicions of their own?"

"True."

"So now what?" Mimi asked.

"We send the hairbrush to my son John. He's a chemist for the Pennsylvania Board of Health. Normally, you'd need a forensic lab to test a person for poisons. But John said he could do many of the same tests in the state lab that tests water samples. If we Fed-Ex him the brush today, he said he can send us results by late tomorrow."

"So the hairbrush is enough?"

"Apparently. My medical texts say that one of the best ways to identify victims of chronic or long-term poisoning is the presence of poison in their hair or nails."

When they finished their coffees, Doc checked his watch.

"Oh," he said, hopping to his feet. "We better get back to work. Want to meet tomorrow night to go over the lab results before the Old First Night program?"

"Great," Mimi said. "What time?"

"How about six-thirty in the darkroom? That's where I'll be spending much of the afternoon."

"That works."

Before they split up, Doc said until they get the lab results, they could probably sit tight.

"Not a lot of reason to keep investigating."

"I guess not."

Chapter Fourteen

That's what Mimi said.

But as Monday morning dragged on at *The Daily*, with her typing up walkers' names, ages and finish times and placing unanswered calls, trying to dredge up more sports to cover later in the week, her mind rebelled.

It came up with many reasons to keep investigating.

Mainly: If the lab tests confirmed what they suspected, that Brad Hansen had been poisoned, the police would get involved. And if the police got involved, finding Brad's killer probably would get harder.

People might clam up. The guilty might become more careful. And key evidence, such as poisons, if they were still around, might disappear.

Restless, Mimi also turned the question on its

head: Why *not* keep investigating? Especially when, at eleven-thirty, a new lead, by way of *The Daily*'s secretary, Linda Richards, landed in her lap.

"Mimi? Mimi?" Linda yelled across the newsroom. "Are you still on the phone?"

"No. I just hung up."

"I've got an Everett Thompson holding for you on line one. Want to grab it?"

After Mimi did, for half a second, she froze.

She couldn't remember the fake last name she'd left on Everett Thompson's answering machine.

So she kept it simple.

"Mimi, here," she said into the receiver. "Thanks for calling me back. How are you?"

"Not bad," Thompson said. "Not bad. Sorry I didn't call sooner. I've been stuck in court all morning. What can I do for you?"

Mimi, after a deep breath, tried to do a better job at play-acting.

"I'm calling from the Chautauqua Institution," she said. "I'm renting a place on South, near properties owned by the late Brad Hansen whom, I understand was your client?"

When Thompson said nothing, Mimi continued.

"I feel a little ghoulish asking this but . . ."

"Go ahead," Thompson said.

"Well, I have some friends from New York City looking to buy property on the grounds. They asked me to ask around, to see if I could see who, well, is inheriting the Hansen properties. So they could make an early offer."

Thompson chuckled.

"I've read about how they are in New York City," he said. "So competitive about real estate that some people search the obituaries for vacant apartments."

"Exactly," Mimi said, feeling like a traitor perpetrating "evil New Yorker" stereotypes. "That's their mindset. As soon as my friends heard the news about Mr. Hansen, they asked me to move fast, on their behalf."

"I hate to think the Chautauqua real estate market is getting as vicious," the lawyer said. "But it sure has heated up in recent years."

"Can you just give me the name of the person my friends should contact?"

More silence.

"I won't even tell my friends where I heard it," Mimi continued. "They'll just pretend they found out the owner's name by themselves."

Thompson sighed.

"I just don't know if I'm comfortable doing this," he said. "Especially on the phone."

Mimi, ignoring any sympathy she felt for Thompson's predicament, kept pushing.

"What I should tell you is that my friends have a lot of money they want to spend on a Chautauqua house," she said. "They've looked at other houses. Even made a few offers. But, I can assure you, they're serious. They plan to buy something soon. And they'd love to contact the right person about the Hansens' properties."

When she sensed Thompson wavering, she tried a favorite tactic of her favorite TV detectives: silence.

It was a struggle for Mimi. But, somehow, she outlasted Thompson.

"All right, all right," he said, eventually. "I'd hate to think that by standing on ceremony, I'm doing a client a disservice. So I'll tell you that, although Mr. Hansen has two grown children and a brother, everything in his will—including the proper-ties—goes to his new wife. Francine Hansen. Your friends can reach her at the listing in the Chautauqua phone book for Bradley Hansen Sr. at 12 Park."

When the bell tower chimed eleven-forty-five, Mimi shot out of her desk like a kid released from detention.

She put on her mirrored shades. And, remembering Francine's plans to be in Mayville at noon, she hurried to 12 Park.

She maneuvered around what amounts to rush hour in Chautauqua—when thousands of adults leave the Amphitheater after the morning lecture and hundreds of kids go home for lunch from the Boys' and Girls' Club.

At Francine's, she saw no car out front. So she hurried to her first target, the rear utility shed.

Racing past the fenced-in trashcans, without stopping or slowing, was a cinch. But Mole's gorgeous garden was different. His roses, in full bloom, were the stars. Mimi could have stared at them forever. And at their trippy reflection in a gazing globe that merged the flowers' reds and pinks, kaleidoscope-like, with the day's rays of golden sunshine.

Aware of the clock, though, Mimi kept moving.

The shed had a lock. But, as she expected, it hung, unlocked, from its hinge. Mimi pulled the creaky wooden door open, stepped inside and gave her eyes a moment to adjust to the darkness.

When she found an industrial-sized flashlight with a long handle, hanging from a peg, Mimi grabbed it and flipped it on.

On the floor, to the right, she saw a small dusty white

refrigerator holding beers and generic soft drinks. Next to the fridge was a metal toolbox overflowing with wires, nails and screws. Next to the toolbox was a coiled-up green garden hose that, crap, at first, looked like a snake.

Behind the hose was a brown pegboard with hammers and screwdrivers of all types and sizes.

Straight ahead were two shelves that looked like they could be in a health food store. They were crowded with bottles, jars, boxes of what seemed to be homeopathic remedies: vitamins, drops, ointments, pills.

Below the shelves were two heavy bags of charcoal, lighter fluid, grilling implements—a long fork, several spatulas—and other odds and ends.

Beach toys. An old lawn chair with two broken slats. A crank ice-cream maker. A broom and dustpan. A tire pump. A battered box that said it held a badminton set.

To the left of the junk, was Mole's gardening equipment. Muddy black rubber boots. Dirty white gardening gloves. A giant forest-green one-piece work suit.

The suit was so large it looked like it could fit Shaquille O'Neal or a circus giant.

Mole, the tenant Mimi saw the least, *was* a giant, she reminded herself. Definitely more than six feet, he was the tallest old person she'd ever met.

Next to the clothes were bags of mulch, soil, plant food, a pail, shovel, trowel, clippers and other gardening tools. A large box of garbage bags. A plastic Aladdin's-lamp-shaped watering can. An old-fashioned silver pump spray of insect repellent.

Mimi, excited by the insecticide, looked for a list of its ingredients. When she found them, in small type, under a drawing of a skull and crossbones, on the side of the pump, she took out her pen and notebook.

Quickly, she scribbled the first three chemical names. At the fourth, she paused. After looking around to be sure no one was watching, she wrote that ingredient, too, in all caps:

ARSENIC.

CHAPTER FIFTEEN

IT WAS ONLY TWELVE-TEN when Mimi left the shed. Francine's car wasn't back. The main house looked empty.

But Mimi's heart thumped wildly when the screen door slammed, as it always did, as she entered the Hansens' kitchen.

Her plan wasn't well formed. She was looking for anything suspicious, whatever that might be. Plus the remains of anything Brad might have ingested before the Old First Night race.

According to Francine, the list could include Tums, vitamins, energy pills, tea or toast.

In terms of toast, Mimi found no bread anywhere. Not on the counters. Or in the cabinets, fridge or freezer. So any loaf Brad's toast came from was either finished or discarded.

In terms of tea, Mimi did better. She found a half-empty box of Lipton bags in a drawer. Doing her forensic routine again, she used tweezers to transfer one bag from the box to a baggie in her purse. Maybe Doc's son or the cops could test it for poisons in the future.

Aside from the tea, though, her kitchen search was a bust. The drawers and cabinets held the usual: dishes, eating and serving utensils and supplies—breakfast cereals, canned goods, pastas, spices, coffee filters and baking supplies.

The refrigerator, too, held nothing unusual. Just milk, eggs, butter, fruits, vegetables, and lots of leftovers (foil-wrapped casseroles, desserts, salads) from last night.

Under the sink, Mimi found cleaning supplies.

If Brad's Tums, vitamins and energy pills were still in the house, they might be upstairs.

While heading for the stairs, Mimi paused in the Hansens' living room. Like the master bedroom, it was really a beautiful space with an antique breakfront, a couch, rocking chair, a coffee table with an oversized picture book of Victorian houses and a giant roll-top desk.

The desk, for some reason, kept calling to Mimi. Maybe because, rolled shut, it looked like a perfect hiding space.

Giving in, Mimi walked over to the desk and tried

to open it. Not easy. The job didn't require brute force. More finesse to jiggle the top backwards along grooved tracks.

When Mimi got the desk open, she browsed everything on the surface. Stacks of bills. Mail. Official-looking documents. Then she peeked in drawers, finding envelopes, stamps, paper clips, a stapler, scissors, tape, a Xerox of the Hansens' wedding announcement and . . .

"Hey, what the hell are you doing?"

When Mimi spun around, she was surprised to see one of the Ryan twins, Jake's friends from Jamestown.

"Oh, Mrs. Goldman," he said. "Sorry. I didn't realize it was you."

"It's B.J., isn't it?"

Strangers' odds guessing identical twins are 50-50. Mimi's were better, she thought, since she was pretty sure she remembered that B.J. was considered "the cool twin." And this guy had longish hair, earrings and a swagger.

"Very good," B.J. smirked. "Very good. Even our own mother can't tell us apart sometimes. Jake said you're super-observant."

"More lucky, I think."

"I doubt that."

If B.J. didn't belong at the Hansens' house, it didn't

show. As he drew nearer, Mimi noticed that his hair was damp, as if he'd recently showered. He wore a tight white undershirt with baggy jeans and no shoes.

"Can I help you with something?" he asked.

"Do you know if Francine left me a grocery list?" Mimi asked, trying to match B.J.'s ease. "She was supposed to. I thought she might have left it on the table. Or on the desk. But I haven't found it. And I was thinking of making a quick trip to the Lighthouse over my lunch break."

Disappointed by her own nervous jabbering, Mimi finally got herself to shut up.

"Did you check if it was pinned to the refrigerator?" B.J. asked.

"I did."

"How about if Francine left it for you on the porch? Maybe stuck between the screen door and the door jamb?"

"I didn't see it there either."

"I give up then," he said, smiling. "Maybe she just forgot. She's so tore up about things, her head's a scramble."

"I didn't realize you two knew each other," Mimi said. "What brings you around?"

B.J. smiled again.

And, for the first time, he seemed briefly caught off guard. Before he recovered.

"We don't know each other well," he said. "I've done some odd jobs for her. So she asked me to come by to, well, move some furniture. She said, with her husband gone, she couldn't stand looking at things how they were. But the things were, you know, too heavy. So she needed a little muscle."

B.J., smiling again, flexed his impressive biceps.

Mimi whistled.

"We got started moving things around this morning. But then Francine remembered she had to go into Mayville. She told me to make myself at home. So, well, here I am. I was about to make some coffee. Would you like a cup?"

"I usually would."

"Then go ahead. Live a little."

Mimi smiled again.

The kid was definitely charming.

"Thanks," she said. "But I have to get back to work. I'm not done typing up the names, ages and finish times of everyone from the race."

"Sounds exciting."

"Pays the bills."

"I'll tell Francine you stopped by."

"Thanks."

When B.J. turned to head for the kitchen, Mimi followed. But when the distance between them widened, Mimi stopped.

She reached over to the roll-top desk—and, in one swift motion, swept the Hansens' phone bill and marriage certificate into her purse.

Chapter Sixteen

For the rest of Monday and most of Tuesday, Mimi kept her nose to the grindstone. She finished typing up the Old First Night walkers' times. She wrote the feature on the teenaged brothers from Amherst, a Buffalo suburb, who finished in the race's top five.

She even got a little ahead—by writing up weekend golf tournament results to use Wednesday for Thursday. And by getting Mike Halloran, the intern, to write up volleyball-tournament results.

She was going to stay put until her six-thirty darkroom meeting with Doc about the lab-test results on Brad Hansen's hairbrush.

But, by five, she felt antsy. And cooped up. And bitter about missing one of the most beautiful days of the summer.

At five-thirty, she couldn't stand it anymore. She got up. She got out. And she was grateful it was still sunny.

She tied her black hooded sweatshirt around her waist. She got her bike from the bike rack near the bookstore.

She walked it through Bestor Plaza, then coasted her way to the lake, down Miller.

Overhead, a bird's short screeches reminded Mimi of a referee's whistle. Which reminded Mimi of how, as a lifelong city girl, she usually compared things in nature to things man-made. (Tall trees were like skyscrapers; extra-straight ones were like telephone poles; and so forth).

Might that change?

At the bottom of Miller, Mimi drove to one of her favorite Chautauqua spots, a green wooden bench near the bell tower and Children's Beach.

She parked. Then she settled onto the bench for a stretch of people-watching and *Daily*-browsing before meeting Doc.

In the sun's soothing warmth, Mimi sighed. Her tensions unclenched. And, for the first time, she wondered if she and Doc might be way off base suspecting the worst about Brad's death.

The scene before her was so innocent, so unlikely a

setting for murder, Norman Rockwell couldn't have improved upon it.

At the beach, wholesome-looking kids swam, chased, skipped stones, built sand castles and shrieked with joy.

A grandfather and grandson carried fishing poles to a dock behind the bell tower.

Where would murder fit in a throwback place like this? Where few people smoke and liquor can't be sold? Where American flags hang from Victorian porches? Where, on the Fourth of July, people celebrate with picnics and ice cream socials? Where car traffic is limited? And the few cars on the grounds observe a 15 mph speed limit?

Where the raging controversy concerns whether knitting during Amphitheater programs is too disruptive?

Where political satirist Mark Russell got a lot laughs recently asking why Chautauqua even needed its own police force.

"To arrest people with impure thoughts?"

Did she and Doc just feed off each other's paranoia? Dark turns of mind inherited from relatives who'd fled unspeakable horrors?

Doc's parents, Armenians who left Turkey first for

Iran, then the Bronx, were so paranoid they discouraged him from becoming a doctor. He told Mimi they were certain that, despite his top grades at City College, he'd never be admitted to medical school. Then they were sure he'd be cheated out of a degree and refused patients.

Doc's dad had constant nightmares about the atrocities of the Turkish military police. He particularly relived the night he watched the police gather the young men of his village, including two older brothers. Doc's dad watched the police bind the men, cover them with brush and set them on fire. The nightmares were so bad Doc's parents panicked whenever they saw New York City cops doing anything.

The grandparents who raised Mimi—Fanny and Izzy Goldman—were Polish Holocaust survivors.

They, too, freaked out at the sight of anyone in uniform. Many nights, Izzy cried out in his sleep. Both grandparents insisted Mimi take endless "precautions"—like altering her route, daily, to and from school; keeping a suitcase packed and ready to go under her bed; and getting firearms training from age ten.

"Every Jew a .22," was the militant Jewish Defense League slogan her grandparents embraced.

From a young age, Mimi realized many of their precautions were nuts but unchallengeable.

She was "ziskeit" (the sweetness) to her adoring grandparents she'd never want to hurt. And, to them, Mimi decided the precautions made a certain crazy sense.

In Europe, Fanny and Izzy had lost virtually everyone. They tried to start over in Midwood, Brooklyn. They made friends. They had a son. They learned some English. They found their rent-controlled one-bedroom apartment on East Eighteenth Street near Kings Highway. Izzy rose to be head buyer of women's coats at Macy's.

Then they lost their only son, Mimi's dad, in a car crash that killed Mimi's mom, too, when Mimi was seven.

When Mimi pulled the *Chautauquan Daily* from her bag, the newspaper seemed eager to join her internal debate.

The front page featured a story on the first lecture in the "The Mystery of Good and Evil" series.

The lecturer, Dr. Houston Smith, a renowned theologian and author, offered a generally optimistic worldview.

He conceded the existence of evil.

"It's there," he was quoted saying. "It's real and it is

heavy. The Holocaust. Infants, innocent dying to their parents' anguish."

But Dr. Smith concluded that good is in ascendance.

"The world's religions say in unison that in this never-ending conflict between good and evil, it is good that has the upper hand."

Mimi hoped that was the case when the bell tower chimed six-fifteen and she left to meet Doc.

Chapter Seventeen

The Chautauquan Daily darkroom was on the north end of Bestor Plaza that, by bike, could be reached in five minutes.

But Mimi, in no hurry, decided to walk her bike there, past several Chautauqua landmarks.

She passed the Athenaeum Hotel that, according to the history books, was one of the first hotels in the United States to have electricity. She passed Miller Park, named for Lewis Miller, who had co-founded Chautauqua with John Heyl Vincent, a Methodist Bishop.

The founders' genius, said the books, was in recognizing the yearning of their generation, the first Americans to enjoy leisure time—a yearning for a guilt-free high-minded family vacation.

Beyond the park, Mimi passed Miller Cottage, a mini

Swiss chalet that Lewis Miller built in time to entertain President Ulysses S. Grant, one of nine United States presidents to visit Chautauqua.

Later, the cottage was owned by Miller's daughter, Mina, who had her own claim to fame. She was married to the inventor Thomas Alva Edison.

Past the cottage, Mimi took Vincent to Bestor Plaza where crowds were soaking up the day's last rays.

Mimi walked her bike past the Refectory. Heading toward *The Daily* office and the bookstore, she had to duck a Frisbee misfired by a teen playing catch with a friend.

Past the bookstore, she turned left at the Colonnade and started to park. But she saw a rack around the corner, across from the darkroom outside the restaurant called "Sadie J's," so she moved there.

Suddenly feeling late, Mimi hurried to the darkroom that Doc called his dungeon.

It was down ten or twelve steps that led to a public men's room to the left and the darkroom to the right.

Twice before, Mimi had visited the darkroom as Doc's guest. She loved watching how happy he seemed working in the dimly lit smelly quarters. How, while washing, fixing and drying this and that, he hummed along with classical music blasting from a boom-box.

Mimi also enjoyed the last step in the process: the magical appearance of images on dark strips of film.

As Mimi approached the darkroom door, she heard Doc's radio, louder than ever.

Classical music wasn't her thing. Mimi loved show tunes, thanks to her best friend growing up who, after starring in everything in high school and college, tried to make it on Broadway—and, after a struggle, became an amazing high-school drama teacher.

The schmaltzy string piece coming from the darkroom sounded familiar. Maybe Mimi had heard it at one of the Chautauqua Symphony Orchestra concerts that, to her surprise, she was really starting to enjoy. Or maybe it resembled something else. Or was part of a movie or TV soundtrack.

Mimi put her hand on the doorknob and, for some inexplicable reason, she paused.

She felt a prickle of fear on the back of her neck. Or just a chill, maybe, from the sun going down.

Whatever it was, Mimi told herself she was being ridiculous.

She turned the knob. She stepped inside. And she recoiled, as if punched in the gut, from the most horrific sight she'd ever witnessed.

Her eyes, seeking relief, darted to the only normal

sight: a dusty naked light bulb illuminating the green trough-like sink and drying shelves with chemical jugs and a black-and-white timer clock.

Everywhere else was drenched in blood.

Tiny blood spatters dotted the ceiling. Bigger splotches of blood and gore stained the walls.

Blood pooled around Doc who lay perfectly still, face down, in the middle of the darkroom. His clothes, good clothes, a sport jacket, dress pants, he'd obviously put on for Old First Night, were soaked.

Mimi desperately wanted to flee.

Given all the blood, she couldn't imagine that Doc was still alive.

Still, she had to be sure.

Steeling herself, she put one foot in front of the next until she reached Doc.

She knelt beside him and, struggling with all her might, she managed to free one of his arms from underneath his body to check for a pulse.

Unsure exactly where to squeeze, Mimi reached below Doc's Timex watch. His skin felt sticky with blood—but motionless.

There seemed to be no pulse.

But Mimi, thoroughly confused, heard the sound of frantic breathing.

How was that possible? Breathing but no pulse?

Mimi knew her mind wasn't working well and her stomach was in full revolt.

Stepping away, she puked in a corner of darkroom and made herself return to try the pulse thing again.

She wiped her bloody hands on her sweatshirt and bare calves. Again, she squeezed Doc's tiny wrist. Again, his wrist felt as lifeless as a doll's.

When it finally sunk in that the frantic breathing sounds were Mimi's own, she collapsed.

"Doc," she wailed leaning against his still warm body. "I'm so sorry. God, I'm sorry."

Chapter Eighteen

An hour later, the killer shivered reaching into the chilly creek to wash another stubborn stain. The water turned pinkish red. Then it flowed clear as it grew wider heading west to polish pebbles, then rocks and then boulders outside the spot in Chautauqua that kids called "Dead Man's Cave".

The second murder wasn't hard.

Just messy.

After two shots, the know-it-all doctor's head exploded like a mush melon spurting blood everywhere.

It took forever to wash away the obvious spots. And it took even more scrubbing with help—from the skinny bar of soap from the men's room—for tricky ones. Like the blood under fingernails and in fleshy folds and crevices.

Other than the mess, everything else went as planned. The gun choice was perfect. So was the decision to start in the empty men's room and sneak into the darkroom unnoticed by the nearly deaf doctor.

So was the decision to turn up the radio and fire through newspapers to muffle the sound. There wasn't a lot of time to dump the rifle, saw or sawed-off stock. But those details shouldn't come back to haunt.

The figure felt weary but safe. No one was around to watch movements between the creek and the maple and beech woods across from Park.

Virtually all of Chautauqua was heading the opposite way. To the Old First Night program at the Amphitheater. To celebrate, many people left on their porch and house lights. Or they strung strands of multi-colored Christmas lights like candy necklaces from their wide porches.

From the creek, it was tough to hear much by way of human activity. Repeated cracking sounds might be early applause from the Amphitheater. Or, more likely, it was the sound of crickets, rustling trees or the figure's own footsteps crunching leaves and branches.

The loudest sounds came from the Chautauqua Belle, the tourist boat that blew its whistle or belched steam, while churning its way up and down the lake.

As daylight drained swiftly from the sky, the night air took on a chill.

The figure strained harder to listen.

Still no sirens.

It was unlikely the doctor's body wasn't found yet. Maybe the cops were slow arriving . Or maybe they were there but didn't want to scare people with their sirens. Or disrupt the big birthday bash.

Most criminals, it seems, end up getting caught because of their own stupidity. Bring some intelligence and a sound game plan to the table and it's the cops, no matter how smart they think they are, who end up looking stupid.

The know-it-all-doctor wasn't as smart as he thought either. He had the degrees. And the books. And the nosy know-it-all-questions.

But he didn't see this one coming. When he realized he had company in the darkroom, his expression was priceless.

Surprised and, yes, annoyed.

"What's this about?" he asked.

It was funny. The man's tone of voice was peevish. As if he was trying to get rid of some salesman on his doorstep.

"What's this about?"

Bam.

Blood gushed from a hole in Doc's forehead. And the man still didn't get it.

Stupidly, he raised a tiny hand, seeking help from his very destroyer.

Bam, away went the condescending smile. Bam, bam, away went the nosy questions.

By the fourth shot, there was the purest most Heavenly silence.

Killing a second person wasn't in the original game plan. But when it had to be done, it had to be done. And it offered some unexpected benefits.

Virtually everything incriminating was hidden or put to good use.

Now, the killer had one more thing to destroy. It might have made a nice keepsake. But having it around would have been dangerous. And this was no time for sentiment.

Out came a matchbook with a plain white cover. Then the one-page single-spaced report from the Pennsylvania Board of Health Laboratory, signed by one John Segovian, obviously a relative.

Eventually, the police would find out the report's conclusions. But why make things easy?

The killer cleared away rocks, sticks, leaves, acorns and brush and set the report down on the sloping dirt.

With a snap, the match ignited. Its bulging flame

caught the corner of the paper and spread with an orange-and-blue fury.

In seconds, the page became engulfed. The flame ballooned as the page crumpled and curled in on itself, leaving behind nothing but smoky black ash.

Obliterated were the words reporting that Bradley A. Hansen Sr. didn't die of natural causes but was a victim of chronic arsenic poisoning.

CHAPTER NINETEEN

AT ABOUT THE SAME TIME, Mimi sat in a darkened conference room at the Chautauqua Police headquarters, five minutes from the darkroom, trying to get a grip.

She'd told her story twice already to a local cop and to the Chautauqua County Sheriff's deputy who happened to be closest to the Institution when she dialed 9-1-1 from a phone at Sadie J's.

While waiting to tell the story a third time to a detective, Lieutenant John Wilson, Mack's boss at the Sheriff's Department, Mimi blew her nose. She sipped some bitter lukewarm coffee someone had handed her.

And, when she saw Lieutenant Wilson, in the doorway, she vowed to try to learn as much from him as he learned from her.

"Hello?" Wilson called. "Mind if I come in, hon? And turn on some lights?"

"Fine."

A giant, maybe six-three or six-four, Wilson had to duck to get under a rolled-up movie screen at the entrance to the conference room where signs on the walls offered bicycle-safety tips.

When he flipped on lights, Mimi had the same impression she had the first time they'd met.

Aging lumberjack.

Tall and lanky, with leathery skin and sharp green eyes, Wilson wore his usual combination: sport jacket, tie and navy-blue dress slacks with heavy work boots.

"Sorry to meet again under these circumstances," Wilson said, taking a seat across from her. "No one deserves to die the way your friend did. Especially a man as fine as I hear he was."

Mimi, blinking back tears, thanked him for the kind words.

Using Mimi's own interview tactics, Wilson started with easy questions. About her friendship with Doc. About the events leading up to her finding Doc's body. About Doc's friends, potential enemies and routines.

"Who would have known that Doc would be working in the darkroom tonight?"

"Lots of people."

"Why is that?"

"Everyone at *The Daily*, or even anyone passing through, could easily have seen Doc's schedule. He posts it—*posted* it— on the bulletin board, first thing."

"Would the bulletin board be the only way someone could have found Doc?"

"No, not really," Mimi said. "Doc was a man of routines. He was usually in the darkroom in the late afternoon. Anyone who knew him or observed him, could have picked that up."

Wilson paused to scribble some notes in a small blue notebook with a sticker on the cover saying, "It's Best to Suspect the Worst."

"Were you the only one scheduled to meet Doc in the darkroom at six-thirty?"

"No," Mimi said. "My son, Jake, was going to meet us, too."

"And is that it? Just you and Jake?"

"No. Jake invited two friends to come along, too. Twins from Jamestown, B.J. and Bob Ryan."

Out of loyalty to Jake, Mimi didn't add that Jake's last-minute invitation to his buddies came over Mimi's strong objections.

"Do you know exactly where the Ryans live in Jamestown? Or have a phone number for them?"

"I don't. I know they live with their mother. But

I can't remember her name. Jake has their number. But I'll bet you could find one or both of the Ryans scooping ice cream at the Refectory. They're working there nearly every night."

After Wilson paused to review his notes, they moved on to questions Mimi had dreaded—about her and Doc's amateur murder investigation.

Wilson summarized accurately what she had told the other questioners about the effort.

"The other guys told me you and Doc were keeping things hush-hush. Is that right?"

"Yes."

"Can you tell me everyone who knew what you were up to?"

"I think just my son and Doc's son."

"Doc's son meaning the scientist who did the tests on the hairbrush?"

"Exactly."

"And no one else?"

"Jake must have told the Ryans. But I didn't tell anyone else."

"How about Doc?"

"I can't speak for him. But, he's generally very private, so I'd be surprised if he told anyone."

"How did you get the hairbrush?"

"I just took it from the Hansens' house."

"With no one, not even Mrs. Hansen, noticing?"

"That's what I thought."

As Mimi described snatching the brush, Wilson shook his head with obvious disapproval.

"This doesn't seem like the best time to scold you, young lady," he said. "After you just lost a dear friend and all. But it has to be said. You can't keep trying to do on your own what amounts to very dangerous police work. It's risky business. And look where it's gotten you."

Ouch.

Mimi had been blaming herself already for Doc's death, for dragging him into her investigation.

"We did try to bring in the police," she said, hating the defensiveness in her voice. "We—"

"I know all about the call to Mack. That's what I told the sheriff to keep him from filing obstruction-of-justice or other criminal charges against you for getting in our way again."

"Against *me*?"

"Yes, the sheriff was furious. And you've always been high on his shit list."

Wow.

Mimi had totally misjudged Sheriff Cunningham. She thought he was a straight shooter. And a fan of hers. And a man going nowhere.

Recalibrating, Mimi decided the sheriff was actually a liar. A gifted liar. So gifted that he, actually, might be destined for higher office.

"Call me if you think of anything else," Wilson said, obviously wrapping up while handing Mimi a business card. "Or hear anything. It's time to leave the police work to the professionals. No more free-lancing."

When Wilson closed his notebook and started to rise, Mimi stayed put.

"Can you tell me anything you've learned so far?"

Wilson narrowed his eyes, suspiciously.

"Just as an interested friend," she said. "Off the record? What you'd normally tell a victim's family?"

"I can't say much yet. Just what I told the Chautauqua officials at our earlier briefing. We believe that Doc was shot at close range at around 6 p.m. with a small-caliber weapon. And we believe we found that weapon, a sawed-off .22-caliber Remington pump-action rifle, under the sink of the men's room next door."

"Any suspects? Or thoughts on a motive?"

"Too early to say. But, of course, we're exploring any possible links between Doc's death and Brad Hansen's. And we're not ruling out the kinds of theories the powers-that-be in Chautauqua seem to prefer."

"Like?"

"That this was an aborted robbery or another crime

committed by an outsider. A non-Chautauquan who came onto the grounds, did the deed and fled."

"Was anything taken?"

"Not that we've found. But Doc had some pretty expensive equipment a robber might have come for. And then, for one reason or another, left behind when scared off."

"What do you think, *personally*?"

"I don't know, of course. But I'm never one for fancy theories. And I'm something of a romantic, I guess. Some guys are always playing the money angle, looking for a money motive. Me? I'm always looking for the love angle. And, in this case, that makes me want to take a closer look at the new Mrs. Hansen."

"Why?"

"Aside from the obvious?" he smirked. "That it's a pleasure to take a closer look at that dish?"

Mimi nodded.

"Every homicide it's worth looking at the spouse. But especially in a case of a wealthy older man who turns up poisoned to death shortly after he gets remarried. And shortly after the man changes his will—to cut out his children and make his sole beneficiary the hot new wife."

CHAPTER TWENTY

STEPPING OUT OF POLICE HEADQUARTERS, Mimi felt like she'd gotten off a treadmill.

Dizzy, she had to pause to get her bearings. It was much darker than when she'd gone inside. But the world, amazingly, was unchanged.

Crowds leaving the Old First Night program were laughing, talking and eating ice cream. Two guards stood silently outside the darkroom door. But there was no crime-scene tape or other sign announcing the horrors inside.

Chautauqua, obviously, wanted its nine-week show to go on.

Desperate to hear Jake's voice, she stopped at *The Daily*'s brightly lit office. After dashing up the steps and hurrying to her desk, she called home.

"How are you, sweetie?" she asked.

"I'm fine, Mom. How are you?"

"Not the best. It's all so awful and hard to . . . I'm done with the cops now. Have you eaten?"

"The cops fed me. Pizza from Andriaccio's. After they asked a million questions."

"Did they take you home?"

"Your old friend Mack drove me. He said you were being questioned in another room down the hall. And that I shouldn't worry, you were fine. He also told me to lock the door here and not let anyone in but you."

"Good advice. You following it?"

"So far."

"Good job."

"Did they catch the killer?"

"Not yet," Mimi said. "When did you get to the darkroom?"

"Around six-forty. I was running late."

"You didn't see anything awful did you?"

"No, the police were there and wouldn't let me in."

"How about your friends, the Ryans? Were they with you?"

"No, they were meeting me there. And I guess they were later than I was. I never saw them. Are you coming home?"

"After one more thing."

Mimi thought she'd do her one more thing, in writing. But, as she gathered her thoughts—to make a case that *The Daily* should let her lead an investigation into Doc's death—Wentworth showed up.

"Mimi?" he called from the doorway, obviously as surprised to see her as she was to see him. "I never expected you to . . . I'm so, very, very sorry."

As he approached, he looked like a wreck. As if he'd pulled an all-nighter at a hospital or an airport. His eyes were red and damp. His clothes were rumpled. His clip-on bow tie was askew.

When he reached Mimi, he looked like he might hug her. But, then, at the last minute he changed course and, awkwardly, just patted her hand.

"How are you holding up?

Mimi, feeling teary again, looked away.

"Not well. I . . ."

"I can't believe it myself," Wentworth said, sitting in the desk next to Mimi's. "I'd known Doc twenty years. Twenty years. The police asked me to come in and gather some of his work things for them. Files. Phone numbers. Schedules. And whatnot. But I can't seem to . . ."

When Wentworth started sobbing, he turned away and hid his face in a handkerchief.

"I'm sorry," he said, when he got a grip. "Excuse me."

"No need to apologize."

Mimi and Wentworth spent some time reminiscing about Doc and trading what they'd learned from Lieutenant Wilson.

Mimi waited for an opening to make her pitch.

But Wentworth, rambling on and on, seemed to be working up the courage to saying something, too.

What?

Mimi, diverted by speculating in her head, thought she heard Wentworth say something about "not wanting to trouble her" but "asking a small favor."

"What was that?" Mimi asked. "I'm sorry. I'm having a hard time concentrating."

Wentworth held her gaze.

"I know this isn't really the best time to be asking anything of you. But, well, I thought you'd be the best person for the job."

Was Wentworth a mind reader?

Could he possibly be asking Mimi the same thing she wanted to ask him? But would anyone call a murder investigation a "small" favor?

"Go ahead," Mimi said. "Ask me anything."

Wentworth removed his reading glasses and started

cleaning them and re-cleaning them, nervously, on his shirttail.

"Well," he said, "I was wondering if . . ."

"Yes?" Mimi asked.

"I was wondering if you'd, well, take over Doc's job of putting together the Old First Night photo retrospective?"

Mimi had to look away.

She felt, not just disappointed, but ridiculous.

Like someone expecting to be offered the job of running an office who, instead, gets asked to clean it.

"I can give you another week to get it together," Wentworth said, mistaking her hesitation for opposition. "I thought it wouldn't be too tough since Doc, supposedly, was almost through. And the Administration has given us until the season ends. Which isn't until August twenty-fourth. Waddya say?"

"Of course, I'll do it," Mimi said. "I see it as a way to honor Doc's memory. To showcase his work. He was really a great photographer."

Wentworth handed Mimi two very fat accordion files that she set down next to her desk on the floor.

When Wentworth started thanking her profusely, she held up her hand.

"I wondered if I could ask you a favor, too?"

"Sure, go ahead."

Mimi coached herself: Stick to the high road. Appeal to logic not emotion. Make a dispassionate case for justice and the greater good. Not some personal need to assuage her own guilt.

"I wondered if you'd let me lead an investigation for *The Daily* into Doc's death?" she began. "See what we can see to help the police?"

"An investigation?"

"Yes, an investigation," Mimi said. "For maybe a week or two? I have some expertise in this kind of thing. And, I think it's, well, the right thing to do, for one of our own?"

When Wentworth started shaking his head, Mimi felt crushed. Then angry. Then desperate.

"And, well, I'm feeling responsible. Personally responsible. I don't know if I could live with myself if I didn't do all I could to help track down the sonovabitch who . . . I need to do it. I need to do it for Doc and for myself."

When Mimi's voice shook with emotion, she stopped.

So much for the high road.

"Mimi, I've lived a little longer than you have," Wentworth said. "And trust me on this. Your guilt isn't rational. It may feel real now. Give it time. You'll see it's part of the grieving process. No matter what you think you've done, or not done, you are not responsible for the actions of some madman. You're not. Our best response at *The Daily* is to do all we can to cooperate with the police. There's no reason for emotion to turn us into vigilantes."

Mimi knew Wentworth sounded more reasonable than she did. But she couldn't help herself.

"I'm not proposing that we go out, find the killer and hang him from the nearest lamppost in Bestor Plaza. I'm just talking about doing a little investigating. To see if there's anything we could turn up that the police can't. To help them ... "

Wentworth's expression hardened.

"I'm sorry, Mimi. We can't. We're not that kind of a newspaper."

"How about if we make my investigation unofficial?" Mimi begged. "You just show me what you're showing the police? And maybe a few other things? Maybe I just take a few days off? No one needs to know why. And I come back, say, Friday?"

Wentworth looked at Mimi with tremendous pity.

"I'm sorry," he said. "Take tomorrow off, for yourself. Beyond that, let's talk. I need you to do your job and fill the sports pages."

Chapter Twenty-One

At the other end of Chautauqua, B. J. Ryan jumped effortlessly from the cracked white entrance block to Dead Man's Cave.

Reaching into the shallow gray water, stirring up mud and water striders, he extracted two beers.

"Ice cold for your drinking pleasure," he said, smiling, while handing one Bud to his twin brother Bob Ryan.

"What are you so happy about?" Bob asked.

"It's so un-fucking-believable," B.J. said while wiping his hands on his jeans. "Two murders on the Grounds of the historic Chautauqua Institution."

He said the last three words—*historic Chautauqua Institution*—the way he always said them.

With a pretentious Masterpiece Theater-like British accent.

"Didn't you think nothing would ever happen here?" B.J. asked, after opening his beer and taking a long sip. "Spending the summer with a bunch of old farts? And preachers and teachers?"

Bob stared, appalled.

"This is too cool to believe," B.J. continued. "A murder mystery—no, make that two murder mysteries—on the grounds of the historic Chautauqua Institution."

Again, he put on the British accent and cracked himself up.

When Bob glowered, B.J. set down his beer. Unlaced his backpack. Removed his CD player. Flipped it on and the words of Tupac Shakur, the dead rapper poet, rocked the sugar maples, birches and hemlocks around them.

After finishing one beer, B.J. grabbed a second and pushed replay.

This time, he rapped along with Tupac, karaoke-style, with gangsta moves and poses.

"Dear Mama, I'm caught up in this sickness," B.J. claimed while pantomiming regret, hand over his heart. "Don't wanna commit murder, but damn they got me trapped. Hawkin' while I'm walkin' and talkin' behind my back."

For the chorus, B.J. strutted or crouched, pretending to fire two Wild West six-shooters.

"Big finish," he yelled, waving for his brother to join him.

Bob shook his head.

"Bye-bye, and I got no place to go," B.J. rapped. "Where they find me? Sixteen on Death Row."

When the song ended, B.J., giggling, turned the CD player off, took a bow and sat next to Bob.

When they were kids, the Ryan twins looked more identical. Especially when their mom dressed them alike.

Of course, they still had the same features—lean frames, blond hair, blue eyes, straight noses, full lips.

But their looks were re-shaped by their near-opposite personalities.

B.J., a gym rat, was more buff and hip. Besides the longer hair and earrings, he typically wore baggy jeans with some kind of black T-shirt, bandana and a smirk.

Bob was skinnier. More fidgety. More conventional in style. wearing his hair short, usually with a baseball cap and T-shirt with a sports-team logo. His default expression was a wide-eyed look of startled panic.

"What's the matter with you?" Bob asked.

Without the music, the place seemed remarkably

silent. A faint wind rustled some trees. A bike rumbled over the closest span known as Thunder Bridge.

"What's the matter with *you*, bro?" B.J. asked.

"I told you, I think we should call a lawyer," Bob said. "The cops spent way too much time talking to us. And, the more I think about it, the more, I don't like the tone of their questions."

"Then stop thinking about it."

"I can't."

"The cops want to scare us. It's their job."

"They've only scared me."

"That's because you're an old lady. You worry way too much. The cops probably spent a lot of time with everyone because this is a big fucking case. It's not every day a doctor gets his brains blown out in the historic Chautauqua Institution."

Same accent, same snickering result.

"I'm worried about your attitude," Bob said. "And some of the things you told the cops without even thinking."

"Like what?"

"Like when you said we went together to Old First Night during our dinner break at work. I didn't see you there until later."

"So what? I forgot. Is that a big deal?"

"How about volunteering your criminal record?"

"Pot, criminal mischief. So what? I got both YO'ed," he said of the lenient youthful-offender dispositions he got.

"Mention any problems and they start looking at you funny."

"Leave me the fuck alone, bro. Are you the only genius around here?"

B.J. hoisted himself like a gymnast back up on the rock. Straddling it, he took out a pack of unfiltered Camels and a purple Zippo lighter. When he thumbed the switch, the flame illuminated his bemused expression.

"You never should have given them permission to search the apartment," Bob said.

"Would you get off my case? Are you my fucking mother?"

B.J. took a long drag on his cigarette.

"I'm just telling you to stop treating this like a game," Bob said. "It's not. They shouldn't be going through our things."

"I'll tell you what I told the cops," B.J. said. "I told 'em, 'You wanna waste your time, that's your business. I've got nothing to hide.'"

Chapter Twenty-Two

Not far away, sitting in front of his TV, Mole also replayed his interview with the cops. But he replayed it alone. And his regret was singular: that he couldn't stop thinking, not about any particular questions or answers, but about the deaths themselves.

The end of two lives of men close to his own age.

Mole would be seventy in October. Seven years younger than the doctor. And two years older than his brother Brad.

Over and over, Mole told himself no good would come from dwelling.

He flipped through channels on the TV—baseball, some silly sitcom, news, more baseball. He waited for something to grab his attention.

Nothing.

What Mole needed, he knew, was activity, any activity to keep his mind from heading where it shouldn't.

At ten-thirty, he made himself get up and go outside. He headed straight for the dark musty utility shed behind his 12 Park.

He turned on the light. Slipped his giant aching frame into his green work suit. Traded sneakers for muddy boots.

Then he put on gloves and dragged plant food, clippers and a plastic bag over to his precious rose bushes.

As he lowered himself to the ground, he felt shooting pains in his back and legs. He was exhausted.

He should have taken the golf cart to and from the Old First Night program. All the walking and stress were getting to him.

But, at the same time, he didn't want to baby himself. And get any weaker.

Mole sighed.

Getting old, he thought, wasn't pretty. But it sure beat the hell out of the alternative.

He chuckled.

Beats the alternative, no question.

On the damp ground, Mole pushed aside some wood chips. Using a rusty spoon, he spread crumbly white rose food at the base of his bushes.

When he rose with some difficulty, he sensed someone nearby.

"Good evening, Mole."

It was Francine, dressed—or maybe he should say, barely dressed—in a red robe and high-heeled red slippers. She held a trash bag in one hand and a tall amber-colored drink, maybe bourbon, in the other.

As Francine dumped her trash in a can and clanked the lid shut, Mole tried not to stare.

Francine was a beautiful woman. And she knew it, standing in the moonlight with her breasts peeking out of her robe. If you could call it a robe. It was more like an undershirt barely reaching the top of Francine's thighs.

And who puts on makeup to take out the trash? Francine's lips were definitely extra red, her lashes extra black around her doe-like eyes.

When Francine fluffed her thick black hair, obviously preening, Mole glanced away.

He never liked this kind of woman.

"I didn't realize I had company," she said.

Mole, ignoring her, returned to his own business. He flipped on the spigot next to the house. Then he uncoiled the hose lying there. He dragged it past his hostas, hollyhocks, cosmos and day lilies, back to his roses.

"Won't you stay and talk a little?" Francine asked. "The news is so unbelievable. I almost need to say it out loud to believe it. Brad was poisoned to death. The doctor shot dead. It's too much too absorb."

As Francine sipped her drink, Mole watered around his roses. When he finished, he walked the hose back to where he'd found it and turned off the spigot.

When he returned to the rose bush, this time Francine followed.

"Did you get the same detective?" she asked. "A Lieutenant Wilson? The man was a sphinx. He kept asking question after question without revealing a thing."

Francine took another sip.

"No, he was worse than a sphinx," she said. "He was a fighter pilot and I was his target. That's what it felt like. He kept dropping bombshells—the poisoning, the shooting—and the man said almost nothing. Not a peep. Worse than you, Mole."

Francine giggled. When her giggles turned into sobs, she forced down more of her drink as if it was some kind of medicine. Then, reaching in her robe pocket, she pulled out a Kleenex and blew her nose.

"I'm sorry," she said. "I'm having a hard time keeping my grip."

Mole, sick of her trying to draw him in, focused on

surveying his prickly hedges for the most beautiful rose blooms.

When one caught his eye, he leaned close. He inhaled. And fingered the softness of the flower's red folds within folds.

Perfect.

Mole clipped the stem below a cluster of five leaflets and dropped the prize into his plastic bag.

As he repeated the process, he sensed Francine drawing nearer still. He smelled her citrusy perfume, heard the rattle of ice cubes in her glass.

When he looked down, he saw a thin gold chain embracing a perfectly formed ankle, tiny red toenails perched like rubies on the slipper ledge.

"Couldn't the poisoning have been an accident?" Francine asked. "That's what I'm wondering. A tragic accident like Legionnaire's Disease? Isn't that possible?"

When Mole still didn't respond, Francine, wobbly on her heels, raised her voice.

"Isn't it possible? Isn't it? I just need an answer, Mole. Please?"

"W-w-w-what you need is some coffee to sober up," Mole said.

Francine giggled. And, as she did, her robe loosened to reveal more of her full breasts and black lace panties.

"Whoops," she said, turning away to get herself

together. "The mysterious older brother speaks. And it leads to my undoing."

Francine, turning back, cinched her belt tight around her thin waist.

"Oh, my," she said. "I'm sorry. You know your flowers are beautiful, Mole."

"Th-th-thanks."

"Are you making a bouquet?"

Mole nodded and continued his methodical work of finding a bloom, sniffing and snipping it and moving on.

"I didn't know you cared so much for my dear husband."

Mole, sorry he'd given Francine any encouragement, just shook his head.

"So if you didn't care for him, why the wreath?" Francine asked.

When Mole's eyes, betraying him, filled with tears, he looked away.

"A t-t-t-ribute you w-w-wouldn't understand."

Chapter Twenty-Three

Next door, Evangeline Warren set her binoculars down on the coffee table next to the worn leather family Bibles.

"What do you think they're talking about?" Evangeline asked.

"It's none of our business," Philomena said. "It isn't."

Without the binoculars, Evangeline continued to stare through a peephole she created by stretching two Venetian blind slats between her bony thumb and forefinger.

"And it's shameful your watching," Philomena continued. "Watching and yet getting on your high horse lecturing people about morals all the time. And —"

"I'm not watching anyone who doesn't expect to

be watched. They're not indoors. They're outside for thirty minutes in an open yard."

"More like fifteen."

Evangeline, scowling, shuffled to the corner of the room. She leaned her cane under the shelf with a walnut clock and antique spoon collection, next to the sisters' latest acquisition: an Amish quilt, with a yellow-and-blue sunburst pattern.

Then she turned, full glare, on her sister.

"I don't know why I listen to a thing you say," Evangeline said. "Or why anyone should. When you're with us, what, half the time? The other half you're gaga, confused, and still you refuse to see a doctor."

"I was wondering how long it would take for you to bring that up."

"I will bring it up as often as I need to," Evangeline said. "The situation is getting out of hand."

Philomena, seated on the couch, reached down for Ezekial, her favorite cat. She pulled the green-eyed tabby into her lap and addressed him.

"There, there, Zeke," Philomena said while stroking his back. "Good boy."

"I won't drop it," Evangeline said, clearing away some throw pillows with needlepoint covers before sitting beside her sister. "I'm worried about you. I think we should move up our appointment with Dr. Abernathy and see him this week. Or, at least call."

"We usually go in October," Philomena said. "That's soon enough."

"Aren't you the least bit concerned? You couldn't even tell the detective how you spent your night. I had to say you were with me. But where were you?"

Philomena, silent, kept stroking the cat.

"A killer could be loose on the grounds and you don't even know where you were," Evangeline said. "I'm worried about you."

"I was walking for some of the time," Philomena said. "I know that. I found myself at one point on Center Street. In front of what used to be the Aldens' place at twenty-six."

"Where we stayed as girls?"

"Exactly. It's canary-yellow now. Used to be white with green shutters. Remember the iceman who used to come to us there? Tall and thin with a big Adam's apple?"

"Like Ichabod Crane."

"Exactly," Philomena said. "I think he was as tall as Mole or that detective tonight. He'd go up and down the narrow streets in his wagon yelling, 'Iceman. Iceman.'"

Philomena's face lit up with the memory.

"This was seventy years ago," Evangeline said.

"I know. But I stood there picturing it. As clear as if it was yesterday. I was thinking about how he'd stop at our place. And all the children in the neighborhood would come running. He'd check the order card in the front window. He'd cut the right-sized piece of ice. And he'd head for the icebox behind the house with his giant tongs. And then—"

"Where are you headed with this?" Evangeline asked, exasperated. "Listen to yourself. You're in some La-La Land. You've got to try to keep your mind in the present. Please. Work at it. You scare me with all this reminiscing. I don't think it's healthy. Can I get you some tea?"

Philomena, lost in thought, chuckled.

"When the iceman would walk to the back of the house with his tongs, that's when you'd shoot me this look."

"What look?" Evangeline asked.

"I was thinking about how you still do it," Philomena said. "How you still give me the same look."

"What look?"

"The look that says, 'I'm too scared, but you do it. please' It's all in your eyes. Your eyes told me, 'Hurry, hurry, hurry; get to the truck and scrape off two ice chunks for both of us to suck on before the iceman returns and anyone gets caught.' Remember?"

Evangeline didn't answer.

"Remember?" Philomena pressed.

"Nonsense," Evangeline said. "But that doesn't explain how you spent the whole night tonight."

"Don't worry about it. I caught up with you at Old First Night in time to enjoy your favorite part, Vesper. And my favorite part, the drooping lilies."

"You say you enjoy the lilies," Evangeline said. "But you have a funny way of showing it. Crying through the whole thing."

"I'm always emotional at that part," Philomena said. "I can't help myself. When I see all of those white handkerchiefs in the dark. And the announcer says, 'Raise and lower your lilies—"

"*Reverently* raise and lower your lilies," Evangeline corrected. "That's how he says it, '*Reverently* raise and lower your lilies'."

"That's right. '*Reverently* raise and lower your lilies to honor all departed Chautauquans.' It's too much for me," Philomena said. "Remembering. The tears won't stop."

"Sister," Evangeline said. "It's been a terrible few days. The news is awful. It makes me feel like I've lived too long. The pure evil of it. Until they catch someone, I think we should stick together or stay home. The whole thing scares me."

Philomena laughed strangely.

"What?" Evangeline asked.

"I don't think we need to be scared."

"And why is that?"

"Don't we both know in our hearts, the killings weren't random?" Philomena asked.

"I suppose we do."

Chapter Twenty-Four

At ten-thirty, Mimi realized there's no way she was going to sleep. And that, in her dazed state, she'd left the files with Doc's photos for the retrospective at *The Daily* office.

So, after making sure Jake was asleep—which he was—she stepped outside, and planned to take the lakeside route back to the office.

She made it to the corner of Fletcher and South. Then she froze. Looking down the street toward the lake, a shadow at the bottom near Heinz Beach spooked Mimi. It looked like a person, lying in wait.

Mimi stared.

And no matter how many times she told herself the shadow was probably a bush—*most likely* a bush—*almost definitely* a bush—she was unconvinced. And she couldn't move.

When the bell tower chimed ten-forty-five, Mimi told herself she couldn't stay there all night.

She could:

A) Talk herself out of her fears and continue past the shadow to *The Daily*.

B) Power through her fears (a la Jake's "Fake it 'til you make it" philosophy) past the shadow, to *The Daily*.

Or C) Avoid her fears altogether and take a different route.

Choosing C, she headed briskly up South, away from the lake, turning right onto Clark.

When she continued past the Hall of Philosophy, to the car- and bike-free redbrick path leading to the Amphitheater and Bestor Plaza, and saw two cops at both ends, she started to relax.

And refocus.

Who the hell would want to kill Doc? The whole thing seemed so unreal. And horrific.

The only plausible suspect Mimi could think of would be whoever it was that killed Brad Hansen—IF they considered Doc a threat. But why would they?

When Mimi reached Bestor Plaza it was still busy, loaded with teens hanging out and families lingering over ice cream.

All the lights were still on at *The Daily* offices. Mimi, while bounding up stairs, heard chatter and laughter. And the music of the teens from the *Corry* (Pennsylvania) *Journal*, who worked nights, pasting up *The Chautauquan Daily*, before driving the pages to their printing plant.

When she entered the newsroom, the teens, a boy and a girl, stared, guiltily, at her then each other.

"We're, uh, sorry about your friend, the doctor," the girl said, while turning down their music. "Very sorry."

She glanced at the boy.

When he didn't say anything, she added: "Jared's sorry, too. He's just shy."

"Yeah, I am, uh, sorry, too."

"Thanks," Mimi said. "I'm just, well, here to pick up something I forgot. Go ahead and do what you have to do."

When the teens, obviously relieved, returned to their work, Mimi saw the two fat accordion file folders of Doc's Old First Night photos exactly where she'd left them, next to her desk.

She could have grabbed them and gone home. But, not eager to leave, she started browsing.

Doc, an incredible neatnik, naturally had everything extremely well organized. The photos were segregated in separate envelopes by era. Post-its gave caption and photo credit information. If the photos were borrowed, also attached were stamped envelopes addressed to their owners for their return.

Flipping through the photos felt like a refresher course in Chautauqua history.

The earliest photos featured founders Miller and Vincent in frock coats and Rip Van Winkle-like beards before earnest-looking gatherings at Chautauqua's first tent retreats.

In one photo, Miller and Vincent celebrated Chautauqua's Old First Night birthday in front of a barge ablaze with light on the silvery lake. In another, they stood near hundreds of Japanese lanterns on the ground or hanging cocoon-like from trees in Miller Park.

In a later Depression-era shot, the Chautauqua president at the time, Arthur Bestor, stood on the Amp stage, waving a dollar bill to inspire contributions to save the near-bankrupt Institution.

This Chautauqua survived, barely.

But hundreds of spin-off "daughter Chautauquas"—that brought great speakers like William Jennings Bryant and great entertainment to remote places, mainly out west—died in the 1920s. Victims, according to the history books, of the Next Big Things: the advent of the automobile, movies and radio that brought entertainment closer to home.

A comeback here in the eighties was evident in Doc's recent photos of Old First Nights with extravagant multi-tiered birthday cakes. Kids releasing multi-colored balloons. And the head usher wearing a wicker collection basket on his head, again, trying to encourage contributions.

Some of the best photos, as Doc had said, were from the Old First Night celebration in 1945.

Many reminded Mimi of the sheer joy in the famous photo of a sailor upending a girl as they kissed in Times Square upon hearing the news of the Allies' victory.

Taken by Doc, there were shots of: a young solder in Army fatigues pumping his fist in triumph from the Amp's front row; a tall young man hugging a redhead in the aisles; the Chautauqua Symphony Orchestra conductor waving his baton with verve; and young children, standing on their seats, howling with joy.

Apparently, Doc had finished all of the caption work he'd been dreading. All Mimi had to do was make her final choices for the retrospective, lay them out and retype Doc's words.

When Mimi reached the last envelope in Doc's file, she expected more photos.

But, instead, she found odds and ends, mostly pages printed out from Doc's computer.

Maybe Doc had left the items. Or maybe they were a set of what Wentworth had made for the police. And maybe, having second thoughts, Wentworth had left them for Mimi.

Either way, a once-over left Mimi thinking the items fell roughly into three categories.

The first set, held together with a rubber band, included fifteen pages of phone numbers that looked like they had been printed out from Doc's computer.

The second set was a collection of Doc's recent schedules from the bulletin board. Yesterday's showed his typical hectic pace:

Monday, Aug. 4, 1997
8:30 Darkroom
9:30 Staff meeting
10:30 Mimi coffee
10:45 Backup for Morning Good and Evil Lecture, Houston Amp
11:30 Opera, Dress Rehearsal, Norton Hall
12:45 Children's School, Old First Night Bake Sale, Bestor Plaza
1 New Yacht Club officers, outside Sports Club
3 Men's Tennis Champ, Doug Reynolds, Main Courts

5–7 Print Photos, finish OFN captions, darkroom

The third group was the most intriguing.

It printed out a file that Doc had labeled SUSPECTS.

A file that seemed to be Doc's personal views on anyone who, conceivably, could have killed Brad Hansen.

It included some things Mimi already knew and random thoughts Mimi was surprised Doc would have left in his computer.

The file began with a general statement.

"Poisoning," Doc wrote. "Is a crime of cunning; an intimate or household crime; requires high degree of knowledge; 3 to 6 percent of homicide cases."

Below that, Doc included his thoughts on potential motives, as well as the means and opportunity available to a list of potential suspects.

No. 1 for him—as it was for Lieutenant Wilson—was Francine Hansen, Brad's widow.

Doc noted that she was in her forties and had married Brad in May. Next to motive, Doc was blunt. He typed $$$. Elaborating, he added, "inherits houses worth $1M and carpet biz worth $6M."

After the letters m and o for means and opportunity, Doc wrote: "Plenty, close to BH's food and drink, educated former teacher."

Mimi agreed with much of Doc's analysis. But she wondered if suspicions, even reasonable suspicions against Francine—as opposed to real proof—would make her want to kill him.

Also if Francine were the type to poison someone, would she also be the type to kill with a sawed-off rifle? A modern-day Annie Oakley? Or was it sexist to think her incapable?

No. 2 on Doc's list was Brad Hansen's kids, Mary Hansen and Brad Jr.

Doc thought each kid was in their thirties. For motive, he wrote: "Cut out of will. Knew it? Past feuds."

Only Mary, according to Doc, had means and opportunity, since she lived on the Chautauqua grounds as a member of the Chautauqua Symphony Orchestra.

Brad Jr., he noted, would have needed a partner because on Saturday he told police he was in Manhattan, ten hours away (by car) or three hours (by plane plus a car ride from Buffalo airport).

Both children, Doc added, "have sufficient education to be poisoners."

But would they be the type to use a rifle? Mimi wondered. What was the type?

If Doc had more proof either Hansen killed their dad, how would they even know it? As far as Mimi knew, Doc had never met either Mary Hansen or Brad Jr.

No. 3 on the list was Millard "Mole" Hansen, Brad's brother, who was seventy.

His motive, according to Doc, was "past differences." His m & o, Doc wrote were: "strong, access to poisons and BH's food. Expertise as a gardener makes him well-acquainted with toxic pesticides."

To Mimi, Mole seemed so detached from people, it was tough to imagine him getting worked up enough to kill two. On the other hand, far more than anyone else Mole fit Mimi's view of someone who might be comfortable with a rifle.

The rest of Doc's list was incomplete. He included the names of all of the other Hansen tenants who might have had access to Brad Hansen's food.

Next to her name and Jake's, Doc wrote: "Where were Jake and his friends before the race?"

Next to Evangeline and Philomena Warren and Violet Greenwood, Doc wrote nothing.

Maybe he had nothing to say. Or hadn't gotten around to writing anything.

Next to Betsy Gates, Doc had an intriguing entry: "Return her call some time on Tuesday."

Chapter Twenty-Five

MIMI, GENERALLY A RULE-ABIDING GOODY-GOODY, was feeling unmoored. In the past few days, she'd broken a dizzying number of rules—maybe even laws—by lying, snooping and stealing.

So, though a fervent believer in not calling people after ten o'clock at night, she grabbed the phone. And she dialed Betsy Gates.

After a few rings, a groggy voice answered.

"Uh, hello."

"Hello, Betsy?"

Silence.

"Betsy?"

"Uh, yeah. Who's this? Who's calling?"

"Sorry to call so late," Mimi lied. "It's Mimi Goldman, your neighbor. Sounds like I may have woken you. Should I call you back tomorrow?"

"Oh, no," Betsy said. "No, no. Just give me a sec to splash some water on my face."

Betsy set down the phone and returned maybe two minutes later.

"Mimi, hey, how are you?"

Betsy's transformation—from dull sleepyhead to her usual perky self—was amazing.

"Fine, fine," Mimi said. "Like I said, I'm sorry to be calling so late."

"Please, don't give it another thought. It's not even eleven. I got the baby down. My husband's asleep, too. And I must have just dozed off on the couch. In fact, I think I should thank you. Now I won't wake up tomorrow in my clothes, without washing my face or brushing my teeth."

Mimi was glad to be let off the hook.

But, really, Betsy was too much—in her Pollyanna search for the bright side.

Would she thank a robber for lightening her load? Or a driver who injured her in a crash for getting her time off work to recuperate?

"What can I do for you?"

Mimi, who did best sticking close to the truth, said that her boss at *The Daily* had asked her to take over some of Doc's responsibilities. She said she had, as a result, been going through his things.

"I saw a notation he'd made to remind himself to call you today," she said. "I wanted to follow up. To be sure we don't miss something that needs immediate attention. Do you know why Doc made a note to call you today? Why was he calling?"

"You're amazing," Betsy said. "How do you do it? Keeping your focus, going to work after so much tragedy? I can barely keep my wits about me. Maybe falling asleep is my body's way of saying, 'Too much. I can't cope. Must shut down.'"

Betsy laughed again.

Mimi said she didn't see much choice for her. She was just doing her job, fulfilling her duties as an employee of a six-day-a-week newspaper. She might have preferred suspending publication for some kind of mourning period. But it wasn't up to her.

"So why was Doc calling you?" Mimi asked.

Betsy grew quiet.

"I guess I can tell you now that he's gone. And you're such a close friend and all."

"That?"

"You might not believe it," Betsy said. "But even before the police realized that Brad Hansen was poisoned, Doc suspected it. He swore me to secrecy. But he said he was conducting something of his own investigation into the death."

"Really?" Mimi asked.

Feigning surprise wasn't that tough because Mimi was genuinely surprised Doc had confided in Betsy. Who else might have known what he was up to?

"Really," Betsy continued. "The man was brilliant. He must have been a wonderful doctor. He recognized the signs. I'm a nurse, you know, and I didn't see it. Brad hadn't been well. He wasn't young. So I just figured it was, like the EMS people said, a heart attack."

"So why was he calling you?"

This was the third time Mimi had to ask.

"Well, this is something I'd rather you keep between us. I didn't even mention it to the police when they interviewed me earlier. I guess I could have. But, at the time, it seemed like I'd be breaking a confidence."

"I won't mention any of this to anyone."

"Doc said he was kind of suspecting Francine."

"As the killer?"

"Yes. Don't be surprised," Betsy said. "It's terrible to say. But most people around here are probably thinking the same thing. Even if they don't say it aloud. Doc asked if I could help him by finding more about Francine. Like where she's from. What kind of teacher she was. Where. Past marriages. Family. That kind of thing."

"And?"

"I was flattered to help."

"Did he ask you because you have any special knowledge about the Hansens?"

"No," Betsy said. "Oh, no. I just met them both in June when I answered their ad to rent this place for weeks seven through nine of the season. Maybe Doc thought I'd have luck, asking Francine things woman to woman. Or he felt comfortable asking me since we are—were—both health-care professionals."

"Did you find anything?"

"Very little. Doc never called me back. But, if he had, I'd have had little to report. I found out that Francine was a teacher originally from Indianapolis. She moved to this area, to western New York, last year. I think in July. To sell real estate. I know she was married at least once before but was either widowed or divorced. I'm not sure. Before teaching, this might not surprise you, Francine had a brief career on the stage. She certainly has the looks for it. As far as what she was doing most recently, before moving here, I couldn't find out myself. And Francine, when I tried asking her, wasn't forthcoming."

"Do you know if Doc shared his suspicions with anyone besides you?"

"I don't think so."

"Do you know if Francine knew about them?"

"I really doubt it."

"So you didn't tell her?"

"Absolutely not."

"Did you tell anyone else about what Doc was doing?"

"No."

When Mimi hung up, she left a note for her boss, Wentworth. Unsure if he had left her Doc's papers intentionally or if they were just in the file, she thanked him for giving her the next day, Wednesday, off.

"I'll check in," she wrote. "After Brad Hansen's funeral."

Chapter Twenty-Six

The ten o'clock funeral the next morning really tried Mimi's patience.

From her seat in the middle of the Hall of Philosophy, she could barely stand anything about the Reverend Franklin Johnson, the minister officiating.

Mimi hated his shiny suit. Two last-names name. Phony toothy smile. And his bs over-the-top eulogy, calling Brad Hansen a "war hero, a great industrialist, a great husband, a great father and a great man."

Was this guy serious?

To hide her disgust, Mimi put on her mirrored shades. She scrutinized the funeral program, starting with the cover that said, "Service of Remembrance. Bradley A. Hansen, 1929–1997."

She looked around.

Francine was front and center, in a black dress and veil, next to the Warren sisters. Behind them were Betsy Gates and Violet Greenwood, a seat apart, and, at the far end of the second row, Mole Hansen.

Brad Hansen's children, who had agreed to talk to Mimi after the funeral, were seated in the last row in the back.

Jake was, thank goodness, where he said he'd be, snapping dozens of photos along with the media, corralled behind a barrier, on the lawn of the Hall of Missions.

Any time Mimi felt herself drifting, she forced herself to read along with Rev. Johnson in the worn black prayer book she found at her pew.

"Let not your heart be troubled: ye believe in God, believe also in me," she whispered. "In my Father's house are many mansions: if it were not so, I would have told you. I go to prepare a place for you."

When Mimi glanced around the Hall again, she noticed far in the back, behind the Hansen children, were—holy crap—Mack and Lieutenant Wilson.

Mack and Mimi's eyes met.

And held.

For maybe five minutes, the two of them just stared at each other, smiling.

Mimi looked away first to join in singing the final hymn:

When peace like a river attendeth my way
When sorrows like sea billows roll
Whatever my lot thou has taught me to say,
It is well, it is well, with my soul

When the hymn ended, she turned around again. But, this time, Mack and Lieutenant Wilson were gone.

As planned, Mimi hung back, waiting for Jake in her seat. When he showed up, she gave him a long hug and, together, they left the mostly empty chapel.

"We don't have to go to the cemetery, do we?" Jake asked.

"Not if you got all the photos I asked for?"

"I did."

"Then, we're fine. We don't have to go."

A van taking people to the cemetery was idling nearby on Cookman Street.

Francine, flanked by Betsy Gates and another woman, was heading for the van. She walked past Jake and Mimi, apparently not noticing them—until the last minute.

"Before I get on the bus," she said, wheeling to face Mimi. "I want to have a word with you, young lady. I have one serious bone to pick."

When Mimi gestured for Jake to get lost, he did.

And Betsy Gates and Francine's other escort, also scattered.

"What's the matter, Francine? The last thing you need on a day like this is to be angry with someone," Mimi said. "What's wrong?"

"I don't mean to speak ill of the dead. But, from what I hear, you and that friend of yours, Doc, were behind some awful whispering campaign that suggests that . . ."

"That what?"

"That I killed my husband," Francine sputtered. "I don't know why you would want to torment me like this. And I want this to stop. NOW."

Mimi, trying to calm Francine down, put an arm around her shoulder.

"Believe me, Francine, we were doing no such thing," she said. "Doc and I were asked by our boss to do some discreet investigating. And consider every possible angle. And theory. And suspect. Neither of us got far enough to narrow it down to a particular suspect. Not you. Or anyone."

When Francine looked skeptical, Mimi continued.

"If you're feeling singled out, I hate to say it, but it's the normal course of gossip in a small town. You might not want to hear it. But whenever there's a homicide, the first suspect is the spouse. Especially when there's a substantial inheritance. And especially when the spouse is an outsider."

Betsy Gates, who'd stepped away, was returning.

"I'm sorry Francine," she called. "But we've gotta go."

"One minute," Francine said. "Please. One minute for me to speak with Mimi, alone."

Betsy re-crossed to the van.

"If you have any questions about me, I'd appreciate it if you asked me directly, instead of skulking around my back," Francine said.

"I have no problem with that," Mimi said. "How about tomorrow?"

"Give me a call."

Mimi, skeptical of Francine's sincerity, tried to keep this conversation going.

"For now, can I ask you one more very quick thing?"

"Go ahead. Then I've really gotta get on the van."

"Okay," Mimi said, recounting how she had encountered B.J. Ryan at Francine's when she came to see about the grocery shopping.

"He was in your living room and—"

"He told you some crazy story about being there to help me move some furniture?" Francine asked.

"Yes. The story wasn't true?"

"No. I'll tell you why he was there. But I trust you'll keep this between us?'

"You have my word."

"I'm tutoring him for the SATs," Francine said. "I've been giving him test-taking strategies, vocabulary lists, math drills, practice tests. You know I was a teacher?"

Mimi nodded.

"Sometimes when I'm not home B.J. comes and takes practice tests on Brad's computer upstairs."

"What's the big secret?"

"It's a teenage thing. B.J. wants to be the first in his family to go to college. But I guess it's not cool at his age to look like you're trying."

Chapter Twenty-Seven

BRAD HANSEN JR., who was supposed to meet Mimi at three on the Athenaeum porch, was nearly an hour late. But waiting for Brad at a linen-covered table with a single rose centerpiece overlooking the lake, Mimi had to admit, wasn't too tough.

The rain had stopped. So she could enjoy watching activities resume on the lake that, hours earlier, had looked nearly as choppy as an ocean.

A few hardy kids were already in, swimming. Two sailboats, battling strong winds, tacked back and forth near the bell tower.

Mimi wondered why Francine had bothered to correct B.J.'s furniture-moving story. Was the new SAT-tutoring tale any more plausible?

She also wondered if Betsy Gates had given Doc

away? Or if Betsy was just so bad at snooping that Francine somehow guessed?

When a waiter offered to top off Mimi's coffee, she accepted. And, while sipping her millionth cup, she turned toward a flock of birds on a power line.

In one instant, they were sitting there in a row. In the next, obviously sensing danger, they scattered. Like black pepper specks in the gray sky.

"Sorry to be so late."

Mimi, over-caffeinated, startled at the sound of Brad Hansen Jr.'s voice.

"Hope I didn't hold you up long."

"No," Mimi lied. "I was late, too."

Brad Jr.'s girth, hidden in his mourning suit, was more obvious in the baggy khakis and striped polo shirt he'd changed into. And, in a word, he looked, well, red.

Given his red hair and oversized florid face.

"I'm very sorry about your dad," Mimi said. "It's terrible to lose a parent, even when the relationship is complicated."

"Thanks."

After a little more small talk, Mimi launched into her spiel about how *The Daily* was conducting its own investigation into the deaths of Brad's dad and *The Daily*'s photographer, Doc Segovian.

"We're hoping we might turn up something the police haven't or—"

"I was under the impression you were working with the police. And could tell us how things were going. They've cut us out of the loop."

"That's because there's little to report so far," Mimi bluffed. "I can assure you, though, they're pulling out all the stops. They've got virtually every officer in the region following leads. And our newspaper probe should, at a minimum, help hold their feet to the fire. And keep them honest."

Brad pulled a metal flask from his pocket, unscrewed the lid and tilted some of its contents into an empty juice glass.

"Sounds like a noble goal," he smirked. "Certainly one worth toasting. Care to join me?"

Mimi declined and wondered how much toasting Brad had already done that morning.

After they both ordered cheeseburger platters, Mimi got under way in earnest.

"At least to start, we're taking as a working assumption that the two deaths may be related. That maybe your dad's killer also killed Doc, too, to cover their tracks."

"Do the police think that, too?" Brad asked.

"It's certainly something they're considering."

"Among other things?"

"Yes," Mimi said. "They're casting a wide net. And we are, too. So I wondered, for starters, if you can think of anyone who might have wanted to see your father dead?"

Brad giggled.

"You're kidding, right?"

"No," Mimi said. "I'm not."

"Well, a lot of people, myself included at times, would have wanted to see him dead. But I'll tell you what I told the police. God's honest truth. I can't think of anyone who'd have the guts to actually do it. To kill him."

"What did you have against him?"

"Where to start?" he asked. "You'll probably hear this from everyone. Or maybe you saw it yourself. But my father was the No. 1 most self-centered person on earth. At all times, he had to be the most important person in the room. To achieve that, he was ruthless. He'd, well, crush the spirit of everyone close."

As Brad spoke, he wiped tears from his eyes.

"Sorry," he said. "I'm a big crybaby. I embarrass my wife all the time."

"Did your father succeed at crushing everyone's spirit?"

"Nearly. He couldn't hold my sister Mary down. She's tough. Fought him very step of the way. When she was eighteen, she ran off to music school in New York City and never looked back."

"How about you and your mom?"

"No contest," Brad said, after taking another sip.

"For both of you?"

He nodded.

"My mom especially. She was no match for him. It got worse in recent years, when my mom got sick, very sick. My dad didn't believe she was sick. Mary and I weren't home enough to judge the situation ourselves. My mom didn't want to complain long-distance and . . ."

Losing it again, Brad stopped and shook his head.

"I'm sorry," he said. "It's all . . . Anyway, by the time we came home last Christmas it was too late. When she went to the hospital in February, the doctors said the cancer had spread too far to operate. They just stitched her closed. And tried to make her as comfortable as they could."

Brad took another long sip of his drink as their order arrived.

"We failed her," Brad said. "And, I'll tell you, that still eats away at me most days."

"Did you blame your father?"

"I blamed myself more."

"Did you ever accuse him for his part in it?"

"I didn't."

"Did your sister?"

"Yes, they had a knock-down drag-out in the hospital. In front of mom. It was awful. After that, my mother made us promise we'd stop blaming and dwelling on 'what might have beens' and focus on her getting well. We promised we'd do that. Even though we all knew it was too late."

"I'm sorry. I understand she died in March. How old was she?"

"She would have been sixty-five on August second," he said aloud. "So she was sixty-four."

Mimi, mid-bite, set down her burger.

"So Saturday was your mom's birthday?"

"Yes."

"The very day your father died. What do you make of that?"

"Probably just an awful coincidence."

They both ate for a while in silence. Then Mimi, after reviewing her notes, decided to shift gears to ask Brad Jr. more about himself.

She learned that he was born and raised in Erie. That he was thirty-nine. That he had been an accomplished flutist who, after high school, considered following in Mary's footsteps and studying music in New York City.

"I chickened out," he said. "And went to SUNY-Buffalo, then law school."

After that, it sounded like most of Brad's decisions were made by Valerie, the Long Island plastic surgeon's daughter he had met and married in law school.

"We moved to Manhattan when Valerie got a job, a very prestigious job, at the U.S. Attorney's office," he said.

He cut back his own hours as in-house counsel to a contractor when Valerie got hired at a big law firm. He quit to become a full-time house-husband when Valerie was named the firm's first female litigation partner and they had two children.

"How old are the kids now?" Mimi asked.

"Jessica's ten. Amanda eight."

"How's life as a house-husband?"

"It's not for everyone," Brad said. "My father certainly never understood it. But I enjoy it. And it works well for my girls."

After the waitress cleared their plates, Mimi returned to more sensitive questions.

"What did you tell the police when they asked where you were Saturday, the day of the race?"

"The truth."

"Which is?"

"That I was in the city all day with the girls. Doing errands. Shopping. Birthday parties."

"Could anyone vouch for you?"

"Hey, what are you trying to do here?" Brad snapped. "You're not accusing me, are you?"

"Please don't take offense," Mimi said. "I'm just trying to be methodical. To rule people out. One by one. It's a standard procedure."

Brad didn't look mollified. But he said he'd get back to Mimi after giving the question some thought.

"Humor me," she continued. "And let me ask this. Did you leave anything for your father to eat or drink on Saturday?"

"No."

"Do you know of anyone who did?"

"No."

"When was the last time you saw or spoke to your father?"

"At my mom's funeral in March."

"Where were you Tuesday at around six when my colleague Doc Segovian was shot?"

He paused.

"Here. In Chautauqua," he said. "To help with the funeral arrangements. So let me think . . ."

After another sip, he said, "At six, I think I was walking the Chautauqua perimeter by myself. Before meeting my sister for a quick dinner at her place, before the Old First Night program at the Amp."

When Brad checked his watch, Mimi said she'd be wrapping up soon. And she decided to end with questions about Brad's will.

"Did you expect any inheritance?"

"I hadn't given it much thought, honestly. The man was unbelievably strong. We didn't expect him to die for years."

"But when he did die what did you expect?"

"I guess I thought Mary and I would at least get the main house."

"At 12 Park?"

"Exactly. I was under the impression our mom had bought it with her own family money. It also was mainly her thing, not dad's. Fixing it up was her greatest pleasure. She studied the archives photos to match what she could. Doing a project each year. Last year, it was the sawn porch railing. The year before the stairway banister. Her first step was painting the exterior, the original gray."

Brad's eyes teared up again.

"Sorry, I warned you. I'm a big baby. Anyway, back to the will. We could understand dad leaving his business and other things to Francine. But the house . . ."

"So."

"Mary and I met with Francine this morning before the funeral. She was kind enough to hear us out. We gave her our perspective on how the main house was really my mom's baby and, well, she agreed."

"She agreed?"

"Yes, she said she'd speak with dad's lawyer, Everett Thompson in Jamestown. And she'd make sure 12 Park ended up with us."

"Just like that? Francine saw the injustice of her keeping it?"

Brad, red in the face, took another long sip.

"Yes," he said softly.

"Do you plan to sell it?"

"Too soon to say," he said. "We may rent it out. We need to find out how much things are renting for, or selling for, these days. My sister, especially, isn't getting as much work as she used to now that the conductors want them younger and younger."

"How about you? Could you use the extra income?"

"Who couldn't?"

Chapter Twenty-Eight

Mary Hansen looked so much like her brother it was uncanny.

They had the same round oversized flushed faces, red hair, green eyes and bear-like builds. But while Brad's girth made him look soft, Mary's—encased in a tie-dyed caftan—made her look like a mountain-sized force to be reckoned with.

"I'm very glad you could join me," Mimi said as Mary set her violin case on a chair between them at the Refectory. "I know it can't be the easiest topic to talk about. And I thank you for—"

"You could thank me most by getting right to the point," Mary interrupted. "I only have twenty minutes until I have to get home. Change into my whites for the concert. Tonight's Bach."

Mimi explained her supposed assignment for *The Daily*. Embellishing some on what she'd told Brad, she claimed to be working, cooperatively, with the police.

Then, either because she, too, felt ornery, or because she wanted to gauge the depth of Mary's antipathy toward her dad, she resumed her excessively sweet expressions of concern.

"Really, how are you holding up?" she asked.

"Are you kidding? I thought you might have done some homework before meeting me. And found out that my dad and I weren't the least bit close."

Mimi, sipping more coffee, just nodded sympathetically.

"I'm sick of the bullshit condolences. Especially at rehearsal today," she said. "I felt like standing up and announcing that I'm fine about my dad's death. What I'm not fine about is the stupid CSO bicycle-chain rotation system that has me sharing a stand tonight with the most annoying woman in my section."

Mimi nodded some more.

"I won't say her name. But let me tell you that when you're near her, it's impossible to concentrate. Today's she's playing too fast. And I'm sure she's also wearing perfume. I confronted her. But she insisted it was just her shampoo. It's so distracting, I couldn't focus on the music."

When Mary paused, Mimi finally re-asserted herself.

"I'm wondering, for starters," Mimi said. "If you have any idea who killed your dad?"

"I thought that's your job," she said. "But me? I have no idea. One thing I can assure you is that it wasn't me or Brad."

She confirmed everything Brad said about her terrible relationship with her dad. And how they hadn't spoken after the fight at the hospital before her mother's death. Mary also agreed with Brad's view that Brad. Jr. and their mother took Brad Sr.'s putdowns the hardest.

"The tough thing for my brother was that, no matter how much he tried, he couldn't stop caring what our father thought. At some level, he still wanted dad's approval."

"And your mother?"

"I was never sure why she didn't just leave him. My dad was so nasty to her. Called her a malingerer, a heifer. It was awful to watch."

"Did you think there was any significance to your dad being killed on her birthday?"

"No," Mary said.

When Mimi just stared, Mary added: "What do you want me to say that it was karmic justice? I don't believe in that numerology crap."

After a few more family questions, Mimi asked

Mary if Brad Hansen had fought with others outside the immediate family.

"The group he *didn't* fight with might be smaller," Mary said. "He was always battling someone. His brother. A former business partner in Erie. Tenants. Ex-tenants. Bill collectors. He never got along with anyone."

When pressed, Mary said she couldn't summon a lot of names of Brad's adversaries. The former business partner she thought she'd remember and call Mimi with later.

"What about Mole?" Mimi asked. "What were their issues?"

"I'm not sure I ever knew. It might go back to the war," she said. "My dad was the younger brother. When Mole couldn't serve because of his stutter, which was apparently shameful back then, my dad went and enlisted. At sixteen or seventeen. Then he came back a hero for leading the Seventh Infantry's storming of the Shuri Castle in the Battle of Okinawa.

"Or saying he did," Mary continued. "I wouldn't be surprised if it was something he lorded over Mole. He never let us forget how he, singlehandedly, helped end the war. Brought the Japs to their knees."

Moving on to questions about the inheritance, Mary agreed with Brad that she hadn't given much thought

192 • DEB PINES

to her father's will but considered 12 Park rightly theirs. She confirmed that Francine had agreed and signed over the property that morning.

"Why?"

Mary didn't get flustered like her brother. But she, too, didn't answer the question directly.

"You'd have to ask her."

"Your brother said that Francine saw the injustice of her keeping what your mother pretty much devoted her life to."

"I guess," Mary shrugged. "I don't need to tell you how to do your job, I'm sure. But it's probably best if you go right to the horse's mouth. And ask Francine."

Mary said there was no decision yet on whether to sell or rent the house that could be worth as much as a million dollars. But she agreed that she and Brad could certainly use the cash.

"You *and* Brad? Not to be too blunt, but, well, I thought his wife was partner at a big New York law firm?"

"Val's a big earner and big spender. Apartment on Park Avenue. Summer house in the Hamptons. Only the best for my nieces. Private school. Camp. Music lessons. Believe me, it all adds up."

As she reviewed her notes, Mary tapped her foot, impatiently.

"Okay, okay," Mimi said. "I'm almost through. I'm just going to ask a few more questions I'm sure you've already answered for the police. Like where you were Saturday, race morning?

"At home in bed."

"Alone?"

Mary smiled.

"Sadly, yes."

"Did you ever bring anything to your dad to eat or drink before the race?"

"No."

"Or have someone bring him something?"

"No."

"How about Tuesday at six when Doc Segovian, my colleague, was killed?"

"You know the practice shacks near the tennis courts?"

"Yeah."

The shacks, mini-bungalows, were where musicians and singers could rehearse, at full volume, without disturbing anyone.

"I was in one of the shacks until I met my brother for dinner and we walked over to Old First Night together."

"Did anyone see you at the shacks?"

Mary nodded.

"Yes, not when I entered or left. But I remember

peeking out the window at some point. And making eye contact with someone entering the shack next to mine."

"And that person was?"

"My standmate Diane Hauser."

Mary gave Mimi Diane Hauser's phone number and said if she couldn't reach her by phone, Mimi could try to intercept Diane after that night's concert.

"You'd recognize her right away," Mary said. "She's the one with the perfume."

CHAPTER TWENTY-NINE

MIMI HAD TO PUT her investigation on hold for the rest of the afternoon to do her *Daily* work and make spaghetti for her and Jake for dinner.

But, after dinner, she got back to it.

She left a message for Diane Hauser as Jake, who had eaten two helpings of spaghetti plus garlic bread, plus salad, foraged through the refrigerator for more to eat.

"Don't we have any Gatorade?" he called.

"Check the shelves on the door," Mimi said.

"I did."

"Then check again. More closely."

As Jake took his time, surveying the refrigerator, Mimi bit her tongue.

She wanted to yell: "Close the damn fridge!"

That's what her Grandma Fanny, an extremely patient but extremely frugal woman, used to yell when Mimi, as a kid, dawdled in front of the open refrigerator.

"Aroysgevorfen gelt," Fanny would then mutter under her breath about the fortune Mimi was wasting on electricity due to the open door.

When Jake finally found a Gatorade, he kept looking. And glancing over at Mimi. And looking.

"Don't you want to tell me to close the damn fridge?" he asked.

"YES! NOW! CLOSE THE DAMN FRIDGE," Mimi yelled. "And stop pushing my buttons."

Jake, giggling, grabbed a string cheese and a handful of chocolate-chip cookies, closed the door.

"Why do you bait me like that?" Mimi asked.

"Just doing my job, Mom," he said. "Doing my job."

When Diane Hauser finally called Mimi back, she was nearly as annoying as Jake.

She spent the first ten minutes explaining how, as a general rule, she didn't believe in speaking to the press. And she also, as a general rule, believed in leaving police investigations to the police.

"I also have nothing to add," Diane said. "I didn't

know either man who was killed. Not the doctor. Or Mary Hansen's father."

"But you do know Mary Hansen, right?"

Silence.

"Is that what this about?"

"Yes. I was just wondering if you could back up her claim that she was practicing at the practice shacks at around six o'clock on Tuesday?"

More silence.

"I'm not going to quote you in any story or anything about this," Mimi said. "Mary says she saw you there. At the shacks. At about six o'clock. Is that true?"

"Let me think," Diane said. "We were both definitely at the shacks on Tuesday evening. I was in number five, the one they call the Gershwin shack because that's where George Gershwin composed his Concerto in F."

"Really?"

"Really. There's a sign in the shack with the history. Check it out. It says Gershwin was there in 1925."

"Okay, but back to Tuesday. Do you remember what time it was when you saw Mary?"

"Did she say six?" Diane asked.

"*Around* six."

"Okay," Diane says. "I'd say it was more like five-thirty or five-forty because I was rushing to get home by six. That's when my kids get home from their tennis lesson."

198 • DEB PINES

"So when you left, Mary Hansen was still in the shack, practicing?"

"Yes."

"And your best guess is that that was around five-thirty or five-forty, not six?"

"That's correct."

Mimi's next call, from Brad Hansen Jr., was more brief.

"I've just got a sec," Brad said. "But I wanted to get back to you like I said I would and tell you what I told the cops. And that's that, in retrospect, I can't think of anyone who'd say they saw me on Saturday morning."

"How about your wife? Or daughters?"

"My wife was away, on a business trip to London. And what I forgot to say when I was talking to you this afternoon, is that my daughters weren't around Saturday morning either. I dropped them off Friday night at a sleepover. At the Drabers', some old friends of ours. And I picked up my girls and the two Draber girls, at around three on Saturday afternoon."

When Mimi hung up, she dialed Francine.

After three rings, the answering machine clicked on.

Then, yow, on came the voice of a dead man.

"This is the home of Brad and Francine Hansen," Brad Sr.'s voice said on the machine. "We're not here. Leave a message."

Mimi hesitated.

She considered leaving a message for Francine. Then, thinking better of it, she hung up.

"What's up, Mom?" Jake asked.

"I can't reach Francine even though she told me she'd talk to me."

"So why didn't you leave a message?"

"I've already left one message. I didn't want to be a pest and maybe scare her off."

"Sounds like you've already scared her off."

"Maybe. Also it now seems like neither Hansen kid has a good alibi. I thought the brother was with his family Saturday morning, the day of the race."

"But?"

"He now says his wife was in London and his kids were at a sleepover until Saturday afternoon."

"And the sister?"

"She says she was alone Saturday morning. She said she was seen in a practice shack at six, the time of Doc's killing, Tuesday. But the lady who saw her says it was more like five-thirty, five-forty."

"What's next, Sherlock?"

"I have a couple of ideas."

"I may regret this," Jake said. "But—okay—is there anything I can do for you?"

"Very kind of you to ask."

Chapter Thirty

As Mimi and Jake headed for *The Daily* offices, Mimi couldn't get the story of the Gershwin practice shack, and then various Gershwin melodies, out of her head.

"I got rhythm, I got music. I got my man. Who could ask for anything more?" she eventually sang out loud. "I got daisies in green pastures—"

"Enough," Jake howled. "Enough. I agreed to do your computer search. Because I know you can't do it yourself. And I'm also curious about the mysterious Francine Hansen. But do I have to listen to you sing?"

"Old man trouble, I don't mind him," Mimi sang anyway. "You won't find him 'round my door."

When Jake shook his head, Mimi raced through the rest.

"I got starlight. I got sweet dreams. I got my man. Who could ask for anything more?"

"MOM!"

"Okay, done," Mimi said. "Sorry. Since the woman mentioned Gershwin, I can't stop. I'll try to keep it to myself."

After walking up South, they turned right onto Clark, the brick path that reminded Mimi of a college Fraternity Row.

Like she'd seen in movies or college catalogs.

A nerdy good student, Mimi had dreamed of going away to college, maybe even to one in the Ivy League on scholarship.

But when her grandparents got sick, she stayed home to care for them, then bury them, while attending Brooklyn College.

The houses on both sides of Clark weren't frat houses. They were modest rooming houses run by various church denominations with their signs out front: Lutheran House, Baptist House, Episcopalian.

Mimi and Jake continued past the walk. Past a plaque at the Amphitheater proclaiming Chautauqua's commitment to being "a center for the identification and development of the best in human values" and "a resource for the enriched understanding of the opportunities and obligations of community, family and personal life by fostering the sharing of varied cultural, educational, religious and recreational experience."

The Daily offices, thankfully, were empty.

So Mimi set Jake up at the one computer in the back with Internet access.

As he punched keys, Mimi went through a pile on her desk. On top were three pink message slips. Each one—from Mack, Wentworth and Violet Greenwood—had the box checked beside the words PLEASE CALL.

Under the message slips, was some mail announcing upcoming Chautauqua sports events. Mimi circled their dates and organized the pile in chronological order.

"How are you doing, hon?" she yelled to Jake. "Ready for me to come look over your shoulder?"

"Not yet. I'm still getting into the NEXIS account. The machine is unbelievably slow."

As Jake stared at the screen, Mimi flipped through Wednesday's *Daily*. She stopped at page three, an account of the second day's lecture in "The Mystery of Good and Evil" series.

And she zeroed in on the words with the intensity of someone consulting their horoscope.

The speaker, Yaffa Eliach, a Holocaust survivor and

expert, discussed the difficulty people have facing hard truths about evil.

"The truth, actually, never has many friends and unpleasant truths are especially friendless," said Eliach, who knew that lesson firsthand.

Like Mimi's grandparents, Eliach was from Poland. And her story, like theirs, featured horrific loss and betrayal.

As a five-year-old, Eliach had watched her mother and baby brother shot before her eyes not by the Nazis—but by neighbors she'd trusted who turned out to be Nazi collaborators.

Disbelieved by Poles at the time, Eliach said, she was facing a new generation of Holocaust deniers.

She urged Chautauquans to "try to understand evil, no matter how painful it is." To study the "story of the dislike of the unlike" or risk having history repeat itself.

"It may happen again," she warned. "And who knows who will be the Jews of the next Holocaust."

Mimi, nearly in tears, reached in her bottom desk drawer for Kleenex. And, on top of the box, she came upon the marriage certificate and phone bills she'd swiped them from the Hansens' desk—and nearly forgotten.

She brought them with her over to Jake.

"I've got six entries for a Francine Hansen," he said, looking up from his screen.

"The most recent are wedding announcements in the Mayville, Jamestown and Erie papers," he said. And three old ones for someone who couldn't be our Francine Hansen."

"Because?"

Jake shook his head, disgusted.

"Because, genius mommy, Francine wasn't Francine *Hansen* until she married Brad three months ago."

"Good point. Good point."

"So are we done here?" Jake asked.

"No," Mimi said. "Why don't you type Francine Rodino, R-O-D-I-N-O?"

"Because?"

"Because, genius son, that's her maiden name on the marriage certificate I found—"

"You mean *stole?*"

"Okay, stole from the Hansens."

Jake, smiling, did more typing and staring at the screen before he paused.

"What?" Mimi asked.

"I've got two-hundred and seventy-three entries for Francine Rodino."

"Let's do it."

Jake sighed.

"The first few," he said. "Are obits for various Francine Rodinos. One Francine L, a homemaker from Boston, survived by eleven children and forty two-grandchildren. Who died at eighty-two and —"

"Move on."

"There's a Francine E. Rodino of Atlanta Georgia. Renowned writer of children's books," he said, reading his screen. "Who died in 1975 after a long battle with cancer, according to *The Atlanta Journal-Constitution*."

"Can't we limit the search further?" Mimi asked.

"Is there more on the wedding certificate?"

Mimi checked and found under date of birth that Francine had been born February 20, 1953 in Indianapolis, Indiana.

"How about typing Francine Rodino and Indianapolis?"

Jake did and pushed search.

"Eighty-six entries," he said.

"It's fewer than two-hundred and seventy-three. Why don't you open the first one from *The Indianapolis Star*?"

With a few clattering keystrokes Jake did. The computer called up a December 6, 1991 news story.

Mimi read over Jake's shoulder, starting with the headline:

Speedway Teacher Arrested
for Alleged Student Rape

Mimi leaned closer to read the text:

SPEEDWAY—A 38-year-old Speedway Middle School teacher was arrested yesterday on charges she had a longstanding sexual relationship with one of her eighth-grade students, a 14-year-old boy she also tutored outside school.

Francine Rodino, a widow who had taught math in Speedway for four years, was charged with statutory rape, a Class B felony punishable by up to 20 years in prison, after the boy's mother reported her suspicions to the police.

Rodino intends to plead not guilty, her lawyer John McAvoy said late yesterday.

"She is the victim of a modern-day witch hunt," McAvoy said.

Later stories indicated that Rodino was suspended from school when more parents complained of alleged inappropriate contacts with boys in the boys' choir Francine Rodino directed.

Rodino's interest in their kids, demonstrated by personal notes, gifts and phone calls, was unnatural, they said.

Rodino never spoke to the press. Her lawyer, throughout, insisted the charges were untrue.

When Rodino ended up pleading guilty to a lesser offense—child molesting, a Class C felony—the lawyer said it was to spare the kids the ordeal of a trial.

The sentencing judge, however, was unconvinced.

Citing an "appalling betrayal of trust," Judge Calloway gave Rodino close to the maximum: seven years in the Indiana Women's Prison.

Later news accounts called Rodino a model prisoner. She tutored fellow inmates, got psychiatric counseling, furthered her own education and helped lead a successful class-action lawsuit to equalize educational and recreational offerings for male and female inmates.

Her first time up for parole, after five years, Rodino apparently wowed the board. In a closed hearing, reports said she promised to relocate and never teach or work with young people again. She noted, among her accomplishments, securing a New York State Realtor's license.

The last stories said that Francine Rodino got out of prison in July 1996—about the same time Mimi's landlady reportedly started selling real estate in Chautauqua County, New York.

Chapter Thirty-One

At home, Mimi couldn't imagine sleeping.

But Jake, of course, dozed right off on the couch beside her as soon as she turned on the TV and found the channel with the Yankees-Mariners game.

That left Mimi to go over all they'd learned by herself. She recalled the facts. Then she moved on to a series of questions.

If Francine, as it seemed, had a kinky thing for teenaged boys, would that make her a murderer? Only if she wanted to get rid of her husband for a boy? Like B.J. Ryan maybe?

Would being an ex-con make her greedier? More ruthless? Susceptible to blackmail?

When Mimi's head hurt from all the questions, she tried to focus on the baseball game.

It was into extra innings: 8-8 in the bottom of the eleventh.

The Yankee pitching was miserable. And Mimi knew her team wasn't going to win a slugfest against power-hitting Seattle. Especially in Seattle.

When Jake, asleep beside her, started squirming and kicking, she had enough.

She'd been lazy about moving him to his room. She'd kept vowing to do it at the next commercial, then the next, then the next.

The problem was that Jake, now five-nine, one-forty, was three inches taller and twenty pounds heavier. She couldn't carry him.

Putting her arms under his arms, she led him, wobbly step by wobbly step, to his bedroom.

"This way, this way," she coaxed. "You're doing great."

When she got Jake into bed, she pulled up the covers and stood there, staring.

Then, seizing the opportunity, Mimi gave Jake a kiss that, if he were awake, he'd resist.

"Good night, sweetheart," she said. "I love you very much."

Mimi was going to stand there, staring, a little

longer. But she heard, or thought she heard, a knock on the front door.

Warily, she returned to the living room, listening for a sound at the door, while glancing at the TV.

The sight of Yankee manager Joe Torre jogging wearily to the mound for a pitching change, made her heart sink.

A bad sign.

Then came a loud knock.

"Just a minute," Mimi called, trying to keep any fear from her voice. "Hold on."

Fumbling through her purse, she removed the .22 she'd owned since childhood and carried since Doc's death.

"Who is it?" she asked. "Who's there?"

"It's Mack. I hope I didn't scare you. When I heard on the car radio that the Yankees were in extra innings I thought you might be up. Can I come in?"

Mimi, after returning the gun to her purse, opened the door. And nearly swooned.

Mack, even exhausted, was breathtakingly handsome.

"Is everything okay?" Mimi asked.

"Sure, yes," he said. "I just wanted to see you."

"Come on in."

212 • DEB PINES

When he stepped inside and followed her to the TV, Mack kept talking.

"I also wanted to give you a lecture," he said. "For someone who earns a living depending on people returning your phone calls, you're terrible at returning calls."

"I know."

"I don't know how many times I've—"

"Okay, guilty," Mimi interrupted. "I confess. I felt awkward and nervous about returning *your* calls. Can I buy you off, Sergeant, with a beer?"

He smiled.

"Absolutely."

As Mimi walked to the kitchen, she felt Mack checking her out. And she hoped, he liked what he saw.

In the female grooming and wiles departments, she always felt inadequate. But her current outfit—ratty black shorts and her good-luck Bernie Williams jersey—at least, showed off two of her best assets: shapely legs and a little cleavage.

When Mimi returned with beers and pretzels, Mack

was sitting on her couch. Awkward about joining him, she stood.

"Sorry again about stopping by so late," Mack said, while accepting his beer. "But, well, I saw your light and I . . ."

"I thought you heard about the extra innings?"

He smiled sheepishly.

"The innings. And the light. And . . ."

"It's good to see you, too," Mimi said. "Very good. How's Kevin?"

"Like I said the other day. He's a miracle. Recovering better than we ever could have dreamed."

The *we* felt like a stab. But Mimi tried to hide it.

"How about Tina?" she asked. "How's she?"

"It's complicated. Let's not go there. I didn't come for that."

They both sipped their beers for a while in silence.

"I wanted to say how sorry I am for the loss of your friend, the doctor," Mack said. "He sounds like he was quite a character. And a special man."

"He was. The photography thing was a second career for him. And he was great at it. Took news photos and nature shots. Beautiful bird photos for the Audubon Society. And flower photos, too. And . . .

Do you have any news about the murder investigations?

When I saw you at Brad's funeral, I didn't know if maybe you were on the case."

"I don't have the big picture, by any means," Mack said. "But from what I'm overhearing at headquarters, I wouldn't be surprised if there's an arrest soon."

"Really?"

"Really. I wish I had more to tell you and I promise I'll call if I hear anything new."

"What makes you think an arrest is imminent?"

Mack, smiling, shook his head.

"You can't tell Wilson I've told you anything. The fact that you're following this, too, is making him nuts."

"I'm not going to take that personally," Mimi said. "I think Lieutenant Wilson's not that comfortable with women, in general. Not just me."

"He talks like a Neanderthal sometimes," Mack said. "But he's actually very good at what he does."

"So what can you tell me?"

"I think they've found the owner of the sawed-off rifle by tracing the serial numbers to a gun sold at the Wal-Mart in Lakewood. And this I'm less sure of, but I think they may also have an eyewitness placing the owner of the gun at the crime scene or nearby."

"You don't know who the owner is?"

Mack was shaking his head when the thwack of a

bat connecting with a ball drew Mimi's attention back to the TV.

Ken Griffey Jr. stood at the plate, grinning, very annoyingly, after hitting the ball out of the park.

Ten-eight, Mariners.

Game over.

Disgusted, Mimi turned off the TV.

"I can't stand the man. I don't need to watch his victory lap," Mimi said, before asking Mack, "Really, why did you come here?"

"Hey, don't take the loss out on me," Mack said. "I came because I wanted to see you. I needed to see you. Especially when you didn't return my calls. I started worrying you were getting yourself into some kind of trouble. Again."

Rising to his feet, he held Mimi's gaze.

"I wanted to look you in the eye. And say be careful. And, remind you, that if you're ever in any kind of jam, you should call."

Mimi, dizzy standing so close, took a step back.

"Thanks for the advice," she said. "It's good to see you, too. It really is. Now I've gotta get some sleep. So . . ."

"Got it," Mack, red-faced, said while heading for the door. "Like I said, I'll call you as soon as I hear anything."

After Mack let himself out and lingered in the hallway, Mimi felt a pang. Maybe she'd been too brusque, too dismissive.

She reached out to give Mack a conciliatory, coach-like pat. But her hands—apparently following their own agenda—didn't stop at the pat. They traced Mack's broad shoulders. Muscled arms. The hollow between his shoulder blades. When they ended up entwined around Mack's neck, that was it.

Surrendering to the same spell, Mimi gave Mack a long lingering kiss that he answered hard back.

When she withdrew, gasping, Mack held her tight.

"I'm sorry," she whispered.

"I'm not."

Chapter Thirty-Two

Eventually, Mimi did get ready for bed, got into bed and turned out the lights.

But, for hours, her mind raced.

She beat herself up for going as far as she did with Mack, a married man. Then she beat herself up for not going further, given her hopeless infatuation for that man.

Done with him, Mimi moved on to far worse self-recriminations about Doc. Why had she dragged him into her investigation, oblivious to the risks?

Had Doc been kinder to her by keeping something damning he'd learned to himself? Not even typing his suspicions into his computer?

Mimi was going over Doc's list, suspect by suspect, when sleep, mercifully, arrived.

But didn't last long.

The next thing Mimi remembered was the jangle of a telephone.

With a jolt, she sat up. Absentmindedly, she reached for the receiver where it used to sit on a nightstand in her grandparents' rent-controlled Brooklyn one-bedroom where she'd lived most of her life.

The phone kept ringing.

Gradually, Mimi remembered where she was. And she ran for the phone on the kitchen table next to her grandparents' wedding photo.

As Mimi picked up the receiver, she noticed the time, 5:25 a.m., on the clock on the tiny kitchen stove.

It was still dark out. In the distance, a dog barked incessantly.

"Hello," she said, thickly. "Hello."

"It's Mack."

"Mack?" she repeated

"Yes, Mack."

"Mack, is everything okay? What happened?"

Mimi felt the groggy panic that accompanies a middle-of-the-night phone call—even though her grandparents and parents were long dead and she could see her son safely asleep in his room.

Involuntarily, her body braced for bad news.

"Everything's fine," Mack said. "I'm just calling

because I said I'd call if I learned anything new. In terms of the homicide investigations."

Mimi said nothing.

"Are you there?" Mack asked.

"Yes, yes. I'm here. And awake, finally. Please, go on."

"I didn't want you or Jake to hear anything first on the news. The press is just getting wind of things. And I was afraid you might get up. And turn on the radio. And hear this and . . ."

"What's up?"

"About twenty minutes ago, Lieutenant Wilson brought two people in for questioning. And, from what I understand, it's only a matter of time before he places them under arrest."

"For both murders? Brad Hansen's and Doc's?"

"No, just Doc's. At least for now, that's what I hear. I can't give you a lot of details because I don't know a lot of details. Much of what we have, in terms of evidence, will come out at their court appearance later today. But I wanted to call with what I . . ."

"Mack, please get to the point. Who are the suspects? Do I know them?"

"I'm afraid you do," Mack said. "It's those friends of Jake's. The twins from Jamestown, B.J. and Bob Ryan."

Chapter Thirty-Three

The killer, sitting in court later that day, knew the space wasn't neutral territory.

It favored the powerful over the weak. The confident over those intimidated by the trappings of power.

Trappings like the courtroom's high coffered ceiling. Heavy oak furniture. Brass light figures. Portraits of dead judges.

In their presence, some guilty people might quake in their boots. Or even confess.

Not *this* guilty party, the killer thought.

The atmospherics don't work when you have two potent weapons on your own side.

A great game plan.

And a calming power that comes from reciting ritual phrases.

The killer could sit in the courtroom like anyone else, waiting for the big show at 1 o'clock. And put on the face desired.

By just reciting something. The best something was the 23rd Psalm.

"Ye, though I walk through the valley of the shadow of death, I will fear no evil: for thou art with me."

It was like a narcotic. Say the psalm a few times and it spreads a sense of comfort and wellbeing through the bloodstream that can't be shaken by a few silly courtroom actors and props.

"Ye, though I walk through the valley of the shadow of death, I will fear no evil: for thou art with me."

Feeling miles away, the killer watched the clock. At 1:22, everyone else seemed to be talking and fanning themselves, trying to get comfortable in the sweltering heat.

The next minute, 1:23, all activity stopped. A hush spread. The crowd turned as one toward a manly looking female court officer.

In what felt like slow motion, the court officer walked to the front door. She banged the heel of her thick palm against it.

"People of the State of New York versus Robert Adam Ryan and Brigham John Ryan," she yelled. "The Honorable Randall Fenterman presiding."

The judge, a tall skinny man in a black robe, marched to the bench.

The courtroom echoed with the sounds of his footsteps and whirs of the loud but inept ceiling fans.

On the bench, the judge was flanked by the American flag and the flag of the state of New York.

Behind him was a giant portrait of the most famous lawyer ever from Jamestown, New York: Robert H. Jackson, a Supreme Court justice who was the top Nazi war crimes prosecutor at the Nuremburg trials.

The killer tried to absorb everything. But there was too much legal mumbo-jumbo.

At some point, the judge explained the charges: second-degree murder for the fatal shooting of one John Segovian on the grounds of the Chautauqua Institution.

He said the Ryans "being seventeen years of age" would be tried as adults. If convicted, he said, they faced a maximum of twenty-five years to life in prison.

The judge kept mopping his sweaty brow with a handkerchief and addressing the lawyers.

Eventually, he turned to the Ryans to ask if they could afford to hire their own lawyers.

"No," said B.J.

"No, sir," said the other one.

Increasingly, the killer had a sense of being underwater,

with everything playing out in muffled tones far away. One minute the killer was present, the next minute not.

Everyone else's names and roles got confusing.

The tall athletic black man was definitely a defense lawyer. So was the doughy-looking white man.

The other lawyer, hopping up and down like a jack-in-the-box with comments and objections, then, had to be the District Attorney. Three defense lawyers would make zero sense.

The heat was the source of a lot of grumbling from the lawyers and the spectators.

But the killer welcomed the heat.

It brought a dullness that helped perpetuate the sensation of the action playing out on a faraway stage. Far from the killer.

The heat helped.

So did the reciting.

"Ye, though I walk through the valley of the shadow of death, I will fear no evil: for thou art with me."

Uneasiness only struck when the killer felt exposed—by the headlight-like gaze of someone watching.

Watching the watcher.

Not subtle or fleeting, the stare came from the nosy reporter, Mimi Goldman. Standing in the back of the courtroom with her son, she was taking her time, sizing things up.

Did she know what Doc knew?

Highly unlikely.

But she still needed to be monitored.

This was no time for slip-ups.

The killer, under Mimi's gaze, was conscious of trying to look as normal as possible. To concentrate on the District Attorney Ed Billings' words.

Playing to the audience, Billings proposed that the case proceed expeditiously and start with the hearing the following Tuesday.

"We should be getting preliminary lab and autopsy reports by Monday," Billings proclaimed.

"Beyond that, I see no reason for delay," he said. "This is a crime that has shocked the conscience of our community. And, judging from the media presence here, beyond as well. Other towns have faced this sort of thing. But this is a terrifying first for Chautauqua County. A first and we hope a last. We may never know the reason behind what seems to be an act of senseless teenaged violence. Whether it's a thrill killing motivated by nothing more than boredom. Or glorification of what can only be called a culture of violence."

The killer struggled to look appropriately somber.

"Ye, though I walk through the valley of the shadow of death, I will fear no evil: for thou art with me."

Chapter Thirty-Four

Outside the courthouse after the hearing, the sunlight was blinding. Mimi put on her mirrored shades. But she still squinted while jockeying for position near the two lawyers who were holding impromptu press conferences on the courthouse steps.

The pair—the DA Edward Billings, and B. J.'s lawyer, Justin Winters—weren't New York City slicksters.

But they were impressive.

Billings, a DA straight out of Central Casting, was tall and silver-haired. His voice, a baritone of righteous indignation, repeated his thrill-kill theory for anyone who'd listen.

"If the murder was motivated by boredom as we suspect," Billings boomed. "Then this is one serious wake-up call for our community. A first sign that all of our institutions and I mean our churches, families, schools and government, need to do more for our young people."

Winters, even taller, was a graying well-built black man who was something of a local celeb—for leading Saint Bonaventure University to the Final Four in basketball in the 1960s.

"It is premature to comment today on the wild allegations leveled against my client," Winters said calmly. "I just hope the community keeps an open mind. And recognizes that a young person like B.J. Ryan, just like all criminal defendants in this great nation of ours, is entitled to a presumption of innocence."

Before moving to Western New York, Mimi had never heard of Winters. But in her year at the *Mayville Reporter* his name came up virtually every time there was some kind of a political opening.

On some anniversary, *The Reporter* ran a multi-page spread on Winters's greatest college basketball feat—breaking an all-time assists record in the NCAA quarter-finals.

Sweating under the bright TV lights, both lawyers looked like coaches doing post-game spin.

A female staffer from the DA's office moved among the reporters, handing out media kits, as if they were party favors.

When Mimi noticed Winters wrapping up and heading back to the sandstone copper-domed courthouse with his gray pinstriped suit coat slung over his shoulder, she and Jake followed.

"Excuse me, Mr. Winters?" Mimi called. "Mr. Winters?"

"I've made my statement a few times," he said, firmly. "Please get it from your colleagues. And if you want anything on behalf of Bob Ryan, call his lawyer, John Swoozy."

"I'm not looking for a statement," Mimi said.

When Winters stopped, she introduced herself and Jake. She explained her link to the murder victim, Doc Segovian, and explained that Jake was a friend of the Ryan twins.

A glimmer of recognition crossed Winters' face.

"I've heard of you. And your son."

"Might we have a minute to talk privately about the case?" Mimi asked.

"Not now," Winters said. "I have to go meet with my client. Judge Fenterman was nice enough to let us use the jury room attached to his courtroom. Which gives us more privacy and saves me a trip to the jail. But . . ."

Winters seemed to be working something out in his head.

"How about this?" he said. "Want to meet me outside

the courtroom in about an hour? Around three-thirty? And I'll see if there's more I can say."

Mimi said that would be great.

"Thanks," she said, shaking Winters' hand.

"By the way," he said. "I don't normally give the press the time of day."

"But?"

"I remember what you did last year. My client B.J. also said you're a sharp one. And that if I can get any help from you, I shouldn't be too proud to take it."

To pass the hour, Mimi was going to make phone calls from the courthouse. But the phones were occupied by the hordes of visiting reporters.

So she and Jake walked across the sun-baked parking lot to her Honda Accord, planning to find different phones.

"Maybe the ones outside Quality?" Mimi proposed, while sliding into her swelteringly hot car.

"Good idea," Jake said, joining her. "But can't you do anything about the heat?"

Sitting in Judge Fenterman's courtroom, it was hard to imagine anywhere hotter.

But Mimi's car was.

She could barely touch the steering wheel. She took off the linen blazer she wore over a button-down blouse and her jeans to court. She'd sweated through the shirt.

"Mom?"

"BE PATIENT," Mimi barked. "Give the a.c. a chance."

"YOU be patient," Jake shot back.

Mimi was tempted to add another, "YOU be patient." But she reminded herself she was the adult in the conversation.

So she drove in silence into the Quality grocery-store parking lot. When she pulled up to a row of payphones, the a.c. was finally working.

Jake turned one vent toward himself.

Mimi flipped on the radio then fished through her purse for quarters for the payphones.

"Today's shaping up to be a scorcher," said a radio weather lady. "We're poised for temperatures to go into the hundreds. A record for this date in Chautauqua County where—"

The woman's gleeful tone was maddening. So Mimi turned her off.

"I've got four quarters here," she told Jake. "You want to make a call? Or just stay here in the air-conditioning?"

"I'll call."

Mimi said she'd try Francine (again). And her boss

230 • DEB PINES

Wentworth. And as many tenants as she could reach, starting with Mole.

She proposed Jake call the Pennsylvania Attorney General's office. She wanted him to find the names of past business partners of Brad Hansen's to see if his demise was, in any way, related to an old business feud.

When Mimi reached Wentworth, she still wasn't sure if her investigation had his blessing.

He said nothing explicitly. But when she finished summarizing the court proceedings, he paused.

"You don't have to rush back this afternoon, if you don't want to," Wentworth said. "Mike volunteered to take care of the sports page for tomorrow."

"The intern?"

"Kid's turning out to be a great little worker. And, well, I thought, you might have something else important to do."

Mimi, grateful, felt her eyes tear up.

"Thanks," she said. "And one more thing?"

"Sure."

"I've been meaning to ask if you know if there ever was a murder in Chautauqua before?"

"I can't answer you for sure," Wentworth said. "Rumor has it that some time in the 1940s one waiter killed another in the kitchen of the Cary Hotel. People say it never got reported because of local snobbery. Since neither party was considered a *real* Chautauquan."

After leaving messages for Francine and for Betsy Gates, Mimi was prepared to leave a message for Mole, too, when—after four rings—he picked up.

"H-h-hello," Mole said.

"Hello," Mimi answered. "It's Mimi Goldman. I was hoping you had a minute?"

Silence.

"I wanted to talk to you about the Ryans' arrest and the death of your brother?"

More silence.

"I promise I won't take a lot of your time."

"Y-y-you won't take any of my time."

"But I wondered if—"

"If the p-p-police say these boys did it, th-th-that's good enough for m-m-me."

"I just—"

"And I w-w-won't help some b-b-b-busybody reporter tear things d-d-down. So sh-sh-she can make a n-n-name for herself. And se-se-sell newspapers."

Before Mimi could protest, Mole hung up.

When Mimi hung up, too, she noticed Jake standing beside her, smiling broadly.

"Looks like you had better luck than I did."

"Nothing to do with luck, Mom."

"What?"

"Pure skill. Finesse. Genius."

"Okay, fine. Did you get the names of any of Brad's ex business partners?"

"The one who helped him open his first carpet store in Erie in the nineteen fifties," Jake said, smugly.

"And the name of that partner was?"

"Henry Greenwood," Jake said.

"*Greenwood* as in our fellow tenant Violet Greenwood?"

"Same last name. Don't know if they're related."

Chapter Thirty-Five

THE SECOND-FLOOR JURY ROOM where Mimi ended up meeting Justin Winters after dropping Jake off at home, was a long windowless, low-ceilinged, fluorescent-lit space.

In the center was a wooden table where countless jurors, seated in the mix-and-match chairs, must have deliberated.

Nearby was an old wooden coat tree. A dirty coffee maker. A stack of old *People* magazines. A few boxes of jigsaw puzzles.

"Well, well, well," Winters said, rising to shake Mimi's hand. "So this is the great Mimi Goldman."

As she sat across from him, she felt herself blushing. "Not what you expected?"

"I wasn't sure what to expect," Winters said. "We

who fight the good fight on a daily basis with what turns out to be little success, took tremendous pleasure in what you did last year. How you showed up the local constables. Embarrassed them for taking the easy way out and not getting justice for your colleagues at *The Reporter*."

"I appreciate the compliments," Mimi said. "But the truth is I wasn't setting out to embarrass anyone. I just—"

"Well, no matter what you intended. That's what you accomplished. For a while you were, like the PD's, Public Defender's Woman of the Year."

Mimi thanked him again. And she saw why he was such an effective trial lawyer. In half a minute's time, he'd charmed the hell out of her.

"I have great admiration for you, too," Mimi said. "And wondered what you think of the DA's case against the Ryans?"

"Tough to say this early on," he said. "I got a copy of a preliminary police report from sources. But the DA's under no legal obligation to share anything with us until the instant before the felony hearing. So we won't really know what they have until next Tuesday."

"That doesn't seem fair."

"Just the rules of the game. Worse than that, is the terrible start I've gotten off to with my client. B.J.

talked his head off with the cops. And now he's either giving me the silent treatment or cursing me out."

"I don't see how he," Mimi said, shaking her head. "It's so short-sighted and . . . The only thing I can say is that teenagers are pretty near impossible. Sensitive to any criticism of them. But then they unleash the nastiest stuff on everyone else. As if it's all a big joke. Got any teen monsters of your own?"

"No, no I don't," Winters said. "My wife and I have been blessed with many, many things in this world. But no children. We never . . ."

"I'm sorry I brought it up," Mimi said. "I didn't mean to . . ."

"Don't worry. I'm just hoping to get B.J. back in my corner. I think I lost him when I explained that, as a matter of course, I always talk to the DA about a plea deal. In no way, does that mean I'm saying B.J. should take one. But I'd be remiss in my duties if I didn't find out what the DA is offering. The quality of the offer usually tells me what the government thinks of its own case."

"Sounds reasonable."

"Not to B.J. He's adamant. Says he's innocent. He admits the gun was his. He says he was at the murder scene. But he says he's being framed and he doesn't want a lawyer who doesn't believe him."

Mimi, finally learning something, didn't want to interrupt.

"He got ticked off when I asked for particulars about the gun," Winters said. "Where he kept it. When he saw it last. And he lost it completely when I asked about his mother.

"I know the state is treating these boys like adults," Winters continued. "But, by my lights, at age seventeen, they're still kids. And I'd like the mother to be there at least for key court appearances."

"I don't know her," Mimi said. "But, from what Jake tells me, she's not around much. She works nights at a bar in Jamestown. I think it's called Charlie's Angels. She stops by their apartment to leave the boys money. But I think she spends most of her time at a boyfriend's. So they're pretty much on their own."

"When I asked B.J. to call his mom, he refused," Winters said. "When I said I'd call her myself, he exploded. He said I should butt out of his personal life. And he sure as hell didn't need any pity from a nigger."

"I'm sorry. I don't think he generally talks like that," Mimi said. "You must have struck a nerve."

"I'm sure."

"My son Jake's very fond of B.J. And, for whatever it's worth, he also thinks the twins are being framed. Is that possible?"

"I guess anything's possible. I'm not usually big on

conspiracy theories. Too many coincidences, especially the coincidence of someone else using B.J.'s gun, get tough to explain away."

"So you *don't* believe him?"

"I'm not saying that. We don't know everything the government knows yet. And we do have some pluses on our side."

"Like?"

"The judge. Fenterman is one of the fairest judges I've ever appeared before. And he's not afraid to do something unpopular. Remember the Reginald Johnson case?"

I nodded, recalling the case of a black man initially accused of beating the police. Fenterman ended up dismissing the charges when he found the police were the aggressors—largely based on testimony from a group of black senior citizens whose nursing home had a clear view of the clash.

"Anything else in B.J.'s favor?" Mimi asked.

"I think the D.A.'s theory of the crime, if he sticks with it, the thrill-kill motive, he might have trouble selling to a jury," Winters said.

"It's vague. Not something like greed or jealousy," he continued. "Motives people have an easier time understanding. Legally, the DA's under no obligation to prove motive. But, practically, it's another story.

Unless they have something more concrete, a better story to tell, I think they've got an uphill battle."

As Winters spoke, he must have detected something troubling in Mimi's expression.

"What?" he asked. "Do you have something to add?"

"I don't know if there's anything to this but . . . Just to put this out there. I had the impression, rightly or wrongly, there might be something going on between B.J. and Francine Hansen."

"Brad Hansen's widow?"

"Exactly."

Mimi recounted the story of B.J. claiming he was at the Hansens' to move furniture and Francine amending the story to say B.J. was there for SAT tutoring.

Winters sighed.

"I hear you," he said. "I wish I didn't hear you. My client insists there's nothing between him and Francine. But if the police have evidence to the contrary, that's bad. Wanting to get rid of a husband who stands between you and his wife and a fortune? And then wanting to get rid of someone who's figured that out? Wow. Those are the kind of motives juries love."

Chapter Thirty-Six

Betsy Gates left six bucks on the table to cover the tip for her lunch after court with the Warren sisters at the restaurant at Webb's, the motel on 394 closest to the Chautauqua Institution.

Then she told the sisters, who struggled walking under normal conditions, to wait on the curb while she got the car in the scorching heat.

At the car, Betsy didn't want to get in. It felt like an oven. She was glad she'd left Max at home, even though Don claimed he wasn't up to watching his own son, alone.

Ridiculous.

Don, nearly twice Betsy's age, had already raised another family. Also if he didn't want to deal with babies, then he should go out and find himself a new

job. Or stop giving away all of their money to his ex
and their spoiled kids.

Don's "kids" were out of high school. Yet Don was
still paying for their school and rent. And their car
insurance. And some vacations and clothes.

When Betsy looked at their recent credit-card
statements, she couldn't believe it.

Don wasn't working. But it was spending as usual
for him—on golf, eating out, etc., etc.

In Don-ial, Betsy called it.

She'd have to get them out of their mess.

Again.

She just needed time to think. To come up with a
new plan.

A new foolproof plan.

When she pulled up to the curb, the sisters were
waiting. Betsy jumped out to open the car doors.

"My goodness," Evangeline said. "What service.
You're doing too much. Driving us to court. To lunch.
And all the way back."

"Well, thanks for treating me. And for the company."

"The least we could do," Evangeline said. "It was
our pleasure."

Betsy helped Evangeline get settled in the front seat
and Philomena in the back. She stowed Evangeline's
cane in the trunk.

After slamming the car doors, she got in, eased into traffic on 394 and headed toward the Institution.

"What a day," Philomena said.

"True," Evangeline said. "Very upsetting. The whole week. Phil, why don't I run my idea by Betsy? See what she thinks?"

"I think you should drop it."

"I will not drop it," Evangeline snapped. "It's a good idea. And I want to run it by someone with sense. Not just you."

The bickering, amusing at first, was starting to wear on Betsy.

"All right," Betsy said, trying to make peace. "All right. What's the idea?"

"I think Chautauqua should put some restrictions on the kind of people they let work on the grounds," Evangeline said.

"What kind of restrictions?"

"Did you see what they said in the papers about the killers? The Ryan twins?"

"What about them?"

"At least one of them, the one with the earrings, has a criminal record. I think it was drugs, fighting and the like."

"I saw that," Betsy said.

"The District Attorney said this case should be a wakeup call," Evangeline continued. "And I think it should be. Chautauqua should stop letting hooligans like this work on the grounds. Years ago, the restaurants used to just hire college boys from the best summer families. I think they should go back to that policy. No outsiders. What do you think, Betsy?"

"I wonder if it would be legal."

"The institution's private. It can make its own rules. And I think places like Israel require special work permits for Arabs to come into their country. They know the risks they're dealing with."

"It's not the same here," Philomena chimed in. "Now is it?"

"I don't know what you mean," Evangeline said.

"That's a country at war."

"I'm just saying the Ryan boys are rough characters. I wouldn't be surprised if they get charged with killing Brad Hansen as well. What do you think?"

"I don't know," Betsy said.

"Do you know what Francine thinks?" Evangeline asked.

"I don't."

"I thought you and Francine were friends?" Evangeline asked.

"Not really. I wouldn't call us friends."

"How about you and Brad Hansen?" Philomena chimed in. "Would you say you two were friends?"

Betsy, glad she was wearing sunglasses, kept her eyes on the road.

"No," she said. "I wouldn't say Brad and I were friends either."

Chapter Thirty-Seven

Bob Ryan was seething.

It was his brother's stupidity and arrogance that landed them in this hellhole—a tiny cinderblock cell with nothing but two cots, a dentist-sized sink, a stinky seatless toilet and one caged lightbulb.

His brother was why their futures were screwed. And why their presents might be screwed, too, trying survive in this jungle.

And B.J.'s response?

Silence.

He just sat there on his cot, wearing a red bandana, tied Tupac-style, around his head, chain-smoking.

"Why are you freezing me and the lawyer out?" Bob asked. "Does it have to do with the gun?"

B.J., after another drag on his cigarette, closed his eyes as if in deep, not-to-be-interrupted thought.

"I think you owe me, at least an answer," Bob continued. "Even if you're not talking to Winters. I'm your brother. What the hell is wrong with you?"

When B.J. still stayed mum, Bob moved closer.

"It's one thing, you want to commit suicide. But you're bringing me down, too. Don't you give a fuck? Who had the gun? I hadn't seen it around the apartment lately."

Bob, usually the patient one, fumed. When he got no answer, he rushed at B.J. and shoved him hard against the wall.

"Hey," B.J. yelled. "Let go."

"No way. Who had the gun?

B.J., much stronger, easily pushed Bob off. But, underestimating Bob's rage, he relaxed and Bob jumped him and pulled hi to the floor.

"You got a fucking death wish," Bob hissed while pinning his wrists. "Fine. But how can you—"

"Hey, hey, look what we have here."

Bob, struggling to keep B.J. down, thought he recognized "Moose," the guard hosing down the corridor where someone had dropped or thrown a food tray.

"There's a coupla sisters here," the guard yell. "Doing the dirty. Right here. Right now."

When Bob looked up, he saw that it *was* Moose. And he gave B.J. an opening to break free. But Bob, relentless, jumped his brother again, as more footsteps, jangling keys and laughter signaled a growing audience.

"Whip it out, man," one guard yelled.

"Give it to her good," yelled another. "Up the rear."

As the brothers grappled, rolling around on the floor, the guards cheered. When they smacked into the wall, B.J. finally took control. He flipped Bob and, from behind, restrained him in a full nelson.

"Calm down, man," B.J. said. "Easy does it. Sit still."

When Bob kept wriggling, B.J. tightened his grip. "Had enough?"

Bob, gasping in pain, didn't answer.

"Can I let you go?"

When B.J. did, Bob repaid him by slamming his own body into reverse, knocking B.J. into the wall again.

B.J., finally enraged, unleashed a volley of vicious punches on Bob's head and face. When the brothers were wrestling again on the ground, Bob heard keys clattering in the lock and running footsteps.

"ENOUGH, hey," Moose yelled. "ENOUGH. Both of you, back off. And go sit on your beds."

B.J. let go.

But Bob, woozy and tasting blood from a split lip and gash above his eye, tightened his grip.

"Damn, I hate to wade into this mess," Moose said. "But I have an idea. Separate. Both of you. Now. Or I'll have to hose you down. Like a couple of farm animals."

The other guards laughed uproariously.

"Let go, bro," B.J. whispered. "They're serious."

When Bob still refused, someone yelled, "Let 'er rip!"

A strong spray of cold water hit Bob hard in the face. His head jerked back.

As B.J. skittered away, Bob, choking and gasping for air, felt like he was drowning. No matter which way he turned, the water blasted him like nails.

When Bob thought he was about to die, the spray stopped.

"Okay, punk," Moose said. "Be a good boy and go to your bed. NOW."

Bob, exhausted, managed to get to his knees.

"NOW," the guard barked.

Crawling, Bob made it five steps before the spray hit him again and he collapsed to the concrete floor.

The guards, loving it, whooped and cheered louder.

When the water stopped, Bob, soaked and shivering, crawled the rest of the way to his bed that, he realized, was soaked too.

Holding back tears, he leaned into the squishy mattress, hoping the guards had finally had their fill.

Instead, he felt the excruciating pain of being yanked from behind by the hair.

"What the —?" Bob squeaked.

"You owe me an apology, kid," Moose said. "Wasting my time with this garbage."

Bob, in agony, said nothing.

"I said I want an apology," Moose snarled in Bob's ear. "NOW."

"Give it up, kid," another guard yelled.

When Moose released his hair, Bob turned, intending to apologize. But when he saw Moose, smirking while straddling the hose like a giant dick, he didn't get far.

"I am . . ."

Moose turned on the hose again, pretending to be peeing on Bob. The crowd loved it.

When the roars and guffaws finally quieted, Moose insisted on the apology again and Bob, totally demoralized, whispered, "Sorry."

Chapter Thirty-Eight

At home, Francine felt nearly as defeated. Keeping it together with everyone staring at her in court had taken more out of her than she had expected.

At the kitchen table, she slipped off her shoes and started kneading her toes.

What she really wanted was a drink. But her watch said it was only three o'clock. Usually, she could hold herself off until six.

Why should she?

She headed to the liquor cabinet, poured herself a generous shot of bourbon, downed it, then drank another. She took a third shot with her into the powder room downstairs.

Staring in the mirror, she saw her mother's

expression: the shame of being caught drinking alone in the afternoon.

By fourth grade, Francine was so embarrassed by that face or worse—finding her mother passed out on the couch—she stopped bringing friends home.

Moving closer to the mirror, Francine noticed the worry lines on her forehead, the puffiness and crow's feet around her bloodshot eyes, the gray at her roots and temples.

Dammit, she was falling apart before her eyes.

Her looks used to be the one thing she could count on.

Even in prison, she didn't lose them. She'd swap tutoring or legal research to get her hair or nails done by some of the younger girls who, despite having little education, were often skillful with a comb and brush.

Now, she needed to spend so much time beautifying just to break even. To look good took forever.

After chugging the rest of her drink , she closed her eyes. And felt the staggering weight of decay. Of her past catching up.

How much longer could she outrun it?

She took out her brush and teased her hair furiously to hide the gray. She applied a new coat of mascara and more blush and lipstick.

She took off her dress-for-success blazer and undid

another button of her white blouse to show some cleavage. She sprayed on perfume. When she added her sunglasses, she smiled.

She still looked like the movie star people used to say she resembled most: Linda Darnell. Or the other real women, with breasts and hips, they used to feature on the big screen. Not today's scrawny, anorexic stars.

Francine brushed her teeth to keep herself from wanting another drink.

After that, she left the message she'd intended to leave on Mimi's machine.

"It's Francine," she said. "Sorry I haven't retuned your calls. If you're free, why don't you come over in about an hour? At four?"

Francine decided to spend the hour walking to the bookstore. To get away from her thoughts and the liquor cabinet. She didn't want to be too sloshed when Mimi showed up.

She stepped outside, crossed the porch, walked down the stairs and, distracted by the screech of the bus on South, nearly walked smack into her brother-in-law.

"Oh my, Mole. I'm so sorry."

"N-n-no problem," he said from the ground where he was pulling weeds and listening to a transistor radio.

"We've got to stop meeting like this," she said.

Though Francine had on her sunglasses, the sun was too blinding for her to stare into Mole's face.

"Is there more news?" she asked.

"N-n-nothing really. A f-f-friend at the diner, Bill M-m-mackey is the s-s-uper in those twins' building in Jamestown. Said they're a c-c-couple of bad apples. Minor scrapes as kids. Sh-sh-oplifting. V-v-vandalism. That kind of th-thing. Not much supervision. Everyone knew it was only a ma-ma-matter of time before they got into serious trouble. B-b-bill thinks they'll be ch-charged with killing Brad, too."

"So you think they did it?" Francine asked.

Mole slowly rose to his feet, massaging his lower back, in obvious pain.

"Y-Y-you're not one of those b-b-bleeding heart liberals, d-d-d-oubting the police at every t-turn, are you?"

"It's not that. I just . . ."

"W-w-what?"

"They said so little in court about the evidence. I couldn't see why these boys would want to kill anyone."

Mole shook his head.

"Also you know Mimi Goldman?" Francine asked. "The tenant who works for *The Chautauquan Daily*?"

He scowled.

"She's someone with experience with these things.

And she isn't acting like the case is closed. She's still asking questions and—"

"M-m-m-aking trouble. Sh-sh-e's a goddamned meddler," he fumed. "Th-that's all. C-c-alled me, too. And I g-g-ave her a piece of my m-m-ind. The p-p-press never wants a story to end. Th-they l-l-ove every twist and t-turn. Whether j-j-ustice is served or n-not. Otherwise how c-c-an they sell newspapers?"

"Maybe. But I thought I'd just hear her out."

"G-g-go ahead," Mole said. "B-b-but I think it's a c-c-complete waste of t-time. Wh-why on earth would the p-p-police go out and arrest the wr-wr-wrong guys?"

"They're only human," Francine said feeling wobbly from the alcohol, the sunshine and her churning emotions. "Lord knows, they make their share of mistakes."

Chapter Thirty-Nine

Violet Greenwood looked happy to see Mimi. But she still didn't let her right into her apartment.

"Shoes off, please."

Violet, dressed in a silky purple pajama-like pantsuit with matching purple sandals, stood like a purple sentry behind her screen door.

"Don't get me wrong," Violet continued. "The rugs here aren't anywhere close to mint. But I'm trying to save what's left. Especially what's left of the Persian Sarouk by the door. The colors are still nice even though the binding is shot."

After Mimi took off her shoes, she stepped inside, accepted an offer of iced tea and engaged in some drawn-out small talk. So drawn-out, she wondered if she had the patience for this kind of sift-through-mountains-of-muck-for-a-single-nugget interview.

For a while, she nodded, smiled and sipped her tea.

Then, increasingly impatient, Mimi explained she was partly there on business.

"Even though the police seem to be concluding their investigation in to the deaths of Doc and Brad Hansen, *The Daily* wanted me to keep asking a few questions," Mimi said. "To tie up some loose ends."

"So you don't believe those boys did it?"

"I'm not saying that."

"That's a possibility?"

"I guess that's more fair, although we haven't reached any conclusions."

From her seat on the couch, Violet Greenwood looked pleased as she reached in her purse for a cigarette, stuck one between her lips, lit up and sucked on it hard.

"Whatever I can do for you, sweetheart, just ask. I'm something of a mystery buff myself. Read 'em one after another. Almost like these," she said, husky-voiced, waving her cigarette.

"And, I'll have to say, " Violet continued. "I'm not bad at solving them either."

"Maybe you can help," Mimi said. "Why don't I start by asking you some questions. Then see what you think?"

Violet, delighted at the prospect, happily answered questions about herself. How she'd spent her whole life in Erie, Pennsylvania. She'd worked many years as a receptionist in a doctor's office. She'd married. Had two sons. Now a widow, this was her first time vacationing in Chautauqua.

"What brought you here this summer?" Mimi asked.

"Mainly pleasure," Violet said. "My sons thought I needed to get away so they paid for the trip. Who knew it would be the hottest week of the summer?"

"Anything else?"

For the first time, Violet, sitting up straighter, eyed Mimi with suspicion.

"What are you driving at?"

"I'm not sure. I'm fishing a little. But I wondered if you had a business purpose for coming here, too. Since, if I'm not mistaken, your husband, Henry Greenwood, was once a business partner of Brad Hansen's?"

"You are good," Violet said, laughing with what seemed to be genuine admiration. "Who told you that? The police?"

"Public records," Mimi said. "Do you know if the police are aware of your connection to Brad Hansen?"

"I don't know. I didn't mention it to them because I was afraid they'd make too much of the past. Now that they've made their arrests, I see no harm in coming clean. And saying that, yes, Henry and Brad were business partners for four and a half years. Back in the 1950s. After the war, they pooled every dime they had to start B & H Carpets in a hole-in-the-wall in downtown Erie. I can't remember the exact amount. But I know the seed money was fifty-fifty."

"And?" Mimi prompted.

"Brad had the business head, no question," Violet said. "He knew a lot of things. How to get the best deals from the mills. What would be popular. And, of course, Brad realized the value of locking up an exclusive on the first nylon carpet. One that didn't fuzz or pill that …"

Realizing she was off on a tangent, Violet stopped and regrouped.

"My Henry, though, was the one everyone wanted to deal with. Employees. Customers. Mill owners. They all said my Henry had a special kind of decency that was his blessing. And his curse."

When the partners split in 1957, Violet said Henry tried to withdraw his half of the profits but Brad refused.

"Brad kept putting Henry off and putting him off," Violet said. "He said Henry should wait until things took off when he opened a new location. Or he should wait until they cashed in on a new TV ad campaign. Or he should wait until they hired a new manager. It was always something."

Violet lit her next cigarette with the previous one and moved on.

"Then Henry made maybe the biggest mistake of his life. He signed papers he thought, once and for all, set a date for him to claim his share."

"But?"

"The papers didn't say what Henry thought they said. Instead of saying he'd hold off until the new manager came onboard. The papers said he'd hold off until much later. Until if and when the business was ever sold by Brad."

"Did he ever try again to withdraw money from the business?"

"A few times," Violet said. "But, frankly, Henry didn't have the stomach for this kind of thing. Conflict, controversy?"

Violet shook her head.

"Henry just asked. He never threatened. When Brad kept brushing him off, Henry gave up. He was one of those people who believe in letting bygones be bygones. But when things got bad, with the Parkinson's and all, I made Henry pick up the phone again and call Brad."

"And what happened?"

"Nothing good. The greedy SOB was sitting on a business we now know was worth six million dollars. And he wouldn't even part with a few thousand. The amount would have meant nothing to Brad. But, for Henry, that would have made a big difference in the end. In terms of getting a decent doctor. And a nursing home with resources to do some things right. Serve the occasional hot meal. Clean the bed linen. Answer Henry's damn bell when he needed to get to the bathroom. So I every time I showed up, he wasn't sitting in his own mess and—"

When tears filled Violet's eyes, she sighed and sucked hard on her cigarette.

"I'm sorry," Violet said. "It still burns me to this day."

"I'm sorry, too," Mimi said. "So what brought you here this summer?"

She said her sons had read in the newspaper about Brad Hansen finally selling the carpet business. When they told Violet, she said she decided to come here, confront Brad and see if, once and for all, he'd honor his commitment to Henry.

"I told myself that Henry didn't live long enough to see any profits," Violet said. "But I'll be goddamned if Henry's sons don't either."

When she rented a unit from Brad Hansen, she was relieved, she said, when he didn't recognize her. Her plan was to show the papers that Henry had signed to Brad, an early riser, on Saturday morning before the race.

"Did you?"

"I never got the chance."

Violet set down her cigarette in an ashtray. She started coughing and coughing, as if gasping for life. Then stopped.

"Where was I?"

"Saying you never got the chance to confront Brad Hansen on Saturday morning. Why was that?"

"Even though I showed up at around six or six-thirty, Brad was already tied up. From the living room, I could hear him at the top of the stairs arguing with someone."

"With Francine?"

"No, I'm pretty sure he was arguing with a man. Or maybe it was one of those boys the police arrested. The Ryans."

"You didn't recognize the voice?"

"Correct."

"Could you make out anything they were saying?"

"I couldn't."

"What did you do next?"

Violet took a long drag on her cigarette, stubbed it out and started hacking again. Her eyes teared. Her face turned purple before the coughing stopped.

"Damn cigarettes," she said. "Like men say about women: 'Can't live with 'em or without 'em.' So now where was I?"

"You were saying what you did after overhearing Brad arguing upstairs."

"I left, thinking I might say something to Brad if he was alone at breakfast. But when I came back for breakfast, only Francine was downstairs. She said Brad was upstairs getting ready for the race. I told her about needing new bath towels. I don't know about yours. But mine were practically rags. Then I had to hurry to meet my friend Alice Weathersby for a full day of antiquing."

"Did you ever see Brad on Saturday?"

"No, I didn't."

"I have to ask you this, like I've asked everyone I've spoken to: You didn't poison Brad Hansen, did you?"

"Of course not."

"Or ask anyone else to poison him for you?"

"What do you take me for? Some kind of criminal? No, I had nothing to do with Brad Hansen's death."

"Do you think if you had been able to meet with Brad that he would have honored his commitment to Henry?"

"It's impossible to say now, isn't it? I did go into this thinking that if he didn't give me the full amount, he might offer me something just to get rid of me."

"Do you think your chances are better with Brad Hansen dead?"

"That I don't know. No one would call their chances good asking Brad Hansen for money under any circumstances. But I don't know how well the documents will hold up with him gone. Signed by two dead people without any witnesses."

"Any reason to think his widow, Francine, would be more sympathetic to your appeal?"

"You'd have to ask her."

CHAPTER FORTY

MIMI THOUGHT HER FOUR O'CLOCK appointment with Francine was definite. Francine had proposed the time and Mimi had confirmed it on her machine.

But, when Mimi showed up at four and rang the bell, no one answered. She rang it again. And a third time before she heard footsteps.

"Who is it?" Francine yelled. "Who's there?"

"It's Mimi. Mimi Goldman."

"Oh," Francine said, opening the door. "I wasn't sure you'd actually . . . Since we never . . ."

Francine, face flushed, smelled like herbal shampoo. In her favorite red kimono and slippers, she had a towel wrapped around her wet hair.

"Should I come back later?"

"No, no. Just have a seat. Grab some coffee and

something to eat. Please. I have way too much food here. And I'll run upstairs and make myself decent."

From the staircase, Francine yelled, "The newspapers are on the counter. If you want something to read?"

Mimi poured herself a coffee. Then she found the copies of the *Jamestown Post-Journal* and *Mayville Reporter* on the counter. The Ryans' arrest was the lead story in both papers.

The accounts were pretty similar. And they told Mimi nothing new.

They both included a photo of the DA pontificating on the courthouse steps. And the mug shots of the Ryans that were included in the DA press kits.

When Mimi moved onto *The Chautauquan Daily*, she followed her usual pattern.

She made sure that her sports page looked fine. Then she flipped to the latest account of "The Mystery of Good and Evil" lecture series.

The third speaker in the series, Carl Goldberg, a psychoanalyst, sounded like the week's biggest pessimist.

Goldberg, whose latest book was entitled *Speaking With The Devil: Exploring Senseless Acts of Evil*, described the world as morally bankrupt.

He said it is marked by widespread cynicism about virtue and steady rises, worldwide, in cases of clinical depression.

"Under conditions of disillusionment and cynicism, everything is allowable," Goldberg said. "Nothing is too wrong to perpetrate, especially if it amuses us. After all, what other dependable standards do cynical and disillusioned people have than amusement?"

Goldberg sounded like the kind of juror Winters hadn't anticipated: someone who would have no trouble believing the DA's theory that the murder of Doc, and maybe Brad Hansen, too, was a thrill killing—committed by bored, cynical, disillusioned teens looking for amusement.

"Sorry to keep you waiting," Francine said, entering the kitchen looking elegant in jeans and a white linen blouse, cinched at the waist with a thin brown belt.

"No problem," Mimi said. "Just catching up on the news."

"Want me to add some zing to your coffee? I'm thinking of having a drink myself."

"No thanks," Mimi said. "But go ahead and have what you want. It's been a terrible week."

Francine's hand trembled as she added ice, then a generous amount of bourbon, to a tall glass.

Mimi tried not to stare as she gave her usual bogus spiel about *The Daily*'s independent investigation.

"I have a few questions," she said. "Some easy. Some, well, not so easy. I'm sure the police have covered a lot of the same ground."

Francine took a long sip.

"Well, hit me with the worst of it," she said. "I'd like to help however I can. I'm having a hard time believing those boys are guilty."

"Okay, here goes," Mimi said, steeling herself for the worst. "For starters, I was wondering if you are the same woman who, under the name of Francine Rodino, was convicted in Indianapolis of, uh, having a sexual relationship with a student, uh, who—"

Francine, raising her hand, gestured for Mimi to stop.

"Let me make this easier for both of us. I don't know how you found this out. That's your business. But if you're asking if that person, Francine Rodino, is me? The answer is, yes. I think the better question is, is that information relevant at all? And the answer to that is, absolutely not. My past is my past. And I can assure you it has nothing whatsoever to do with the current situation.'"

Responding to follow-up questions, Francine said, as far as she knew, her husband and Chautauqua neighbors were unaware of her conviction.

"The police, of course, asked me about it. And

I told them the same thing I'm telling you. NOT RELEVANT. At. All."

"So you're saying it's wrong for people to think someone guilty of one crime might be more likely to commit another?"

"Now, hold on there," Francine said, slamming her glass down on the table. "Hold on. I told you I was the person convicted. I never said I was guilty. It's a battle I quit fighting long ago. But, believe me, I was wrongly accused. And wrongly convicted."

"Then I have to ask you this: Why did you plead guilty?" Mimi pressed. "Most people, myself included, find a claim of innocence tough to reconcile with a guilty plea."

Francine said that was her only choice.

"The dozens of experts who examined me said I have 'unresolved issues' or misplaced affections. Whatever. And the fact that I'd spent time with these boys, as a friend, a caring friend, put me in a tough position. Legally. I couldn't win. I knew it from the get-go."

Francine took another long sip.

"Believe me, it was a lonely thing being a woman accused of sex charges in the Midwest back then," she said. "My principal didn't support me. The union ran scared. The more I denied the charges, the more

268 • DEB PINES

parents came out of the woodwork with accusations. One wilder than the next."

Francine shook her head.

"My main accuser, Joey Hathaway's mother, Julie Hathaway, was relentless. I got a letter in prison from someone saying Julie didn't stop with me. She supposedly went on to destroy more lives. Of a boy scout leader and an uncle she claimed molested Joey, too. I considered checking that story out and adding it to a last-ditch appeal. But, by then, I was nearly up for parole. And, for my own sanity, I needed to let this fight go. To move on. And make sure the past is past."

If Francine's story was true, it was one of those nightmares, Mimi didn't want to believe.

She took down the names of key Indiana figures in it, including Francine's principal, Tom Bell, to double-check what she could. Then she returned to her other questions.

Echoing virtually everyone, Francine said Brad Hansen had numerous potential enemies. He fought with his children, his brother, his tenants and various creditors, she said.

"You know how most of us need coffee in the morning to get going?"

Mimi nodded.

"Brad needed a good fight," she said. "In person or on the phone. If he couldn't provoke someone he knew, he'd call the talk shows and rant about the Bills."

"What bills?"

"The Buffalo Bills. The football team. But he did have a bitter phone fight going recently over a bill. I'm not sure who was on the other end. But Brad was relentless, saying he wasn't going to pay."

When Mimi asked about Violet Greenwood's recollection of a quarrel early Saturday between Brad and a man, Francine looked briefly lost in thought.

"Now that you mention it," she said. "I think that's right. So much happened since then, I forgot about that fight. But I remember being half-awake in bed thinking Brad was already at it and it wasn't even six-thirty."

"Was he fighting with someone in person?"

"I'm not sure. It was loud. Maybe in person or on the speaker phone."

"You heard another voice?"

"I did."

"A man's voice?"

"I think so."

"Could you make out anything said?"

"If I could, it didn't stick with me. I don't remember the substance of the fight. Just that Brad was in a fight."

Mimi moved on to other questions she'd asked

everyone, including whether Francine had killed her husband.

"I did not," she said. "We all know he wasn't the easiest man to be with. But, believe me, we had something special between us. Something I never thought I'd find again after the death of my first husband."

She chugged the rest of her drink.

"I know people are whispering about me being after Brad's money," she said. "Well let them whisper. Yes, I'm coming into a lot of money. But let me tell you this: With Brad alive I also had a lot of money. Without him, I don't have more money. And I'm alone."

When Francine's eyes teared up, Mimi stared into her notebook.

"I just have a few more questions," she said, moving to the bottom of her list.

"From what I'm told, the will names you Brad's sole beneficiary. So you get everything, including his properties. But I also hear you've agreed to sign over the deed to this house to Brad Hansen's children."

"They knew," Francine whispered.

"What?"

"My past. I didn't want it coming out. So I figured, what the hell? I've got more money and houses than I can use in a lifetime. Why not?"

Mimi was tempted to end it there. But, staring at her list, she decided to cover one more point.

"I know we've discussed this before. But can I ask you again why B.J. Ryan was in your house, alone, the other day?"

"I'll repeat what I said before. He was my pupil. I was tutoring him for the SATs."

"Didn't your sentence in Indiana require you not do any more teaching or tutoring? And not associate with young men?"

She nodded.

"Then why would you take that risk?"

"To tell you the truth, I didn't give it that much thought. It wasn't like I'd taken a teaching job with regular hours and a salary. But that's a big part why B.J. wasn't straight with you when you asked what he was doing here."

"This is a little off the point. But I was wondering if B.J. ever left any belongings here?"

Francine didn't answer.

"Like maybe a rifle?" Mimi pressed.

"No," Francine said, staring into her empty drink glass. "No, he didn't."

The answer wasn't convincing.

But Mimi, not pressing further, finished her coffee, packed up and washed her dirty coffee cup in the sink.

"Is there anything you think I should have asked you about that I missed?" Mimi asked.

"You're pretty thorough but . . ."

"But what?"

"I'm surprised you never asked about the Warren sisters. Evangeline and Philomena."

"What about them?"

"They were among the most recent people to fight bitterly with Brad."

"I'd never heard about it. What were they fighting about?"

"They've been on the rampage since July when Brad went and poisoned one of their precious kitties."

CHAPTER FORTY-ONE

LETTING MOMENTUM CARRY HER, Mimi went right from Francine's house to the Warren sisters' apartment.

Again she had to ring the bell multiple times before she got a response.

"Hello," she called. "Hellooooo."

Inside, Mimi heard Philomena ask her sister.

"Is that someone at the door? You know I don't hear as well as you do."

"We're not expecting anyone."

"Why don't you check?"

"Why don't *you* check yourself?"

When Mimi didn't hear more, she raised her voice.

"LADIES, HELLO. It's Mimi. Mimi Goldman. Your neighbor."

Now, she heard slow shuffling steps approaching.

"Is there anyone there?" Evangeline asked.

"It's Mimi Goldman, your neighbor."

Evangeline opened the door and invited Mimi into the sisters' dimly lit living room that smelled like cats.

"To what do we owe this unexpected pleasure?" Evangeline asked. "What can we do for our favorite investigative reporter?"

Mimi began by apologizing for arriving so late and unannounced. She said *The Daily* wanted her to continue investigating the deaths of Brad Hansen and Doc Segovian. So she had a few questions for the sisters.

"Didn't you hear the news on the radio and TV?" Evangeline asked. "What's the matter with you? The police arrested those brothers, the friends of your son. They were charged with killing Doc. We went to the courthouse even though it's been hotter than blue blazes. And now the talk is they're going to charge those hooligans with Brad Hansen's death, too."

"I know about the charges," Mimi said. "I was there, too. But my paper wants me to forge ahead anyway. Even if I end up at the same place as the police."

"It's their nickel, I guess," Philomena said. "But it seems like a complete waste of time and I hate to see—"

"Let's hear her out, sister," Evangeline interrupted. "Have a seat. Want some tea? The kettle's whistling."

Mimi sat where she was told, on a brown plastic-covered couch, opposite Philomena.

She accepted a tea from Evangeline in a dainty teacup on a saucer that also held two butter cookies. She waited for Evangeline to make another trip to serve herself and her sister before starting in again.

"As you may know a key part of investigating is eliminating suspects," she said. "I'm no expert. But I've found it's good to keep an open mind. Consider every conceivable person a suspect. Then go down the list, marking people off until—"

"So you're saying *we're* suspects?" Evangeline interrupted. "Like the old church-lady murderers in *Arsenic and Old Lace?* You know the old movie?"

Mimi took a swallow of bitter tea.

"I'm not saying you're suspects any more than anyone else around here is a suspect. Myself included."

Evangeline snorted contemptuously.

"We certainly don't belong in the same category as those hooligan criminals the police have arrested and —"

"Didn't you say hear her out?" Philomena asked. "Let's see why we're on the list and get ourselves off. Tell me, Mrs. Goldman, why you might think two elderly God-fearing women would use violence to settle any disagreement?"

"Was there a disagreement?"

Philomena, smiling, wagged her finger at Mimi.

"You must know there was," she said. "Brad Hansen, you surely know, was a disagreeable man."

"It's wrong to speak ill of the dead," Evangeline said, shooting her sister an angry look. "Wrong and sinful."

"Wrong but true," Philomena countered.

"Wrong, nonetheless," Evangeline said.

"Excuse me," Mimi said. "I hear what you're saying about gossip. Mean-spirited gossip. That's not what I'm looking for here. What I want is more like what the TV detectives used to say: 'Just the facts.'"

"We loved that show, didn't we Phil?" Evangeline said, smiling.

And, for once, Philomena agreed.

"So, if you wouldn't mind, could you share the source of disagreement between you two and Brad Hansen?"

"We had several disagreements with the man," Philomena said. "He harbored a grudge, I'd say, about the time, oh, four years ago, when we called the Chautauqua Police on him. His first wife, Margaret, was making a racket, calling for help, as if Brad was doing who knows what violence to her. We asked the police not to say who called. But somehow Brad found out. And he told us in no uncertain terms to mind our own business or find another place to live."

"Was there something more recent?"

The sisters exchanged a look.

When no one spoke, Mimi did.

"Didn't Brad poison one of your cats?" Mimi asked.

"Yes," Evangeline said. "Yes, he did. He'd asked us to get rid of the cats during the season."

"How many do you have?"

"Four. I mean we had four. We have three now. There's Ezekial here, old Zeke," Evangeline said, pointing to a gray furry lump beside her. "Usually we've complied with Brad's wishes. And board the cats for the nine-week season with friends at Point Chautauqua. This year, Elijah wasn't well. Had a touch of ringworm. It seemed unfair to send him off in June."

"I wish we had," Philomena added.

"What happened?"

"We kept the boy under wraps as best as we could. Elijah never went out. He was strictly an indoor cat. Very quiet and neat. No problems. And a handsome gent. Black coat with white scruff at the neck."

Evangeline said Brad Hansen must have found out about Elijah when they stupidly left some empty cat food tins at the curb for the recycling pickup.

"The next day we came home from church services," Evangeline said. "And found the cat dead in a box. With a note signed by Brad Hansen."

"It was the cruelest thing," Philomena said, sniffling.

"He said something like, 'Defy the rules and you pay the consequences.'"

"Did you think of reporting him to the police? Or the ASPCA?"

"Thought about it," Evangeline said. "We definitely did. But we were afraid of losing our apartment here."

"Did you save the note?"

"No," Evangeline answered. "We buried it with Elijah, outside our friends' house on the other side of the lake."

"Did you consider retaliating? By, maybe, poisoning Brad Hansen?"

"Absolutely not," Evangeline said.

"Retaliating, I have to say, crossed my mind, once or twice," Philomena said.

"Shame on you," Evangeline scolded, before turning to Mimi. "You'll have to excuse her. Sometimes what my sister considers humorous. Especially lately."

Evangeline shook her head.

"She hasn't been herself," Evangeline said. "I'm speaking for both of us when I say that, as daughters of a man of God, you have our word. We were taught, and we believe, that it is God's place, and God's place alone, to mete out justice."

The sisters said they were together Saturday morning, getting ready to watch the race. And they were together

Tuesday night eating dinner and then heading over to the Old First Night program early to get good seats. They said they didn't quarrel with Brad Hansen very early Saturday and didn't hear anyone else quarreling with him.

"Did you see anyone leaving or entering the Hansens' house before breakfast? At maybe six or six-thirty?"

Mimi thought she saw Philomena glance at her sister before answering, "No, no we didn't."

"Did you leave anything for Brad Hansen to eat that morning? Or ask anyone else to leave him anything?"

"Like my sister said," Philomena said. "It wasn't our place. We're not in the justice business. If those boys did the crime, they will be judged first by man's laws, then the Lord's."

Chapter Forty-Two

IN THE NEXT FEW DAYS, Mimi obsessed about the case. But she had little time to devote to it.

She had to fill the sports pages.

She got some help from Mike Halloran, *The Daily*'s eager-beaver summer intern.

But on Friday, Mike announced that he had to go home—that very day.

Mike hadn't realized that his marching band in Columbus, Ohio, was starting practice the following week—a week before school started.

So all weekend and on Monday, Mimi busted butt—trying to stockpile enough stories so she could attend the felony hearing against the Ryan twins, starting the following day, Tuesday.

Late Monday, she was still at the office finishing a

feature on the 36-hole Chautauqua Golf Club for a preview of a celebration there next week.

Happily, Mimi got to include one of her favorite Chautauqua tidbits in her story: that Amelia Earhart, on her way to delivering a lecture at Chautauqua, had landed her plane on what is now the Lake Course's seventeenth hole.

Mimi also proofread golf and tennis tournament results, softball box scores and a story on the weekend lawn bowling competition.

"Do you have the lawn bowling caption?" Wentworth, also working late, yelled to her.

"Not yet, I forgot."

In a hurry, Mimi put together a caption, pushed "send" and walked over to Wentworth's desk.

"You should have it," she said.

He tapped a few keys and confirmed that he did.

"Thanks," Wentworth said. "So this means you're covered through Thursday, right?"

"Yes. I'll check in every day to be sure you're okay. But I'm glad you're letting me sit through the hearings."

"No problem. You haven't forgotten the Old First Night retrospective, have you?"

"No," Mimi lied. "I've gone through Doc's photos. He had so many good ones. I just have to make choices."

282 • DEB PINES

"Is there any chance the hearing tomorrow will be postponed?"

"I'll double-check with one of the lawyers before I leave."

When Mimi dialed the Public Defender's office, Justin Winters, B.J.'s lawyer, answered the phone himself.

"Hey, I'm glad to see someone else is working as late as I am," he said wearily. "Misery loves company."

"At least you're doing something important," Mimi said. "I hate to tell you what's keeping me here. A story about lawn bowling. I'm hardly out there saving the world."

"I hope you don't think that's what I'm doing."

After they exchanged a few pleasantries and small talk, Mimi asked if the hearing was still on for the next day.

"It is. Tomorrow at nine."

"Anything new?"

"Not since we spoke yesterday," Winters said. "Like I explained, the DA will hold out on giving us what he's got until a nanosecond before the start of the hearing."

"And, like I said, that doesn't seem fair."

"Just the rules of the game. He plays the ones favoring his side and I play the ones favoring mine."

"How are the twins?"

"Surviving. They've got a few bruises, they say they put on each other, mixing it up in jail."

"But you suspect the guards?"

"No, not this time. I believe the brothers were fighting. I got them cleaned up. We have jackets and ties here for them to wear to court. The tough thing is that B. J. is still stonewalling."

"Stubborn."

"His mom's worse. I left her maybe six messages. She returned one to say she can't make it to court tomorrow."

"I'd call her myself if I knew her."

"Not your problem. I'll try her again later. I'm just sitting here wondering why some people go to the trouble of having children, if they don't give a damn about them. It leaves me . . ."

After a pause, Winters resumed.

"I'm sorry," he said. "I'm gonna have to run. But one more thing I wanted to tell you, is that you shouldn't be surprised by the strategy I'm using tomorrow."

"Which is?"

"Frankly, different than what my client wants and what I thought I might use. B. J. wanted to me to come out punching. Challenge everything. See if I can get the charges dismissed. But the more I thought about it, the more I thought I'll just handle this felony hearing the way I usually do."

"Which is?"

"Basically, I'll be a spectator taking notes."

"Really?"

"Really. I will fight one procedural battle. But that's it. The rest of the time you won't even know I'm there. I could do some grandstanding for the crowds and media. I could poke tiny holes in the DA's expert and police testimony. But why?"

He sighed.

"I'm not fooling myself," he said. "Combined, the tiny holes won't sink their case. And my efforts would only reveal my hand, the little I've got. I'd rather bide my time. Listen. Take in the government's evidence. And come to trial armed for bear."

"So you're conceding there will be a trial?"

"Unless my one procedural gambit pays off."

Chapter Forty-Three

As the felony hearing played out the next morning in Judge Fenterman's packed-to-the-gills Jamestown courtroom, Mimi was glad for the heads up.

Glad Winters had shared his plans and the reasoning behind them.

Because, otherwise, his plans looked a whole helluva lot like surrender.

When Judge Fenterman walked in, everyone rose. Including Winters. And John Swoozy, Bob Ryan's lawyer, who sat next to Winters at the defense table along with both Bob and B.J. Ryan, dressed like prep-school kids in navy-blue gold-buttoned blazers, khaki pants and striped ties.

But, after that, both defense lawyers, for the

most part, didn't budge starting with the DA's first witness Chautauqua County Coroner Thomas Love.

Love, like coroners in most small places with little violent crime, was a funeral home director. He wasn't a professional medical examiner. But he was still a great witness.

A small man with thick brown hair, glasses and a teacherly manner, Love spoke plainly, with little jargon. He also clearly knew his stuff—due to a passion for reading about forensics, attending conferences and teaching a forensics class at the State University of New York campus in Fredonia.

"Together, there were six gunshot wounds to the victim," Love said, while pointing to the wounds in a blow-up of a gruesome crime-scene photo. "Four entrance wounds and two exit wounds."

Entrance wounds, he explained, are smaller in size and more circular and regular in shape.

"Exit wounds are larger because when the bullet exits the body, not only the bullet exits," Love said. "It takes with it particles of flesh and soft tissue."

Under gentle prodding from the DA Ed Billings, Love went on to say that Doc had been shot at fairly close range. He estimated the time as between 5:45 p.m. and 6 p.m. on Tuesday.

"To a reasonable degree of medical certainty," Love

offered the conclusion that the cause of Doc's death was gunshot wounds to the head and chest.

To Mimi, the conclusion seemed ridiculously obvious.

Still, she felt disappointed when neither Winters nor Swoozy rose to rip the witness to shreds.

When Winters did get up, he announced: "I have no questions for this witness, Your Honor."

"No questions either," Swoozy added.

The next witness was Donald Yee, a ballistics expert.

In response to Billings' questions, Yee said two .22-caliber bullet fragments were retrieved from Doc's body and two passed through the body.

All four were fired by the same .22-caliber Remington pump-action rifle recovered in the men's room next door to the darkroom where Doc's body was found, Yee said.

Yee went on to say that sales records indicated that the recovered rifle had been sold three years ago at a Wal-Mart Store in Jamestown.

"Do you know the name of the purchaser of that weapon?"

"Yes."

"Can you tell the court the purchaser's name?"

Yee referred to his notes.

"Brigham John Ryan," he said, using B.J.'s formal name.

After a buzz spread through the courtroom, Judge Fenterman asked for quiet.

"I'm done with this witness," Billings said with a hint of triumph.

When the judge glanced at the defense table, Winters rose.

"I have no questions for this witness, Your Honor," he said before sitting.

"No questions either," added Swoozy, hopping up and down.

Mimi had to remind herself she wasn't there for personal entertainment. For the thrill of watching two legal gladiators do fierce battle. Two teens' lives were on the line. And their lawyers were using every tactical advantage to save them.

The final morning witness was Theresa Vitale, a fingerprint expert.

A small plump woman with graying curls and big black-rimmed glasses, Vitale looked relaxed as she spelled her name for the court reporter and swore to testify truthfully.

Mimi browsed a copy of Vitale's preliminary report, given to her by Winters, as Billings led Vitale through a list of her impressive expert credentials.

Those included her participation in several State Police and FBI training programs, her authorship of dozens of scholarly papers and a textbook chapter and her prior testimony in thousands of cases in state and federal court.

When Judge Fenterman admitted Vitale as an expert, Billings helped her place on an easel two blow-up black-and-white photos of fingerprints that looked like modern art.

With enthusiasm, Vitale explained how her lab uses powders and chemicals to develop a latent or inked print that is visible to the naked eye.

Pointing to the photo exhibits, she noted comparisons between the print on the right, taken from the suspected murder weapon, and the one of the left, taken from the defendant, Brigham John Ryan, also known as B.J. Ryan.

"You can see multiple points of comparison," Vitale said, pointing to whirls and ridges that looked identical.

"So is it your expert opinion, then, to a reasonable degree of scientific certainty, that the prints on the gun belong to the defendant, Brigham John Ryan?" Billings asked.

"Yes, it is."

When Billings finished, he sat. And the whole courtroom, Mimi included, turned with anticipation toward the defense table.

Winters rose with tremendous grace.

"I have no questions of this witness, Your Honor," he said.

"None from me either," added Swoozy.

"Then this seems like a good natural breaking point for lunch," Judge Fenterman said.

"Mr. Billings, are your witnesses available for the afternoon?" the judge asked.

"Yessir."

"Then, let's resume at two."

Mimi hung back. As she watched the courtroom empty, she noted the presence of virtually anyone she ever considered a possible murder suspect.

B.J. and Bob Ryan, of course, were front and center. In the spectator section were: Francine Hansen, her brother-in-law Mole, her step-kids Brad Jr. and Mary Hansen, and all of the renters—the Warren sisters, Betsy Gates and Violet Greenwood.

Downstairs, she scanned the area for her lunch date, Mack. And she found him at the bottom of the courthouse steps, talking to Theresa Vitale, the fingerprint expert.

Chapter Forty-Four

"Lucky for Terry, she's done," Mack said after introducing the women who shook hands. "Now she can go back to work."

"Lucky me."

As Vitale turned to go, Mimi asked if she wouldn't mind waiting one sec.

"I don't know if you're in a big hurry. But I was wondering, well, if you could answer one question for me before you leave?"

"Mimi," Mack scolded. "Mimi. Have some mercy. This woman deserves a lunch break like the rest of us."

"Hey, I don't mind," Vitale said. "I'm a geek who loves talking shop. Especially for a friend of yours whose heroics I followed last summer. I thought I recognized your name. You're not still at *The Reporter*, are you?"

292 • DEB PINES

"No, that job didn't last. But I'm still in the area, working at *The Chatauquan Daily*. At least until September."

Vitale's face softened.

"Then you must have known the deceased?"

Mimi, teary-eyed, tried to keep her voice steady.

"He was a dear friend."

"He sounded like a wonderful man, too. I'm sorry. I didn't realize. This has gotta be tough. What can I do for you?"

"I have a hypothetical question."

"Go ahead."

"If a hypothetical shooter wore gloves while handling a gun, whose prints would you expect to find on the gun?" Mimi asked. "The owner's prints? Or the shooter's prints?"

"That's an excellent question," Vitale said, smiling as if Mimi were her star pupil. "I'm kind of surprised the defense didn't ask me that themselves. Winters is a sharpie. So he's probably just holding back, waiting to ambush me with the question at trial."

"I remember a case from years ago when I was a reporter at *The New York Post*," Mimi said. "There were multiple shootings by a gloved gunman. I remember there was something tricky about the fingerprints issue. But I can't remember what it was. If the other prints—earlier ones under the gunman's—were obliterated by his handling of the gun. Or—"

"Not necessarily," Vitale said. "If a gunman wears gloves, earlier prints, typically an owner's, can survive on the gun for years."

"*Years?*" Mimi echoed.

"Years," Vitale repeated.

"So, hypothetically, a shooter wearing gloves might have fired B.J. Ryan's rifle and left behind none of his or her own prints?"

"That's correct."

"The other thing I was wondering," Mimi said. "Was—"

"Hey, you said one question, Mimi," Mack cut in.

"Sergeant Mackenzie, back off," Vitale said. "I said I don't mind. And I mean it. I don't mind."

"Okay, the other thing is hypothetical, too."

Mack sighed.

"It starts with a reference in your report on the bottom of page four?"

Mimi flipped to the reference and showed it to Terry and Mack.

"It says something about a microscopic trace of powder found on B.J.'s gun," Mimi continued as Vitale nodded as if she knew where this was heading.

"Does this powder make you think it's possible or likely that someone handled B.J.'s gun while wearing latex gloves?" Mimi asked.

"She's good," Vitale said. "Maybe you should take her with you when you go back to law school."

Mack laughed.

"Too many women trying to run my life," he smiled.

"If you'd just let us," Vitale responded.

"So what do you think?" Mimi asked.

"You're right, " Vitale continued. "Latex gloves worn by the shooter could be one explanation for the residue."

"Other explanations?" Mimi asked.

"The powder might have been left by someone wearing talcum powder, before the shooting, then touching the gun. Or it might have been left by someone in law-enforcement after the fact. Say a cop or lab tech wearing latex gloves, as we all do, while processing the gun."

"Or a hypothetical latex-gloved shooter?"

"That's correct."

When Mimi finally finished with Vitale, Mack was standing off to the side, listening intently to his police radio.

"Want to just meet me at the diner?" he whispered to Mimi. "I'll be there in five. I promise."

Five minutes didn't give Mimi enough time to make any of the calls she wanted. Especially to Jake whose morning mission was going through the Hansens' phone bills.

So she just walked over to the diner, across from the courthouse and sat in a red booth near the back.

While sipping coffee, waiting, she reviewed her notes from court that morning, circling or under-lining key phrases. Then she went through one of *The Daily*s she'd brought along as downtime reading material.

She checked the sports page. Fine. Then she moved on to divining any lessons she could from last Thursday's "Mystery of Good and Evil" lecture.

The speaker was Lance Morrow, a senior writer at *Time* magazine. Evil, according to Morrow, is a "strange and versatile and dangerous word. I say it is dangerous because it can be used to describe a genocide and it can be used to justify a genocide."

Near the end of his talk Morrow said, "Many writers have said that one of evil's higher accomplishments has been to convince people that it does not exist."

As Mack slid into the booth across from Mimi, she wondered if the Ryans were the evil ones convincing her they weren't? Or if someone else was doing an even better job of concealing the evil in them?

Chapter Forty-Five

"STILL DOUBT we've got the right guys?" Mack asked while getting settled and loosening his gun belt.

"Not sure," Mimi said.

"That hypothetical you went through with Terry? It's just a hypothetical. So that under some crazy far-fetched scenario, it's POSSIBLE—not LIKELY—possible, that someone other than B. J. Ryan, wearing gloves was the shooter. It doesn't mean that—"

"I realize that."

"So do you have something more substantial? Like evidence? Or a confidential source? That you should consider handing over to the police?"

In her head, Mimi went over what she had.

And she made a calculation something like the one made by Winters.

Her ammo—wisps of threads of rumors of Brad Hansen's business and personal feuds—wasn't much.

So she was better off saying little.

"I don't have anything conclusive," she said. "Just a number of hunches and leads—*good* hunches and leads—that I'm chasing."

"Hunches and leads?" Mack repeated.

Mimi nodded.

"Hunches and leads that are more persuasive than forensic evidence and eyewitness testimony?" Mack asked. "Stronger than B.J. Ryan owning the murder weapon? Leaving his prints on it? And other damning stuff that will come out against both brothers later?"

"Maybe."

Mack shook his head.

"The evidence is strong already and just gonna get stronger."

"I'll see," Mimi said.

"And you don't see that already? Jesus Christ," he huffed. "Your stubbornness scares me sometimes. I'm afraid of where it might take you. And what you miss sitting right before your eyes."

Before Mack could lecture Mimi more, the waitress took their orders: hamburger-deluxe platters, with fries, lettuce, tomato and onion, for both of them. A Coke for Mack. More coffee for Mimi.

As Mack spoke to the waitress, Mimi noticed again how tired he looked. And unbelievably handsome, with his gray-specked blond hair, blue eyes and perfect swimmer's build—broad shoulders, narrow hips, muscled arms.

And sad.

Since Mack's son's accident, Mack had lost the uncomplicated, forever-sunny surfer-dude look he'd had when they'd first met.

"Are you feeling okay?" Mimi asked him. "You look tired."

"I *am* tired. We'll get a break after this hearing wraps up which could be today or tomorrow. You can imagine with such a high-profile case the sheriff is all over Wilson. So Wilson is all over the rest of us to keep pushing pedal to the medal. How about you and Jake? How are you holding up?"

"Jake's great. Or, at least, he seems to be. This is definitely an occasion when being a teenage boy, not in touch with your emotions, is an asset. I'm a little shaky. But my investigating—even if you don't approve—is helping me. I feel like I'm trying to do right by my friend. To get justice."

Mack, obviously biting his tongue, just nodded.

When their hamburger platters arrived, they both ate hungrily. They were aware they just had twenty more minutes until they had to be back in court.

When someone put money in a jukebox up front, next to the carousel of spinning pies, out came one of the few country music songs Mimi knew—because she'd heard it, for the first time, last summer when she met Mack.

The chorus was catchy.

And poignant.

"It's been a while since I felt this feeling that everything that you do gives me," it went. "It's been too long since somebody whispered, 'Shut up and kiss me.'"

Mimi, embarrassed by the whole business, blushed. Mack, apparently oblivious, kept eating.

To distract herself, Mimi switched the conversation to safe ground: baseball.

"Did you see how the night after you came by, my Yankees won the next two games against the Mariners in Seattle?"

"Maybe I'm bad luck, " Mack said.

"Doubt it."

Mack asked the waitress for his own coffee. Mimi asked for a refill.

When they grew silent, of course, the Mary Chapin Carpenter jukebox song reached the chorus again.

"Oh baby when I get this feeling, it's like genuine

voodoo hits me," she crooned. "It's been too long since somebody whispered, 'Shut up and kiss me.'"

When the check came, they rose, Mimi a little unsteadily.

"Why don't we split this?" Mimi asked.

"*Please*," Mack said. "Let me get it this time and you get it the next?"

Chapter Forty-Six

EVEN AFTER MAKING one stop at the courthouse payphones to call Wentworth, Mimi was still able to claim her same second-row courtroom seat. The space was crowded but not overcrowded.

And, as Mack predicted, the evidence against the Ryan brothers just kept getting stronger.

The afternoon's first witness, Lieutenant Wilson, began by testifying about finding a saw and the murder weapon's sawed-off stock in a Dumpster.

"And where exactly was this Dumpster?" the DA Ed Billings asked.

"Next to a building at 403 West Fourth Street in Jamestown," Wilson said.

"Can you tell us who lives in that apartment building?" Billings asked.

"The defendants Bob and B. J. Ryan," Wilson said.

Later, Wilson went on to describe how B. J. Ryan told him about how he'd gone to the darkroom to meet the deceased, Doc Segovian, at six o'clock, instead of at an initial agreed-upon meeting time of six-thirty.

"A half hour earlier than the initial meeting time?" Billings asked.

"Yes."

"Did he say why he went that early?"

"Yes."

"And why was that?"

"He said the friend who had invited him, Jake Goldman, called his brother Bob to say the meeting time had changed. To the earlier time."

"And what did the Goldman boy say about the purported call?"

"He said he never made it."

"And what did Bob say?"

"He backed up B. J., saying Jake called him with the revised time."

"So let me make sure I'm understanding you right," Billings said. "B. J. and Bob Ryan both said Jake Goldman had called to tell them to come at six, not six-thirty. But Jake said he never called?"

"That's correct."

Mimi, of course, believed her own son. But did that mean that the Ryans had invented the call? Or that someone else had called, pretending to be Jake, as part of a frame-up?

After a short break, the government called its next and final witness, Millicent Houghey.

A tiny lady with a halo of cotton-candy-like white hair, Houghey took one step into the courtroom, surveyed the crowd and, wide-eyed, stopped.

When a giant male court officer offered his arm, Houghey gratefully grabbed it. And she let the court officer escort her, like a wedding guest, up the courtroom aisle to the witness stand next to Judge Fenterman.

There, Houghey, pink-faced, light blue eyes darting around the room, looked like a scared rabbit.

"Mrs. Houghey?" Billings asked.

"Yes," she said, whipping her head in Billings' direction.

"I know, for most people unaccustomed to being in a courtroom, it's scary to testify in front of so many people," Billings said. "Are you nervous, sitting up there?"

She nodded.

"Well, just a few reminders," Billings continued. "All you have to do is answer my questions to the best of your ability. This isn't school. You won't be graded on your answers."

When friendly laughter erupted, Houghey smiled and Billings won points for trying to put her at ease.

"You also have to answer my questions with words. No head shakes or nods. As loudly as possible. So let's try that again. Mrs. Houghey, are you nervous, sitting up there?"

"Yessir, I am," she said, softly. "Or, let me say, YES, I, AM," she repeated louder.

More laughter.

"Very good," Billings said.

Next, Billings led Houghey through a description of herself: That she was eighty-four years old and a widow from Cleveland. That she had spent parts of her summers in Chautauqua since she was five years old. That, this year, she came for Weeks 7 and 8 because that was when her grandchildren from New York City would be there with her daughter-in-law. She also tried to plan her visits to attend Old First Night, Chautauqua's birthday celebration, she said.

After a little more scene-setting, Billings moved on to the case at hand.

"May I direct your attention to the evening of Chautauqua's birthday celebration, Old First Night? Which was this past Tuesday, August fifth?"

Houghey nodded.

"I mean, yessir."

"Can you tell us where you were at around five or five-thirty?"

"Yessir, I can."

"And where was that?"

"I was standing outside the restaurant that used to be the Star Cafeteria, across from the Colonnade building."

"Do you know what the restaurant is called now?"

Houghey frowned.

"It's Sadie something," she said. "I'm sorry, I can't think of the full name."

"Is it Sadie J's?"

"Yes, I believe that's right."

Houghey went on to say that she stood outside the restaurant for a long time, waiting for her grandson who was late. At around six, she said, she noticed a young man exit the darkroom in the Colonnade building and check his watch. Then, she said, she saw the young man "run like the dickens toward Bestor Plaza, as if in some kind of foot race."

All eyes followed Billings as he stepped away from the witness, walked to the prosecution table and grabbed a paper on top of a pile. When Billings returned to the witness, he dragged the moment out by reading the paper to himself.

When he finally looked up, he asked, "Do you

remember giving a description of that young man to a police officer that very night?"

"I do."

"Do you remember saying that the young man in the foot race was about five-foot-eight?" he asked, reading from the report. "Muscular. With light eyes and blond hair in a ponytail?"

"Yessir, I do."

Mimi, like most people in the room, turned toward B.J. and went down the list.

About five-eight?

Yup.

Muscular?

Yup.

Light eyes?

Yup.

Blond hair in a ponytail?

Yup.

There were a few more questions about what Houghey had told the officer before Billings swooped in for the kill.

"And do you see here in court today the young man you saw hurry from the darkroom Tuesday at around 6?"

Houghey was so conscientious she didn't answer right away. She did a full 360-degree gaze around the room—checking out the reporters and sketch artists up front, the spectators in the middle, the local lawyers seated in the jury box, then everyone at the defense table.

"Yessir, I do," Houghey said.

"Could you please point him out to the judge."

Houghey pointed a bony finger at B.J. Ryan, whose usually impassive face colored slightly.

"Let the record reflect the witness is pointing at the defendant, B.J. Ryan," Billings said.

After a brief pause, Judge Fenterman asked Billings, "Are you through with this witness?"

"Yes, Your Honor," I am.

"Well, given the late hour," Fenterman said. "I would usually propose that we break for the day and start again tomorrow morning. But I have another idea. From what I understand, the defense doesn't plan to put on its own case. And it has no legal obligation to do so. So, unless they have questions for this witness, I propose we take a short break. Then push through to the end. If both sides give relatively brief closing arguments," he said, pointedly staring at each lawyer, "then I believe I can gather my thoughts and rule from the bench. And we can be out of here by six o'clock, the latest, tonight. What do you say, gentlemen? Why don't I ask you, individually?"

The lawyers nodded.

"Mr. Winters, for starters, do you have any questions for this witness?" the judge asked.

"Yessir, I do."

"And Mr. Swoozy?"

"I have a few questions as well."

A murmur spread through the courtroom.

If the judge was surprised that, for the first time in the proceedings the defense lawyers would be asking questions, he didn't show it.

"Then let's break for the day. And meet back here, starting at nine o'clock sharp tomorrow."

CHAPTER FORTY-SEVEN

At home, Mimi and Jake made quick work of a pepperoni pizza she'd brought home from Andriaccio's.

Mimi had one slice. So, as Jake did most of the eating, she filled him in on what happened in court. When he finally finished four slices, plus leftover chicken wings, plus string cheese and two glasses of orange juice, Jake cleared the table.

"Did you have an interesting day, too?" Mimi asked while washing the dishes.

"Definitely."

"So you found something in the phone bills?"

"Yes," he said, pulling out the marked-up bills.

"Did they show incoming *and* outgoing calls?" Mimi asked.

"Yes."

"And these were recent calls?"

"Yes."

"How about patterns? Did you see any that—"

"MOM!"

"What?"

"Stop interviewing me. I can tell the story myself."

"Okay, okay," Mimi said. "Sorry. It's hard to turn the interviewing thing off. But I will. Tell the story your way."

"Okay," Jake said. "I'd say one of the most interesting things I found was that, over the course of the past two months, four parties were called from the Hansen house ten times or more. Name those parties?"

"Do I have to?"

Smiling, he crossed his arms.

"This is *my* way."

Mimi sighed.

"Brad's business? How about that? I'll bet he called his business a lot."

"Ding, ding, ding," Jake said. "Good guess, mom. There were nineteen calls from the Hansen house to Big Brad's Carpets in Erie, according to the phone bills. Who else?"

"Brad Hansen's children?"

"No, sorry," Jake said. "I don't see any calls in the

312 • Deb Pines

past two months from the Hansen household to Brad's kids."

"Not to Brad Jr. or to Mary in New York or in Chautauqua?"

"That's correct. Move on, lady."

"Okay, how about Brad's brother, Mole? Were there calls from the house to him?"

"Nope. Bzzzt. Guess again."

"I don't know, Jake. Just tell me."

"Fine. There were eleven calls in the past two months to Everett Thompson in Jamestown. That's the lawyer, right?"

"Right."

"There were sixteen calls to someone in Erie named Phyllis Angelides. I looked her up and she's a stockbroker. And the number called the most, you want to guess?"

"No."

"You don't?"

"I don't."

"It's a number that was called a whopping forty-two times from the Hansen house?"

Mimi shook her head.

"Give up?"

"Yes."

"Okay, I'll give it to you then. The party called

forty-two times was—get this—the billing office at WCA Hospital in Jamestown."

"Seriously?"

"Seriously."

"Do you know why?"

"Not yet."

"Interesting."

"But not the most interesting thing I found."

"Which is?"

"That there was an incoming call to the Hansen house at five-forty Saturday morning, the day of the race."

"What can you tell me about that call?"

"I know it lasted two minutes and forty-two seconds."

"And?"

"I know it was made from a room at Webb's, the motel on 394."

"And?"

"I don't know who made it. But I have a scheme for trying to figure that out."

Chapter Forty-Eight

When Mimi reclaimed her same seat in court the next day, Millicent Houghey was already back on the witness stand.

The judge reminded Houghey she was still under oath. He complimented her previous day's performance. But, as Justin Winters approached, Houghey looked terrified.

"Good morning, Mrs. Houghey," Winters said sweetly. "My name is Justin Winters. And I am representing one of the brothers charged in this case, B. J. Ryan."

"Good morning," she said warily.

"Just as the District Attorney reminded you of your duties as a witness—to answer questions as truthfully and loudly as possible—I'm going to remind you of my duties, as well. Okay?"

Houghey nodded.

Winters, smiling, wagged his finger at her.

Laughter spread through the courtroom. And Houghey, realizing her mistake, raised her hand.

"I'm sorry," she said. "I didn't mean to nod. I meant, yessir."

"No problem," Winters said. "Just as you have your role, my role, under the U.S. Constitution, is to provide that boy," he said, glancing at B.J. Ryan, "the best defense I can humanly offer. No matter what my opinion of the facts might be. Or what your opinion might be. Understand?"

"Yessir."

Satisfied, Winters pulled the same stride-across-the-courtroom-to-pretend-to-be-getting-very-important-documents trick that Billings pulled the day before. And, same as when Billings did it, all eyes followed Winters to the defense table, then back to the witness.

"Mrs. Houghey," he said. "What I want to ask you about and all I plan to ask you about, is the process the police used to get you to—or should I say, help you to—identify my client."

Houghey nodded that she understood. And, gradually, she let Winters take her through the identification steps, starting with her talking to a young Chautauqua County Sheriff's Deputy named Riggs.

"I don't remember his first name," she said. "Just Riggs."

"That's fine," Winters said. "Better than fine. I'm more concerned with what you told Deputy Riggs than his name."

"Just what I said yesterday," Houghey said. "About waiting for my grandson outside the restaurant. Then seeing the young man run away from the darkroom."

Wilson nodded.

"When you told Deputy Riggs what you told us, about the young man being about five-eight, muscular with light eyes and blond hair in a ponytail—what did Deputy Riggs do?"

"He wrote it all down."

"And, Mrs. Houghey, did he then do anything with that description and a computer?" Winters prompted.

"Oh, yes," she said, catching on. "Yes, he did."

"And what did he do?"

"He made a sketch of the suspect by having me pick the features—facial features, hair, nose, etc.—from choices on his screen, that most matched the young man I'd seen. Very clever."

"So it sounds like Deputy Riggs, with the help of his computer, was able to make a composite sketch of the suspect without using a sketch artist? Is that correct?"

"Yessir."

"Do you know if he had a name for the computer program that created the sketch?"

"I can't remember."

"Did he call it Mr. Potato Head by any chance?"

"Exactly," Houghey said, while smiling for the first time. "I remember the name now because my grandchildren have the plastic Potato Head toy."

"Do you know what Officer Riggs did with the composite sketch you helped him create?"

"I believe he showed it to other people in the police department. To see if anyone recognized the youth."

"When was that?"

"Tuesday night."

"When was your next involvement with the case, after speaking with Officer Riggs?"

"Very early the next morning, Wednesday. No, two days later, Thursday. At around seven-thirty in the morning."

"What happened then?"

"The same officer, Deputy Riggs, came to my room on the Chautauqua Institution grounds at the Lakeside Lodge. And he drove me to the police station near here in Mayville. He took me to a room with a two-way mirror. And that's where I picked out the boy."

"How?"

"I looked through the mirror into the room. And I

saw him handcuffed to a chair. And I said something like, 'Yes, that's him. That's the one.'"

"Was there just one person in the room?"

"Yessir."

"And, to recap, Deputy Riggs said something like, 'Is that the young man you saw outside the darkroom?'"

"Yessir."

"And, again, for the record, you said?"

"Something like, 'Yes, that's him. That's the one.'"

Mimi knew Deputy Riggs had screwed up: that a proper identification procedure requires a witness be shown more than one suspect, either in photos or a lineup.

But she didn't know the significance of the screw-up.

A glance at the lawyers didn't help.

Billings, a pro, smiled, as if embarrassed by a minor misstep, no biggie.

Winters and Swoozy—maybe acting, too—looked jubilant, leaning close to their clients, whispering, before Winters hopped to his feet.

"May we approach the bench?" Winters asked the judge.

"Absolutely," Fenterman answered.

As the lawyers and judge carried on a fairly heated sidebar conversation, the spectators chattered, too. The volume in the courtroom got louder and louder.

So Mimi could make out little from the lawyers besides a few "But your Honors" and "If you pleases."

The judge, obviously annoyed, turned his anger on the spectators.

"PLEASE! Can we have a little order here?" he snapped. "If you want to carry on side conversations, step outside. Or I'll have to ask my deputies to remove you."

The threat worked.

In an instant, the spectators went silent.

The debate at the bench, though, continued for ten more minutes. Then the lawyers, looking humbled and weary, returned to their desks.

Fenterman whispered something to his legal secretary, a young man with a soldier-like crewcut and bearing. The secretary returned with a fat legal reference book.

For a few minutes, the judge copied notes from the book, ignoring the crowd following his every pen stroke.

When Fenterman finished, he set down his pen.

"Ladies and gentlemen, thank you for your patience," he began solemnly. "Though we're approaching our usual lunch break, I see no reason to prolong these proceedings any further."

He whispered something to the court reporter.

"Ready," the reporter said, while sitting taller, hands on his mini-keyboard.

"Will the defendants and their counsel please rise?" Judge Fenterman said.

When all four were on their feet, the judge began with a civics lesson.

"The legal standard at this stage of a criminal proceeding is a very low one. I don't need to be convinced beyond a reasonable doubt that these young men committed a felony in order to hold them for trial. I only need to find that a preponderance of the evidence weighs against them. That it's more likely than not that they committed a felony. After that, it would be up to a jury to weigh their fates, their guilt or innocence, based on a much higher standard of proof—beyond a reasonable doubt."

The judge took a sip of water.

"That said," he continued. "Even given that lower standard of proof, I find that, at this juncture, the government has failed to meet it."

When a murmur spread through the crowd, the judge raised his voice.

"Ladies and gentlemen, please," he scolded. "Hear

me out. I am not saying these boys are innocent. Nor am I barring the government from re-filing charges in the future with a stronger legal foundation. I'm just saying that the testimony I've heard these past few days is not enough."

When the room quieted, the judge resumed.

"A reliable eyewitness placing the defendants or one defendant at the crime scene might have carried the day. But today's eyewitness testimony was so tainted as to be meaningless. The court cannot accept an ID based on showing a witness one young man in the highly suggestive pose of being handcuffed to a chair. There is a right way and a wrong way of doing things. And unless charges are filed in a proper manner, they will not be sustained by this Court.

"Therefore, I order the charges in criminal information number ninety-seven dash, oh, one, six, six, be dismissed immediately. Without prejudice. And the defendants be released."

Chapter Forty-Nine

The killer didn't come to court with a plan. But, when one presented itself, well . . .

It was too easy to shadow the nosy reporter out the courtroom. Downstairs. To the parking lot. And halfway back to the Institution.

When Mimi Goldman and her son made a stop that was the opening. The chance to send a message.

The killer continued, slow and steady, back to the Hansens' rental property and still reached it before anyone.

Changed.

Grabbed a bag of tools.

And ended up in little time standing in front of Apartment No. 1 on the ground floor.

On came the latex gloves. A turn on the knob

revealed the door was locked. Surprising but not a deal breaker.

Few people locked their doors in Chautauqua. So the locks tended to be unsophisticated. Nuisances more than barriers to entry. Not like in big cities where pickers and locks were probably more evenly matched.

Reaching into the bag, the killer removed the smallest tool: a paper clip.

A few twists and turns straightened the clip. A few more reshaped it into an "L."

One end of the L went into the lock. After a few jiggles and pushes against the pins, the killer felt good.

The job was almost done. And then, bloody hell, the paper clip snapped.

The killer took a deep breath.

Then a second breath.

Relax.

Relax.

It was only 12:30, the killer noted. Plenty of time.

When the killer felt like fleeing, the reciting began:

"Ye, though I walk through the valley of the shadow of death, I will fear no evil: for thou art with me."

"Ye, though I walk through the valley of the shadow of death, I will fear no evil: for thou art with me."

"Ye, though I walk through the valley of the shadow of death, I will fear no evil: for thou art with me."

Three times did the trick.

The killer reached in the bag again. This time, the tool of choice was the next size up: a nail file.

After extracting the broken paper clip, the nail file went in, pointy end first, as deep as the file's lime-green plastic handle.

Ever so slowly, the killer twisted and turned the file. And twisted and turned it more.

One final twist and, like magic, the tumblers were fooled into thinking the file was a key.

The cylinder turned. The killer was in.

Now what?

Just leaving the door ajar was enough of a message for Apartment No. 1.

Then, wanting to look like an equal-opportunity burglar, the killer repeated the same assault on the other two units downstairs.

Even though little time elapsed, the killer felt harried.

Apartment No. 4, the Warren sisters', posed the greatest challenge. They were the only tenants who'd changed the original locks. Their sturdy new Medeco couldn't be fooled by a paper clip, nail file, bobby pin or the next tool up, a thin screwdriver.

Frustrated, the killer decided to improvise, by leaving a similar message with force. A few whacks at the doorknob with a small hammer didn't break it and only left skid marks.

The killer tried wedging the screwdriver between door and frame.

Better.

The fork-like striations looked like a failed break-in.

On the way to the reporter's apartment, No. 6, the killer jiggled the knob to Doc's old apartment, No. 5.

Locked.

The killer smiled.

Locked *now*?

What more did the know-it-all doctor have to lose? Were his relatives more protective of his belongings than the doctor was of his own damn life?

Outside No. 6, the nosy reporter's apartment, the killer felt energized.

The thrill of a hunter closing in on its prey.

This door was locked, too, probably because the reporter came from New York City. Or had something to hide.

Thankfully, the lock was the original ineffective cylinder lock on every door but the Warren sisters' door.

Out came the nail file. But the twisting movements were too rushed. The pins weren't fooled.

The killer's heart was beating too fast and loud.

To drown out the beats, the reciting began anew:

"Ye, though I walk through the valley of the shadow of death, I will fear no evil: for thou art with me."

"Ye, though I walk through the valley of the shadow of death, I will fear no evil: for thou art with me."

"Ye, though I walk through the valley of the shadow of death, I will fear no evil: for thou art with me."

By the third recitation, the reporter's lock gave way.

The door was open.

The killer felt a sense of triumph, of being smart and in control.

But, aware of the passing of time, the killer walked through the small one-bedroom apartment.

On the one table, were piles of newspapers, magazines and mail. No work. There were also no signs of work in the drawers or closets of clothes. Or anywhere in the kitchen—in drawers, or cabinets or on counters. Or in the boy's room.

If the reporter had any work in connection with the case, it was elsewhere.

Now, it was time to leave a calling card. Something that would get this woman's attention. That would get her to back off and mind her own business.

But what?

When the phone rang, the killer jumped.

When it kept ringing, loudly and incessantly, the

killer exploded, taking a hammer from the bag and smashing everything in sight.

The nosy reporter's TV. Dishes. Glasses. Table. Chair. And, lastly: a wedding photo of some foreigners, maybe grandparents.

Chapter Fifty

"Okay, I love your plan," Mimi told Jake as they approached the main entrance to Webb's from the parking lot. "I just have one amendment."

"Of course you do."

"Here," she said, handing him the Ryan twin mug shots from the DA's press kit.

"I don't think I need them but . . . Okay," he said, accepting the photos anyway. "Couldn't hurt."

The motel, designed to look like a giant farmhouse, had gray shingles on the exterior, a rooster windmill on the roof. Inside, there were numerous hanging flower baskets and a fake fireplace, with a painted-on chimney.

As planned, Jake approached the severe-looking woman at the desk as Mimi hung back, near the door.

"Young man, may I help you?" she asked.

"Uh, I'm not sure," Jake said, softly.

"Well, come here, and speak up. What is it you want?"

"Uh, well, the truth is my mother over there didn't want me to do this but . . ."

The woman, clearly no fan of defiant sons, kept shuffling papers.

"We were at the Chautauqua Institution for a wedding over the weekend of August second," Jake said. "Two weekends ago. And, well, you see my mom's a widow. And I think she may have had a secret admirer staying in your motel."

The woman stopped the paper-shuffling.

"You see, my mom got a big bouquet of flowers," Jake continued. "Beautiful roses and daisies. And those tiny white ones?"

"Baby's breath?"

"Exactly," Jake said. "Baby's breath. The flowers came after the wedding and . . ."

As Jake reeled the woman in, Mimi felt proud. And appalled.

In the lying department, Jake was definitely his father's son, able to tell minor fibs or giant whoppers without any telltale catch in the voice, guilty twitch or sidelong glance.

"Didn't they have a card?"

330 • DEB PINES

"No, ma'am. That's the problem. The card must have fallen off. My mom wanted me to drop the whole thing. But I finally convinced her to let me call the florist whose name was on a ribbon around the vase."

"And?"

"The florist apologized. He said he couldn't find his records with the name of the person who sent the flowers. He could only say they were ordered by someone who was staying at Webb's."

Mimi thought the story had some gaping holes. But the woman, swept up by the tale of thwarted romance, didn't notice them.

"Like I said, my mom wanted me to drop it. But I had an idea."

The woman, now firmly in Jake's camp, waited.

"I brought some pictures of people we met at the wedding," Jake said, while pulling out an envelope of his photos from Brad Hansen's funeral, plus the Ryans' mug shots.

"I took most of these myself," he said. "And I thought maybe you could take a look? And see if anyone looks familiar? Unless I'm catching you at a bad time and we should come back? If I can get my mom to agree to drive me here again?"

"No, no," said the woman, thrilled to be part of the

matchmaking conspiracy. "Stay put. Now's as good a time as any."

The woman explained that she just works weekdays, so she'd only recognize the guest if they were there on the Friday night, August first. If they were just there on Saturday or Sunday, she said she'd have to summon her son, Dallas, who mans the desk nearly every weekend.

"Is he around?" Jake asked.

"As a matter of fact he is."

After the woman summoned her son, she repeated Jake's bogus flowers-from-a-secret-admirer story. She proposed that she look at the photos first, then step aside for Dallas to look.

Meanwhile, Jake laid out the photos, side by side, like cards in a solitaire game. There were shots of Francine, the Hansen children, Mole Hansen, the Warren sisters, Betsy Gates and her husband Don, Violet Greenwood, Bob and B.J. Ryan, and, for good measure, Wentworth, Mack and Lieutenant Wilson.

If the desk lady thought there was anything odd about women's photos being in the mix, she didn't say anything.

One by one, she examined the shots, pausing in front of a few to hold them close to her face.

"I'm sorry," she said when she was done. "I didn't recognize anyone."

Dallas, a gentle giant with long blond hair, denim coveralls and boots, stepped up for his turn.

Walking from one photo to the next, he studied them like an art lover studying paintings in a gallery.

Mimi was impressed by the care mother and son were devoting to the effort—but skeptical it would go anywhere.

The son was near the end of the array when—amazingly—his eyes lit up.

"Here's the one," he said, triumphantly grabbing a photo. "He was here that Saturday. I remember him. He stayed in Room 34, around the back. If you want, I can get you his name and phone number?"

"That would be great," Jake said. "I don't know how to thank you."

"An invitation to this wedding might be nice," the mom said laughing.

Mimi and Jake were out the front door, heading for their car when Jake handed her the photo.

And she saw that the mystery guest who had called Brad Hansen from Webb's the morning of the race was —his son, Brad Hansen Jr.

Chapter Fifty-One

Justin Winters stared at the plastic champagne flute on his cluttered desk and the party in Legal Aid's outer office celebrating his victory.

He'd mixed a little with the crowd and even delivered some formal remarks. But the celebrating was more for others' benefit than his own. The young people especially needed to see that in this burnout business of constant defeats, there was an occasional triumph.

The losing used to wear Winters down, too. Until he replaced his athlete's win-loss mentality with a greater emphasis on process. On the significance of his role of just being there to test the government's proofs against the best evidence and arguments he could muster. If their proofs held up, so be it. He'd done his job.

Winters watched the party switch from champagne to beer in the bullpen shared by secretaries, paralegals and the newest lawyers who didn't get tiny perimeter offices like his

"Hey, Justin," his No. 2, Chantelle Redmond yelled. "Join us."

Winters, waving his phone to convey that he needed to make a call, yelled, "Just a sec."

"We're going to finish this all without you," she yelled. "Go ahead."

Winters had already called home and accepted congratulations from his wife.

Now, he had to finish his "withdrawal of counsel" motion to submit to Judge Fenterman tomorrow.

His client, B.J. Ryan, had made it clear he wanted Winters off the case. And, for B.J.'s protection, he needed new counsel appointed as soon as possible.

The legal community of Western New York thought Winters had scored a big victory. B.J. didn't. He thought the win made him look guiltier, because it was based on trickery, not a head-on attack on the evidence.

Winters turned on his computer and waited for the screen to come to life.

He rested his hands on the keyboard. Then he withdrew them and did what he really wanted to do—dial the Ryan brothers' home number.

They should be home by now even if, as Justin suspected, the mom never showed up and they hopped a bus.

After a few rings, Bob Ryan picked up.

"Hey, Bob," Justin said. "How are you?"

"Great. Glad to be home."

"Is your brother there?"

"Hold on."

When Bob put the receiver down, Justin heard rock music and arguing.

"No, I refuse," B.J. said loudly. "Tell that nigger I don't want to talk."

When Bob returned, he was very apologetic.

"I hope you didn't . . ."

"Don't worry about it," Winters said.

"My brother doesn't want to talk now."

"Or ever," B.J. yelled.

"He's had too much too drink, celebrating. But I want to thank you for all you did for us. And my brother may talk to you tomorrow—"

"I appreciate what you're saying, Bob. And I know I'm not your lawyer. Or B.J.'s anymore. But I want to remind you, both of you, not to talk with anyone about the case. And I mean *anyone*. Not family. Not friends. Not the press. And certainly not the police. If the police call and start asking questions, you both should politely—and I mean politely—refer them to your lawyer. You understand?"

"Yessir."

"Also I don't know if Swoozy told you this. I'm sure he did. But I'll mention it anyway. Both of us expect, despite what happened in court today, that the DA will re-file charges against both of you. I'm not sure when. But Swoozy said he will try to arrange it so, as a courtesy, you two can just surrender and skip the whole scene of the police dragging you to jail in handcuffs."

"That would be better."

"I'm not sure if it will happen that way since Billings is so pissed. But Swoozy will definitely ask."

Winters realized that he was blathering on and on, hoping something he'd say to Bob would somehow change B.J.'s mind and let him keep the case. But he couldn't stop himself.

"I don't know if your brother told you," Winters continued. "I have some perspective of what it's like to be an outsider in Chautauqua. The kind of person people suspect the worst about."

Bob didn't respond.

"My mother was a domestic on the grounds in the fifties," Winters continued. "She cooked and cleaned for some of the finest religious families who, by the standards of the times, treated her very well."

He said Chautauqua was progressive in that it had some prominent black speakers, including Thurgood Marshall and Ralph Bunche.

"But the place still kept a separate rooming house for colored people," he said. "Near the practice shacks. Called the Phyllis Wheatley Cottage."

When Winters was in junior high, he said his mother brought him to the grounds to hear her idol, Thurgood Marshall, speak at the Amphitheater.

"And that did it for me," Winters recalled. "I had been wanting to maybe play ball professionally. After that, I wanted to go to law school."

"I was the only black kid in the audience in August 1957. And everyone was looking at me. Including Justice Marshall when he complained about the hypocrisy of white liberals who denounced Jim Crow and school segregation but don't want to live among Negroes or send their kids to school with them. When I graduated from Howard Law School, my mother gave me the text of his remarks I have framed right here in my office."

When he finished his story, he felt like both he and Bob were embarrassed.

"Mr. Winters," Bob said. "Lemme see if I can get my brother to talk to you."

After more bickering in the background, B.J. finally did pick up.

338 • DEB PINES

"Listen Winters, I don't want to talk to you. I don't want to hear your boring Black History Month stories. I don't want you representing me—when you don't trust what I'm saying and go and do some sneaky-ass shit in court. Why are you bothering me? Didn't you get paid?"

"I'm not sure why I'm bothering with a punk like you either. Except that I think I'm in the best position to get you justice. You talk about me not trusting you? What about the reverse? You've been holding back on me since Day One. And if you're still protecting that woman Francine by denying you left your gun at her place, you're the fool. At this moment, my sources say she's downtown rolling over on you."

"Is that right? That bitch, she —"

"No, it's not right," Winters said. "But I wanted to verify my hunch and show you how vulnerable you are without me."

Chapter Fifty-Two

MOLE KNOCKED on the Warren sisters' door with a sense of dread.

After hearing bustling in the apartment, there was zero chance of him getting in and out without talk.

"Who is it?" Evangeline yelled. "Who's there?"

"M-m-mole."

When Evangeline opened the door, she just stared at Mole and at the coveralls, work boots and tool belt he'd put on after court.

"My word," she said. "What brings you around?"

"N-n-new locks."

"We don't need a new lock. Ours is perfectly fine. That burglar or whoever it was, got in everywhere else. Not here. He just put a few dents in our frame."

Evangeline pointed out the damage.

"I think it was just four years ago, maybe five when we replaced our lock," Philomena chimed in. "Shortly after we moved here year-round."

"That's right," Evangeline said.

"F-f-francine . . ."

Mole, frustrated by the effort, stopped.

"So she's behind this?" Evengeline asked. "She put you up to replacing the locks?"

"Or ch-ch-checking them."

"Some people might think she's concerned about our safety. But my bet is the lawyer put her up to it," Evangeline continued. "Covering her you-know-what in terms of liability."

Mole didn't respond. But that didn't stop Evangeline.

"Or maybe she's worried now that they cut those hooligans loose. What a travesty," Evangeline continued. "My oh my! What is this country coming to?"

When neither Mole nor Philomena answered, Evangeline continued.

"If that judge was saying he didn't believe old Millicent Houghey, that's—excuse the expression—malarkey."

Mole shrugged.

"That woman wouldn't make things up. She's in our church group and sings in the choir. Has sung for years and years. And you know what they say about people in the choir, don't you?"

When Mole didn't answer, Evangeline and Philomena answered together.

"They pray twice," they said.

"People in the choir pray twice," Evangeline repeated. "If Millicent says she saw that boy outside the darkroom, she saw that boy outside the darkroom. No doubt in my mind."

Mole jiggled the Warren sisters' doorknob.

"Look okay?" Evangeline asked.

"L-l-l-et's see."

He locked the lock from the inside then stepped out, closed the door and tried jiggling the knob.

"O-k-kay. Open up."

Evangeline opened the door.

Mole took out a screwdriver and tightened the screws attaching the lock to the door and frame.

"C-c-an I try your key?"

"I don't see why not," she said, shaking her head. "Or why you should for that matter."

After fishing through her purse, she found her front-door key, handed it to Mole. He inserted it in the lock, twisted it left and twisted it right several times.

"F-f-fine," he said. "C-c-cylinder's fine."

After skipping Doc's apartment, declaring it low

342   •   DEB PINES

priority, Mole continued to the last unavoidable stop: the apartment of the nosy reporter, Mimi Goldman, and her son.

Mole hoped no one would be home.

But as he approached, he heard conversation and the scritch, scritch, scritch of a sweeping broom.

"So did you reach Brad Jr.?" the son asked.

"No," the mom said. "I wasn't sure if he was still in Chautauqua or if he'd gone back to New York. So I left messages at both locations. At his sister's and his own home."

"Did you say what we learned about Webb's or did you—"

The son stopped when, in the hall, he saw Mole.

"Hey, Mom?" he said.

"What?" she said, straightening from where she'd been sweeping broken glass into a dustpan.

"We have company."

In his usual halting speech, Mole explained that he was there, at Francine's behest, to install a new lock.

The reporter tried to engage him in small talk or questioning. But he ignored her. And, eventually, she gave up.

In silence, Mole did his work as Mimi and her son cleaned up the damage in silence, too.

Chapter Fifty-Three

"DOESN'T HE GIVE YOU THE CREEPS?" Jake asked when Mole finally left.

"A little," Mimi said. "Was he just standing outside our door, eavesdropping?"

"I wasn't sure," Jake said. "Maybe he was listening. Or maybe he showed up to change the locks, heard us talking and didn't know how to interrupt. I don't know."

"So what's your plan?"

"I was hoping to hurry over to the library, to see if anything on file about the Hansen house might shed some light on possible hiding places. For the poison. Or anything else incriminating."

"It's almost four-thirty. Want to wait and see if I get anywhere with the hospital billing office? Now's

344 • DEB PINES

when the boss, Mark Hammerschmidt, was supposed to be in."

Jake said fine.

He sat at the table where his mom had thrown out everything broken—except her grandparents' wedding photo. She scraped off the shards of glass and set the photo aside.

Then he listened as his mom dialed the billing office at the WCA Hospital in Jamestown and put the call on speakerphone.

"Is Mark Hammerschmidt there?" she asked.

"Please hold."

Mimi and Jake stared at each other until someone picked up.

"Hello, may I help you?" a man asked.

"Is this Mark Hammerschmidt?" she asked.

"Yes," he said. "What can I do for you?"

His mom launched into the truth, or near truth, explaining that she was a reporter at *The Chautauquan Daily*. She said she was investigating any disputes, even seemingly unimportant disputes, that Brad had with the hospital in the year before his death.

When Mark Hammerschmidt went silent, Jake wished he could grab the phone.

He'd love to start over with a better ruse.

He didn't have one. But he was sure if he were in

charge one would come to him. And it would be way better than his mom's straightforward rambling.

"I understand Brad Hansen made dozens of calls to the billing office in recent months," she said. "So I figured there might be some kind of dispute. And I also hoped that you'd agree that any possible claims to confidentiality ended with Mr. Hansen's death?"

Mimi, sensing Jake's disappointment with her lack of creativity, shrugged and crossed her fingers.

"I'd like to help you any way I can," Hammerschmidt said. "The man was a holy terror."

When Mimi smiled, Jake high-fived her for having the good fortune to find someone who put personal grievances ahead of rules and protocol.

"Why did he call your office so often?"

"I wondered that myself."

"Was there some kind of billing dispute?"

"That's an understatement. The man owed us fifty-two thousand dollars for the care in the oncology unit and then in our hospice for his deceased wife, Margaret O'Brien Hansen. She stayed with us for something like thirty-four days and was given the works. Top-notch treatment in our new top-notch facility. We made her as comfortable as anyone could be under the circumstances. If you're writing an article, maybe you could work that in. That our hospice has been ranked in the top ten in Western New York, for the past five years, in a survey by APRA."

"APRA?" Mimi asked.

"The American Patients Rights Association."

Jake, smiling, caught his mom's eye. But she looked away to focus on the call.

"I'm not writing on that subject now. But one day I might."

"Well, I could put a press packet together for you. With the ranking. And some other articles about the hospital that have appeared in the Jamestown and Buffalo papers that might interest your readers. Okay?"

"That would be great," Mimi lied. "I'll share the stuff with my editor who would be the one to make the assignment and . . ."

"Maybe I should talk to your editor?"

"Of course, absolutely," Mimi said, "I'll set that up. I promise. But, for now, if you wouldn't mind I'd like to get back to Mr. Hansen."

"Oh, sure, sure, sure. Sorry."

"So was he calling to dispute his wife's bill?"

"It was crazier than that."

"What was the problem?"

"He said he wanted to know who had brought his wife into the emergency room when she first sought treatment. Until he got that information, he refused to pay."

"*He* hadn't brought her in?"

"Apparently not."

"And you wouldn't tell him?"

"*Couldn't.* We couldn't tell him. We certainly tried. No one on the staff remembered who had dropped off Mrs. Hansen on . . ."

His voice drifted as if he were consulting a record somewhere.

"That's Mrs. Margaret O'Brien Hansen, who was dropped off on February twelfth of this year," he said, reading from something official. "Our records show the emergency-room nurse, handling admitting that night was what we call a traveler. She was here as a temp. Left no forwarding number with the agency that placed her. And we've been unable to find her."

"What's her name?"

"Our records just say it was Regina Jackson."

Chapter Fifty-Four

Jake didn't want to get roped into his mom's locate-Regina-Jackson mission. So he grabbed a notebook and jacket to head to the library to learn more about possible hiding places at the Hansens' house.

To him, 12 Park seemed to include a maze of secret nooks and crannies. A map of the secret nooks and crannies would be great.

The archives with that kind of information was in the Smith Memorial Library. But in the quieter, less-visited basement of the library.

When Jake stepped inside, it felt like a mega-event. The three researchers, taking notes at a long table, looked up. So did both librarians at a microfiche machine.

Everyone seemed to be wondering what might be Jake's next move.

Jake wondered, too.

Before him was a small, musty room jammed with shelves of history books and bound back issues of Chautauqua publications. There were also glass cases of memorabilia. A grandfather clock. A tape player. Two large Xerox machines. A box of tapes labeled ORAL HISTORIES. A glassed-in office with climate-sensitive materials.

"May I help you?" the younger of the two librarians whispered.

"I hope so," Jake whispered back. "I'm looking for information about a house on the grounds. Maybe blueprints, history, that kind of thing."

"Of course."

The librarian led Jake to a set of tall wooden card-catalogue drawers.

"We've got files on around seventy-five properties on the 750-acre institution," she said. "Organized numerically. By street. Just pull out what you need. And if you run into problems, ask."

When the woman left, Jake flipped through the top drawer. And he saw the system was very straightforward: brown envelopes with tabs indicating street addresses.

With little effort, he found a tab that said 12 Park. He pulled out the corresponding envelope.

To make things easy, he decided to make no big decisions. He'd just Xerox everything inside so he could mark up his pages and show everything to his mom.

He found the helpful librarian.

"Should I pay you for the copies?" he asked.

"After," she said. "When you're done."

The woman set him up at the machine and, without giving it much thought he kept feeding things into a noisy humming machine.

Old photos. A brief history of the house. A four-page "Building Structure Inventory" form that the first Mrs. Hansen, Margaret O'Brien Hansen, had filed with the State Historic Trust in Albany.

When Jake was about halfway done with his Xeroxing, he paused to read Mrs. Hansen's description of 12 Park.

She described it as a privately owned residence. Using check marks on the form, she also indicated, among other things, the house's building material (clapboard), structural system (wood frame with interlocking joints), condition (good), color (gray) and date of initial construction (1874).

She also noted on the form that the house is a typical Victorian cottage with a gothic peaked roof, gingerbread trim and two porches with railings of sawn art.

When asked if owner can "relate any interesting

anecdotes about the house," Mrs. Hansen wrote, "See attached on back."

Flipping the form over, Jake found a copy of a faded news clipping from the August 9, 1877 edition of *The Chautauqua Daily Assembly Herald*.

The story was about a weird anti-alcohol ceremony organized on the porch of 12 Park by its original owner, John Howell, a Pittsburgh minister and Temperance leader.

The story was told through the eyes of one of Chautauqua's founders, Dr. Vincent.

He said it all began when "one of our keen-eyed, strong-handed policemen" captured a couple of young men who'd brought contraband —a large square box filled with bottles of whiskey—to that year's Chautauqua gathering.

In the story, Vincent wrote that he sent the young men home. He turned the whiskey over to Howell and Francis Murphy, two flamboyant Temperance speakers.

That's when Howell, apparently, took over. He invited the entire Chautauqua Assembly to gather outside his home. Then he delivered a fiery funeral oration for the whiskey he called "as out of place in Chautauqua as Satan among the sons of God."

At his cue, four young men smashed the bottles with shovels. And Howell proceeded to bury their remnants in a full-sized wooden funeral casket in his front yard.

352 • DEB PINES

A blurry copy of an archives photo of the event was also attached to Mrs. Hansen's submission.

Jake was finishing Xeroxing the last of the file when the librarian returned and he paid her.

"Find everything you were looking for?" she asked.

"I hope so."

When Jake got home, he went right to bed and to sleep. Mimi stayed up reviewing all of the stuff he'd found in the library.

She glanced at her own notes about the thirty-nine Regina Jacksons she'd called, in vain. None were nurses in Jamestown. Or knew any Regina Jacksons who were nurses in Jamestown.

Frustrated, she looked away, at the wedding photo of her grandparents.

They looked impossibly young. And happy.

Her Grandpa Izzy had a full head of curly black hair, like Jake's. Her Grandma Fanny smiled shyly in an elaborate silk dress with shiny beads and veil.

Mimi blinked back tears.

In the context of her grandparents' lives, the broken frame was nothing. They'd endured so much worse.

Mimi never heard the details from them. But after their deaths, Mimi researched what she could.

And she was able to find the bare outlines of a tale like the "Mystery of Good and Evil" lecturer's Polish Holocaust tale. And different.

Amazingly, both Izzy and Fanny survived the death camps. And, amazingly, after straggling home to Kielce, Poland, they found Izzy's mom, Mimi's namesake, alive, too, in a Jewish shelter.

The reunion, though, was brief. A mob, inflamed by rumors of Jews holding kidnapped Christian kids in the shelter, stormed the place. And the "rescue" turned into a bloody massacre.

There were no kidnapped kids. But that didn't matter.

Forty-six Jews, including Izzy's mom, were shot or beaten to death with sticks, fists and stones.

Not by the Nazis, but by their Polish neighbors.

Not during the war, but a year later.

The Kielce massacre was horrible in and of itself. But, for Mimi, almost worse was knowing that virtually no one was ever held accountable. As if the killings had never happened.

Eventually, Mimi dozed off on the couch with Derek Jeter at the plate on TV. Until she was roused by the sound of a loud knock on her door.

Chapter Fifty-Five

"Helloo? Are you there? Hello?"

Mimi tried to identify the woman's voice. But her preoccupation with finding her .22 in her purse and, after finding it, hurrying to the door, made it tough.

"Hello."

"Oh, hello," Mimi said when she finally recognized Mary Hansen and, opening the door, found Mary and her brother Brad Jr.

"I hope we didn't wake you," Mary said. "You said call no matter how late. And we thought this was better handled in person. So we just . . ."

"Oh, no, no," Mimi said. "I must have dozed off on the couch. I'm glad you came. C'mon in."

When they did, Mimi was struck again by how much the Hansens looked alike.

"Can I get you something to drink?" Mimi asked while leading them to her table. "I'm gonna get a beer for myself. But I've got juices? Wine? Water? Gatorade?"

"Beer for me," Brad said.

"Just water," Mary said, shooting her brother a dirty look.

When Mimi returned with the drinks, she sat, too, not far from her purse with the gun and tried to act commanding. Fake it 'til you make it.

"So, as you heard in my latest message, my questions are really for Brad."

A glance his way found Brad spending more time than necessary popping his beer top. And then, red-faced, studying the can.

"So I mainly wonder why you didn't tell me or the police that you were in Chautauqua on Saturday, August second, the morning of your dad's death?"

Brad took a long sip of beer.

"Because I wasn't," he said softly.

"You sure?"

Mary sighed.

"Listen if you're trying to bluff or bully us, it won't work," she said. "You can't make things up, throw it in our faces and expect us to go along with your crazy fiction. To distract people from blaming the real killers.

Who are probably your son's friends. And maybe even your son for that matter because—"

Mimi put up a hand.

"Let me put it this way. Brad, do I need to call the desk clerk at Webb's to confirm that you were staying there?"

Brad didn't answer.

"That you were in room thirty-two in the back?"

When tears welled in Brad's eyes, Mimi steeled herself to proceed without pity.

"Why don't you tell your sister who's making things up?"

When Brad burst into sobs, Mimi looked away.

"Mare," he said after he got a grip. "I was at Webb's. There's no use protecting me. I was there."

"Then let's go," Mary said, hurrying to her feet. "End of interview. Now."

When Brad didn't move, Mary tried to drag him.

"C'mon, Brad. Get up. The way I see it, no harm's been done. We get you a good lawyer. The best. And it's her word against ours. Just stop talking. Let's go."

Brad shook his head.

"What?" Mary asked.

"I don't need a lawyer," he said. "You're not understanding me. Yes, I was at Webb's. But, swear to God, I didn't kill dad. I never mentioned the trip because, well, at first, I was embarrassed. Then when I didn't mention it, I thought bringing it up would make me look bad. But, now that you know I was there, I have nothing more to hide."

Mary sighed.

"Maybe I will take a beer," she said.

When Mimi returned with it, Mary said, "My brother seems to want to talk this out. I think it's a bad idea. But it's his show."

"Okay," Mimi asked. "Brad, why were you here?"

"To borrow money from my dad. We had a plan to meet early at the house before the race."

"And did you meet?"

"We did."

"And what happened?"

"My sister will call me a fool," he said. "And I guess I was. On the phone, when I asked my dad for a loan, he said he'd think about it and agreed to meet at five-thirty or six. I told him about how Valerie and I are in a cash-flow crisis. She gets most of her salary in January in the form of a bonus. We've maxed out on the credit cards and have a lot of bills coming due. For summer camp. The kids' tuitions. And all and . . ."

"And in person?"

"Same old thing," Brad said. "He said he wouldn't give me a dime unless I demonstrated, in a formal business plan, how it would be repaid. And the plan had to include me getting what he called a real job outside the house. I'm not sure why I even came."

"Me, neither," Mary said.

"That's not helping," Brad said, before returning to his narrative. "When I told my dad the money was for his grandkids, not me, he laughed. We argued and I ended up storming off when he said something like if I were any kind of man, I'd go out and support my kids myself."

"What'd you do after that?"

"I checked out of Webb's, drove to the airport, got drunk in an airport bar and flew home."

"You didn't poison your father?"

"Absolutely not."

"Or put someone else up to it?"

"No way."

After a few more questions, Mary finished her beer and took the empties to Mimi's sink.

"Done?" Mary asked.

"I just have one more question that will seem like it came out of left field. But do either of you know who took your mom to the hospital in February when the doctors found the cancer?"

"We just assumed it was my dad," Mary said.

When Mimi summarized the hospital billing

department guy's account of the billing dispute with Brad, Mary chuckled.

"The old cheapskate," she said. "He probably drove my mom himself and trumped up the controversy to avoid paying the bill."

"So neither of you drove her?"

"No," Mary said.

"No," added Brad.

"Could anyone else have driven her?"

"Philomena Warren has a car and drives," Mary said. "My mom also could have called 9-1-1 and gone by ambulance."

Mimi walked the Hansens to the door. When Brad stepped out, Mary lingered.

"When are you going to drop this?" Mary asked. "I know the police don't want your help. And lots of people around here don't appreciate you stirring up trouble. Why don't you think about your own safety? And your son's?"

Mimi, chilled, tried to hide it.

"Is that a threat?" she asked.

"More like a friendly warning."

Unable to sleep, Mimi stayed at the table reviewing her notes, plotting her next move.

Her surroundings were extremely quiet. Quieter

than she was used to as a city girl. And quieter than she realized until, at 3 a.m., the quiet was broken by footsteps in her hallway. And Mimi froze.

She tried telling herself the sounds weren't footsteps. But they obviously were.

And, being the only adult around to deal with them, she took a deep breath. Heart pounding, she stood. Tiptoed to her purse. Removed her gun. And, with shaky hands, aimed it at the door.

She had no idea who was out there. Or why. But she prayed hard that she'd locked up. In what felt like slow motion, the doorknob turned left, then right. Like a living thing. Then it stopped.

Mimi wanted to make a move, any move. But paralyzed by fear, she just stayed put. And stared.

On the other side of the door, she heard a brief rustling and tap-tapping. When that stopped, footsteps sounded like they were leaving.

Mimi kept the gun pointed at the door for what felt like forever. She was afraid to check the hallway, in case she was wrong, and someone was still there.

Gradually, the world got lighter and filled with familiar morning sounds.

Birds chirped. Bottles crashed, like a bowler's strikes, into the recycling truck making its rounds.

Mimi, feeling braver, walked to her front door. When

she heard nothing, in one swift move, she opened the door while pointing her gun.

No one was right there.

So she stepped into the hallway and, back to her door, glanced left, then right.

Again no one.

About to return inside, Mimi felt something sticky on her shoulder. So she turned. And gasped.

Tacked to the middle of the door was a blood-caked necktie that Mimi recognized.

It was Doc's. What he wore the first time they'd met in June at a preseason organizational dinner at the Athenaeum for *Daily* staffers. And what he must have worn the night he was killed.

Below the bloody tie were three spray-painted words: "Death to meddlers."

Chapter Fifty-Six

DURING THE FINAL WEEK of the Chautauqua season, Mimi hadn't, officially, given up meddling.

But she was drowning in chores—filling the sports pages, putting together Doc's Old First Night photo retrospective and considering her future.

Wentworth said *The Daily* could pay Mimi for one more month, if she wanted to spend September filing photos, closing up shop and doing some "strategic planning."

She jumped at the offer. But she also started making calls for leads on longer-term employment.

In terms of investigating, Mimi told herself she wasn't chickening out, that she'd just hit a brick wall.

Maybe.

The leads were, indeed, going nowhere. And the

big break she'd hoped for, that would tie everything together, had never materialized.

The Warren sisters and Mole and the local ambulance corps had all denied taking Mary O'Brien Hansen to the hospital.

More calls to more Regina Jacksons in the national phone listings went nowhere.

The Warren sisters conceded that they had seen Brad Jr. over at the Hansens' house the morning of the race. Evangeline said they never mentioned anything because they didn't want to "get that nice young man in trouble." Mimi wondered if they thought Brad Hansen had poisoned his dad and they were secretly grateful.

Jake was pursuing his own leads from the Hansen house blueprints. He circled possible hiding spots. Then, when Francine was out, he started exploring.

So far, he'd checked out two spots: the site of 12 Park's original furnace, under a rug and false panel in the living room floor; and a crawl space under the front porch.

And, so far, all Jake had found were cobwebs and dirt.

Mimi had double-checked Mrs. Greenwood's alibi and found that she was, as she'd said, antiquing the full day of the race.

On Friday, Mimi spent the morning writing stories

and captions about men's and women's softball-league championships. Before she moved on to the winners of a shuffleboard tournament, she took a break.

She decided to make one more stab at trying to reach Tom Bell, the principal of the Indiana school where Francine had taught.

Bell hadn't returned calls to his home or school. With fall approaching, Mimi thought she might have better luck catching him at school.

The school secretary transferred Mimi's call. After two rings, Bell picked up.

Mimi introduced herself as a reporter for a newspaper in western New York. She said she was doing a background check on the former Francine Rodino who now goes by the name Francine Hansen.

"She's not teaching, is she?" Bell asked.

"No, she's not."

"Is she in some kind of trouble?"

"No, not that either. She's possibly a witness with information about a crime. And I'm trying to gauge her trustworthiness. It's a sensitive matter. And I'm looking for a little guidance."

"I'd be more comfortable if we spoke off the record," Bell said. "I don't want to be quoted. We've finally put this thing behind us. And the last thing I need to do is stir things up again."

"That's fine with me."

"Then what can I do for you?"

"Well, I've read old newspaper stories about the sex-abuse case against Francine. Her conviction and all that. I've also spoken to her recently. And I don't know if you've heard this. But, six years later, she claims she was innocent. She says she pled guilty to end the ordeal. And she says her main accuser, a Mrs. Hathaway, is, well, imbalanced. And that she's, subsequently, accused an uncle and scout leader of abuse, too. Claims, Francine says, were as bogus as the claims against her."

"Is that so?"

"Yes, I was wondering what you thought?"

There was a long pause.

"Mr. Bell?"

"What do I think of Francine's claims?" he asked. "Baloney."

"You still think she's guilty?"

"Absolutely. Mrs. Hathaway is our school board president and a highly regarded member of the community. She has not made any further accusations since Francine left town. I can also tell you, and this never came out in court, that her son Joey had reported his relationship with Francine, not only to his mother, but to multiple parties. And a guidance counselor caught the two of them in the act. In a classroom. The counselor was prepared to testify had there been a trial. But she was grateful she didn't have to."

"So there is no doubt in your mind that Francine was guilty?"

"None."

"How's the boy?"

"I haven't seen him recently. He seemed to be doing fine. He'll be a senior this year."

"So if Francine says she was railroaded—"

"Don't be taken in. She's a beautiful and charming woman who has, I'm afraid to say, a bit of evil in her heart."

Chapter Fifty-Seven

With three days left of the nine-week season, Chautauqua's population seemed to reduce itself by half each day—like a city under evacuation orders.

On the way home from *The Daily* at six, Mimi passed many families packing up.

One, at Fletcher and Foster, looked like it was trying to win a competition for lashing the most to a minivan. After suitcases went in a trunk, a turtle-like cap on top held other belongings. Three bikes hung from the back. The dad was trying to attach a stroller and high chair to the cap.

When Mimi reached Park, she heard voices and saw her neighbors having a party on Francine's porch.

The Warren sisters were sitting on the wicker furniture. Betsy Gates and her son, Max, were swinging on the courtship swing. Violet Greenwood was ladling a pink punch from a cut-glass bowl into a glass cup.

"Mimi," yelled Francine who was circulating with a tray of vegetables and dip. "Mimi, if you have a minute, why don't you join us?"

Mimi stopped in the yard where Mole, of course, was busy at work.

When she stepped onto the porch, Mimi felt like she was putting a damper on things. Heads turned. Conversations stopped.

"Still working?" Francine asked.

"I've gotta fill the sports pages a few more days," Mimi said. "Then I can coast with administrative stuff, clean-up, etc. I think I told you we'll be staying one more month?"

"Of course, yes. I forgot."

Mimi accepted a paper plate from Francine that she'd loaded with carrots, celery, cauliflower pieces and sour cream and onion dip.

She moved to the punch bowl where Violet Greenwood served her some punch.

"What are you celebrating?" she asked Francine.

"Some of us aren't celebrating," she said. "We're mainly saying farewell to Violet and Betsy and dear little Max. They're all leaving tomorrow. We've been through so much together this summer. It's almost like we've known each other longer."

Betsy pointed to an open notepad and pen under the globe light near the door.

"We're also trading addresses and phone numbers," she said. "So if you are ever in Erie, you can visit. We have room for you and Jake."

"Thanks," Mimi said. "We're not sure where we'll land after all of this."

"Take our addresses, in case," Betsy said.

Mimi balanced her plate on the porch railing under the hanging plates. She spent some time eating and drinking and watching the crowd.

Eventually, Evangeline Warren, leaning on her cane, shuffled over.

"Some of us *are* celebrating," she told Mimi. "Did you hear the news?"

"What news?"

"A grand jury this afternoon voted to re-charge those Ryan boys with Doc's murder. Mole heard it on the radio and told us to turn it on. The newscaster said they're supposed to turn themselves into the police tomorrow."

Mimi stood there, eating and listening.

"What's Mole up to now?" Violet Greenwood asked.

"He says he's putting in some tulips," said Francine.

"Why so late? It's getting dark."

"I thought the better question was why so early?" Evangeline said. "I thought tulips didn't go in until the fall. But Mole said, after getting the bulbs from friends, he wanted to get them into the ground while it was still soft from the rain."

As the women chattered more about gardening, their travel plans and plans for the fall, Violet Greenwood approached.

"You're still doubting that the Ryan boys did it?" Violet Greenwood asked.

"Yes," Mimi said.

"I am, too," chimed in Francine.

"Any idea who did?" Violet Greenwood asked.

Mimi felt all eyes on her.

"I'm starting to think I just might."

Chapter Fifty-Eight

At home, Mimi and Jake ate breakfast for dinner—omelets, bacon and toast.

"I can't believe they arrested the Ryans again," Jake said.

"The lawyer told us that was going to happen."

"You know how I said I was through," Jake said. "I'm changing my mind. Got any new leads you want me to follow?"

"I've gotta face up to the Old First Night retrospective. But I had a new idea, if you want to chase it?"

"What?"

"I was wondering if the temporary nurse, Regina Jackson, might be a skier. Maybe she was here in the winter to be near a ski resort. And, it's a long shot. But maybe calling around to hospitals in Colorado, Utah maybe, near ski resorts, might turn something up. And maybe you can find those hospitals at the library while I do the Old First Night thing?"

"You don't have a *better* idea?"

"I don't."

"Okay, see you later."

When Jake left, Mimi pulled out Doc's Old First Night file. She laid out a number of the photos on her table.

Then, weary from everything, including Francine's punch that must have had alcohol in it, she decided to make a pot of coffee to focus her thoughts.

She ground some beans, added the water and turned on the machine. Standing next to it, as the coffee brewed, she noticed something Jake must have left for her on the counter: a clear packet labeled "Natural Super Anti-Oxidant Energypac."

The product called itself a "highly potent" mix that boosts energy, stamina and mental focus and offers anti-aging and anti-cancer and anti-weight-gain benefits, too.

What else?

Inside the stapled-shut pack, were three capsules. A red-and-white one, according to the label, was a multi-mineral. An orange one said it included bee pollen and propolis and royal jelly—whatever the hell they were. A brown one said it was Korean ginseng with herbs.

Mimi usually mocked products with these kinds of names and claims. But, desperate for an energy boost, she downed the pills with her first cup of coffee.

Then she decided to be methodical about the Old First Night assignments. She'd pick five photos from each era. Anything Doc didn't have a caption for, she'd write by hand. Then she'd retype the info into the computer at the office.

She zipped through the early shots, taking captions from the backs. She chose two that included the founders, Miller and Vincent. One had them standing by the illuminated boat, the other by thousands of Japanese lanterns in Miller Park.

On the back of both photos was Vincent's poetic description of the first Old First Night gathering in 1874.

"The stars were out," he wrote, "and looked down through trembling leaves upon a goodly, well-wrapped company, who sat in the grove, filled with wonder and hope."

Mimi next chose the photo of Arthur Bestor leading the Depression-era crowd in waving dollar contributions to Chautauqua. And a more recent shot of a lavish Old First Night birthday cake.

As Mimi reviewed Doc's many photos from the 1940s, she started feeling dizzy.

Maybe she needed more coffee, she thought. So she got up and, feeling shaky, grabbed the table to steady herself.

On the way to the coffee machine, she wondered if she'd gotten up too fast. She paused. Then she refilled her cup, stirred in milk and returned to her task.

The photo on top of the fat pile from the night World War II's end was announced from the Amphitheater stage was of the orchestra.

A caption gave the date, Aug. 14, 1945. And it said the exuberant conductor was Franco Autori.

Mimi, dizzy again, closed her eyes. When she reopened them, she felt a sharp stab of pain in her gut.

She put her head down and, in a few minutes, the pain passed.

Was she getting a flu? Or food poisoning? This was the worst possible time. She had to get this job done, tonight or tomorrow.

Willing herself to continue, she focused on the next photo in the stack: of a tall young man with a crew cut, smiling with a pretty red-haired girl in the Amphitheater aisle.

On the back, the names, for some reason seemed

garbled. There was a Hansen and a Margaret O'Brien. But something was wrong that Mimi's dulled mind couldn't reason through.

She tried sipping her coffee. But, again, she felt dizzy. Very dizzy as if experiencing the spins from drinking too much.

For the first time, she wondered if there was something seriously wrong and she should call 9-1-1 or the library for Jake.

Again, she tried closing her eyes, hoping the feeling would pass.

When a wave of nausea hit, she got up to head for the toilet but collapsed on the kitchen floor.

When she tried to call for help, she couldn't do that either. Too weak, she gagged then threw up.

Was she drugged? Could she rouse herself and reach the phone?

To stay sharp, she tried to remember Bishop Vincent's words. The crowd in the grove definitely was filled with two things. Wonder and hope?

Those felt right. If she could remember that kind of trivia, didn't that mean she was fine? That her mind was working, even if not one hundred percent?

Again she tried closing her eyes. She thought she heard a phone ring. Then stop. Then ring again.

Should she try to answer it? She thought she should. But, eventually, sounds grew fainter, then faint, then faintest. And Mimi drifted into a thick heavy sleep.

Chapter Fifty-Nine

Jake, STANDING AT THE PAYPHONES closest to the library, listened to the phone ring and ring.

Was his mom in the bathroom? Had she gone out? Was she, for some reason, not hearing the phone?

He hung up and stood there, staring at the Methodist House, one of few church houses off the brick walk, across from the Amp.

He could hear the music of Kenny Rogers. The last Friday night concert of the season often got a big name, Jake was told.

Besides the concert sounds, Jake heard an older man on the phone next to his, speaking loudly to someone named Jessie.

When the old man hung up, Jake faced him.

"Excuse me," Jake said.

No answer.

"EXCUSE ME, SIR?" Jake said louder.

"Are you speaking to me, young man?"

"Yes."

The man stepped closer.

"What is it you need?"

"I was wondering if you were speaking to someone on the Grounds. I'm trying to reach my mom and it keeps ringing and ringing. So I was wondering if there might be something wrong with the phones everywhere."

"My call went through," the man said. "I know it's hard for the young. But you should dial again and try to be a little more patient."

Jake re-dialed, listened to the phone ring some more, and hung up. He could go home. Or he could stop at the concert.

By this hour, there were usually many free seats, vacated by older people who, overwhelmed by the volume, went home.

It was a close call. But Jake decided to go home. And, as soon as he opened the door, he knew something was wrong. The place was dark. His mom, a tremendous workhorse, wasn't at the table working.

"Hello?" he called. "Mom, hello?"

He flipped on the kitchen light and looked all around before he saw his mom on the floor. His first thought was that she had been shot like Doc.

But there was no blood. And when he approached he realized that, thank God, his mom was breathing. Shallowly. But breathing.

"What's the matter, mom? What happened?"

When Mimi didn't answer, Jake ran to the phone. He dialed 9-1-1 but got nowhere.

The phone was dead.

He hung up and listened again.

Shit.

Still no dial tone.

Panicky, he tried to make himself think. Where could he get help? Maybe at Francine's if her phone worked?

He sprinted out the door, onto Francine's porch, through the banging screen door, inside the kitchen.

"Francine?" he yelled. "Mrs. Hansen? I need help. Can I come in?"

When he got no answer, Jake ran for the kitchen phone. He picked it up. When he heard no dial tone here either, he felt frantic.

"Shit," he said, slamming the receiver down and heading toward a light upstairs. "I'm sorry," Jake called as he dashed up the stairs, taking them two at a time.

"It's an emergency. My mom is very sick. Mrs. Hansen? Can you take her to the hospital?"

At the top of the stairs, Jake paused.

"Mrs. Hansen?" he called again. "I'm sorry to bother you. But I have an emergency. I need some help."

As he raced toward the bedroom, Jake heard voices he presumed were on the TV.

"I'm sorry, Mrs. Hansen," he said, knocking on the door, out of breath. "My mother is . . ."

When Jake entered the bedroom, he froze, embarrassed.

Francine, naked in bed, reached for a patchwork quilt, to cover herself. The guy beside her reached for his boxers on the floor.

"Oh, my God," Jake said. "I'm so sorry."

He turned his back so the couple could get decent.

"I've got an emergency," he repeated. "Or no way would I have just barged in. I need a car. Or a phone. Or I don't know. My mom is passed out on the kitchen floor, barely breathing and—"

"Jake, sweetie, hold on," Francine said. "Of course, we'll help. Give us a sec to get dressed."

As Francine ran past him, carrying clothes, B.J. Ryan put on his jeans, sneakers and "Grateful Dead" T-shirt.

Chapter Sixty

Jake was so relieved to be getting help, he didn't question anything—like if he was putting his mom's fate in the wrong hands—until after he and B.J. eased his mom into the backseat of Francine's BMW and they were off to the hospital.

Francine and B.J. seemed sincerely eager to help. But could he be falling into a trap?

At the South Gate, Francine asked one of the guards if his phone was working.

"No, everything's down in Chautauqua. The phone company's on the way."

"Do you have some walkie-talkie link to the police? Or the hospital?"

"Yes," the kid said.

"We have a sick lady, a very sick lady, in the backseat. Could you tell WCA we're on the way?"

"I can. And I will. But maybe you should wait here for an ambulance. I can . . ."

Francine, not waiting for the kid to finish, floored it and they zoomed past the gate.

"How is she?" Francine called over her shoulder.

Jake, in the back next to his mom, inched closer. Mimi's eyes were shut as she leaned against the car door. But she was definitely breathing.

"She's breathing," he said. "God, I hope . . ."

"I'm going as fast as I can," Francine said. "We'll be there in no time."

As they flew along 394, B.J. turned to face Jake.

"Your mom's a tough one," he said. "If anyone can tough it out, it's her. I mean it, Jake."

Jake couldn't believe how corpse-like his mom looked.

"Mom," he whispered. "You're gonna be okay. Hang in there. Please. I still need you."

When he felt tears forming, he tried to tell himself it wasn't serious. And, what B.J. said was true. No one in the world was more stubborn.

Francine, who might have been a race driver in a previous life, drove like a madwoman. Past the Chautauqua golf course. Past the usual farm stands. Past Mimi's favorite used bookstore.

When Francine took the turnoff onto 17 East toward

Jamestown, they crossed Chautauqua Lake and were, by far, the fastest car on the road.

Bumping over a series of rumble strips, they took Exit 12 to Jamestown.

It was reassuring when they started seeing signs with a white H on a blue background, signaling they were nearing the hospital.

"Your mom mentioned something earlier about being close to figuring out who killed Doc," Francine said. "Do you know who it was?"

"I don't," Jake said.

"Boy, if she found something, that would be great," B.J. added. "Did you hear they re-charged me and Bob this afternoon? We're supposed to surrender tomorrow."

"My mom gave me the news but she didn't fill me in on her suspicions. I'm sorry."

"So you don't know a thing?" Francine asked. "Not even what she was working on?"

As they passed a giant cemetery and followed more hospital signs, Jake started to feel cornered.

"I wish I did," Jake said. "I certainly owe you both big-time for helping me out tonight."

It was extremely reassuring when, ahead, Jake saw the letters WCA on a tall gray-and-white column. They turned at Prather Avenue, continued past the main hospital and past parking for doctors and dialysis

384 • DEB PINES

patients. They followed signs to the building marked EMERGENCY and OUTPATIENT.

"I know this isn't the time to talk things out," Francine said. "But could we just keep this between us? The fact that you saw the two of us together and all? It doesn't mean anything in terms of the murders. Believe me."

"Sure," Jake said. "You have my word. I won't tell anyone."

Even this close to the hospital, Jake felt paranoid. He tested the back door handle, in case he had to pull some kind of James Bond stunt—and roll out of the car, dragging his mom.

He didn't stop questioning Francine and B.J.'s motives until they pulled into the circular ER Room driveway and stopped under a sign saying, "Emergency Room Patients Only."

CHAPTER SIXTY-ONE

NEARLY FORTY-EIGHT HOURS LATER, Mimi, finally, opened her eyes.

She had two primary sensations: that she was surrounded by white—hospital-white sheets, hospital-white walls, hospital-white curtains, a hospital-white gown. And that someone was watching her.

"About time you got up, slacker."

It was Jake, sitting in the chair beside her bed.

"Who's the slacker?" she whispered. "My body's exhausted. But my mind's been racing. Busy, busy, busy."

Mimi was surprised by how hard it was to talk. And how nonsensical her words sounded. As if she were on heavy drugs—which she probably was.

"If I could reach in the blur," Mimi said. "I think I know something new. But I can't seem to—"

"Give it time, mom. The doctors say you're not going anywhere soon. You need to rest."

Mimi stared at the tubes running from her arm to an IV pole, then at her son.

"Tell me what happened again?" she asked. "I barely remember."

"Arsenic poisoning," Jake said. "The hospital flushed your stomach with water. And they gave you a drug called dimercaprol or something like that. You're still getting fluids in your veins."

"Did I almost die or something? You look so serious."

"Maybe. I'm not sure they're telling me everything here. They're treating me like a kid."

"You *are* a kid."

"Do you have an idea what the poison was in?" Jake asked. "Lieutenant Wilson keeps asking me. And I keep saying I have no idea. I think they've tested everything in our apartment."

"I don't know," Mimi said. "I had punch and a few things to eat at Francine's party. Did anyone else get sick?"

"No, just you. And the police tested everything at Francine's and found nothing."

When Mimi closed her eyes, an idea seemed to be floating past, like a fish, she couldn't grab.

Then could.

"The health food pills?" she asked. "Did you leave them for me by the coffee machine?"

"What health food pills?"

"They were in a plastic packet that said something like Energy Boost or Energy Pack. The label promised all kinds of bs like clearer thinking and stamina and . . ."

"Not familiar."

"So you didn't . . ."

Mimi was glad to be alive and talking but the effort was exhausting.

When she started to doze, she thought she heard Jake.

"Mom? Should I leave you alone? Mom?"

"Yes, you should, baby."

The nurse who came for Mimi's vitals stepped between them.

"Your mom needs her rest," the nurse said. "And so do you. I've never seen such a devoted son, staying by her side, night and day. When she wakes up, I'll tell her how proud she should be that she raised you right."

When Mimi opened her eyes the next day, the same nurse was there.

"Don't pay me any mind," the nurse said as she

wrapped a blue blood-pressure cuff around Mimi's arm, inflated it and made some notations on a chart.

When the air hissed out, the nurse removed the cuff.

"Open your mouth," she commanded. "You don't even have to wake up for this, dear. You can nail it in your sleep. You're that good."

When Mimi opened her mouth, she felt the electronic thermometer slide in.

When the nurse removed it, Mimi opened her eyes. She was barely conscious, between awake and asleep. So she wasn't sure if she was dreaming when she saw the nurse's nametag said "L. Jackson." And her mind wrestled with what that meant.

Hours later, Mimi woke up and, feeling more alert, rang for the nurse, Lydia Jackson. Lydia turned out to be the sister of the mystery nurse Regina Jackson now Regina Jackson Ford.

Regina had worked nights for a short stint in WCA's emergency room to supplement her paycheck from her day job as a nurse in a local nursing home, her sister said.

"Where is she now?" Mimi asked.

"Home, with her newborn, Jamal."

Mimi, newly energized, dialed a home number for Regina.

The phone rang five times.

"Hello," a woman said, as a baby screamed in the background. "Hello."

"Hello," Mimi said with what she feared might be too much enthusiasm. "Is that little Jamal?"

"Yes, yes it is. Who's this?"

Mimi hadn't realized how hard this would be without all of her mental faculties.

She needed substance and form—to ask the right questions in the right tone.

"My name is Mimi Goldman," she said, trying not to sound crazy or threatening. "I'm in the hospital now. At WCA. That's where I met your sister, Lydia. And got your number."

Regina just listened.

When Mimi finished describing the newspaper she worked for and its murder investigation, she paused, exhausted.

"What's all this have to do with me?" Regina asked.

"It's kind of a long crazy story, but . . ."

"I'm in no hurry. I'm nursing the baby."

Mimi prayed for strength.

"The murder victim was named Brad Hansen and his wife—"

"Maggie Hansen, right?"

"Exactly. So you remember her?"

"I do. She was my last patient at WCA. I remember her well because the next day I had complications. One thing led to another. And the doctor said I could no longer work. I had to stay in bed, off and on, the next six months until I had Jamal."

Mimi wasn't sure how to fashion the next question.

"This won't seem like much. But I'm trying to find out who brought Mrs. Hansen to the hospital. Normally, it would seem like nothing. But someone is keeping this a secret. So I'm wondering if they're concealing a friendship. Or something else that, well, might have put them at odds with Mrs. Hansen's husband."

"I can't remember a name, if that's what you're looking for."

Mimi tried not to get too discouraged.

"How about something else? Can you remember what the person looked like? Male? Female? Old? Young?"

Of course, at that moment, Jamal started working himself up to a big cry.

"Hold on a sec?" Regina said. "I've gotta switch sides."

When Regina came back, she said, "Where were we?"

"I was asking if you could remember anything about the person who left Mrs. Hansen at the hospital?"

"It's funny," Regina said. "But I think I do remember

the guy because I wondered why he never came to visit after dropping Mrs. Hansen off."

"What do you remember about him?"

"He was white," she said, slowly. "White and old."

"Anything else?"

"Yes," Regina said. "Very tall. He was very tall and spoke with a stutter."

Chapter Sixty-Two

Jake liked the deputy who drove him home from the hospital. So he didn't quarrel when the man told him to go right inside and right to bed.

Jake just waited for the deputy to drive off. Then he went back outside and made a beeline for the utility shed behind 12 Park.

After grabbing a flashlight and shovel, Jake headed for the Hansens' yard, to the last potential hiding spot he'd circled on his Xerox of the original blueprints for 12 Park.

He tucked the flashlight under one arm. He stuck the walkie-talkie the deputy had given him (because the phones were still down) in his pocket. Then, using both hands, he jabbed the shovel tip into the soil. He stood on the edge to drive the tip in deeper. Then, with tremendous effort, he scooped out a heavy load of dirt and rocks.

Five minutes of digging and Jake was breathless. He paused. He set the flashlight down, feeling like it was getting in his way. And he listened.

It was midnight. The streets were nearly silent. Most of the summer people were gone. The year-round people seemed to be in bed. It was just Jake and the crickets.

When Jake returned to work, he mainly heard himself. The thud of the shovel. His labored breaths and grunts. The plop of each dumped load.

It wasn't cold. But since this was hard, sweaty work, each time a breeze picked up, Jake felt a chill.

Trying to pick up his pace, he stabbed, stood, shoveled, stabbed, stood, shoveled.

But it didn't help.

Working faster, Jake's loads were smaller. And left him more exhausted.

Catching his breath, while doubled over, he gave himself a pep talk.

This wasn't a race, he said. He just had to make progress, a little at a time.

Slowing down, he dug out one, two, then three medium-sized loads. When he aimed for a fourth, his shovel struck a hard object.

Heart racing, Jake traded shovel for flashlight. He aimed the beam into the hole and, by hand, cleared away rocks and dirt.

The hard object, as far as he could tell, was the lid of a long coffin-like box.

A long coffin-like box in the same spot where the blueprints said that John Howell, the Temperance leader, had buried a long coffin-like box. Loaded with the whiskey bottles he'd seized from nineteenth-century sinners.

Jake felt conflicted. He wanted to tell his mom what he'd found AND he wanted to keep going and finish the job.

Choosing the latter, he reached into the hole. He tried to pry open the box's lid with his hands, then with the shovel tip.

But the lid wouldn't budge.

Maybe the box was wedged too tightly in the soil.

Jack tried digging a moat-like crevice around the box. He still couldn't open the lid with his hands. He tried driving the shovel tip between lid and box.

And, hallelujah, this time the lid creaked open.

Inside, the red crushed velvet-lined box looked like an old coffin. But it didn't hold any hundred-year-old whiskey bottles. It held dozens of plastic bags of modern-looking red-and-white capsules.

Excited, Jake quietly lowered the lid and called his mom at the hospital on the walkie-talkie.

"I've got a giant clue that could break this whole thing open," Jake whispered.

"I can't hear you, hon," Mimi said. "You have to speak up."

"Just a sec," he whispered warily when he heard a cough and whirring sound nearby.

"Jake?" his mom asked. "Are you there?"

Quietly, Jake set the walkie-talkie on the ground. He picked up the flashlight.

He aimed its beam at Park as the source of the whirring came into terrifying focus: Mole, approaching on his golf cart, with a giant shotgun in his latex-gloved hands.

Chapter Sixty-Three

Mimi stayed quiet, not wanting to jeopardize Jake's safety if he was trying to hide. But she also leaned closer to the walkie-talkie on her bed, hoping she was wrong.

"W-w-w-what do you think you're doing digging up my garden?"

Jake didn't answer.

Mimi, disappointed to hear Mole's voice, closed her eyes. The deputy on duty at her bedside, who happened to be Mack, squeezed her hand.

"F-f-found what you w-w-w-anted?"

When Jake still didn't answer, Mole laughed.

"T-t-t-t-oo b-b-ad. Not the k-k-ind of knowledge you c-c-c-an walk away with. The n-n-osy doctor l-l-learned."

"So you killed Doc?" Jake asked loudly, obviously for their benefit.

"Of c-c-course."

Mimi, fighting tears, grabbed her clothes and started, frantically, getting dressed.

"And you framed my friends?" Jake asked.

"Th-th-thugs who were d-d-d-estined for p-p-prison. I j-j-j-ust made it s-sooner, not l-l-ater."

"Want to put down that gun?" Jake asked. "Or frame someone for my murder, too?"

When a cry escaped Mimi's throat, Mack grabbed the hospital phone, pounded the keys and spoke urgently.

"I need someone to get to the Chautauqua Institution immediately," he said. "Immediately. A killer, armed and dangerous, is holding a teen-age boy at gunpoint."

Mack gave Jake's and Mole's names and descriptions.

"For now, they're at 12 Park," he said. "Yes, 12 Park at the far south end of the Institution. I'll call you back if I hear of any change. And I'll be on my way there soon myself."

"Not yourself," Mimi whispered as she slipped on her shoes. "I can't sit here . . ."

Mack vigorously shook his head.

But when Mimi, after grabbing the walkie-talkie and her purse, chased after him out the door, he didn't try to stop her.

Jake, sure his mom was listening, wasn't sure how long it would take for her to summon help. So he decided he should stall AND come up with other escape strategies.

When Mole didn't answer his last question, Jake fired another.

"Why did you kill your own brother?"

Again no answer.

"Are you just some kind of a psycho?"

Silence.

"You don't have a reason? You just wanted to kill him?"

Mole scowled.

"Y-y-you're almost as nosy as your m-m-mom. It was all about a g-girl."

When Jake waited for more, Mole laughed again.

"An old b-b-bachelor like m-m-m-e, never f-f-figured for a r-r-romantic?"

"What was the story?" Jake asked.

"M-m-m-aggie was my g-girl, you see? A b-b-beauty. Thick red hair. G-g-green eyes. S-s-summer of forty-five, we'd get off w-w-work at the Athenaeum. R-r-row across the l-l-lake for a picnic and swim. W-w-ar time and Brad was away. When h-h-he came b-b-back, he told me M-m-maggie preferred him."

As Mole described the past, he seemed dreamier and, Jake hoped, less attentive. So, taking a risk, Jake grabbed a rock from his dirt pile and stuffed it in his pocket.

"Th-th-that's how he was," Mole continued. "S-s-saw something he w-w-wanted and just t-t-took it. From birth, he f-f-felt entitled to more th-th-things than anyone. Y-y-you may be too young to understand. M-m-maybe I was, too. I n-n-never challenged Brad. N-n-never. It made s-s-sense to me she'd w-w-want the war hero. M-m-maggie tried to r-r-reach me. Sh-sh-she called. But I never answered. I just s-s-surrendered, thinking she had no f-f-feelings for me."

"But she did?" Jake asked. "She did have feelings for you?"

Mole nodded solemnly.

"In the end," he said. "When sh-sh-she was t-t-too sick to move, I f-f-finally picked up the goddamned ph-phone. F-f-f-fify years later. I was s-s-surprised to hear her v-v-voice. She needed someone to t-t-take her to the h-h-hospital. Brad, the b-b-bastard, wouldn't. He said she was a c-c-crybaby f-f-faking the wh-wh-whole thing. The s-s-sonovabitch. You sh-should have seen h-her. Skin and b-b-bones. L-l-less than a hundred pounds."

He choked back emotion.

"Sh-she asked me to l-l-leave her in emergency at WCA. T-t-told me she'd cared for m-m-me her entire l-l-ife. Wondered if, w-w-when she got w-w-well, if we might still make a g-g-go at it."

He paused again.

"The k-k-kids are the ones who c-c-called to say the c-c-cancer had spread t-t-too far. D-d-d-octors just stitched her up and tried to m-m-make her comfortable. Th-th-that's when I d-decided."

"Decided what?" Jake asked.

Mole laughed.

"Enough t-t-t-talk."

"But what about—"

"Enough."

"I just wondered—"

When Mole started raising his gun, Jake made his move.

With as much force as he could muster, he threw his rock at Mole's face. And, bingo, it struck beneath Mole's left eye.

The distraction gave Jake time for two things.

He whistled one quick verse of "I Got Rhythm"—"I got rhythm. I got music. I got my man. Who could ask for anything more?"—in the direction of the walkie-talkie.

Then he sprinted past Mole, hoping to God that his mom got the hint—and knew where he was heading.

Chapter Sixty-four

The scheme delighted Jake for, oh, about the first two minutes he was into it.

Running full out, he did get past Mole. And up Park. Onto Fletcher. Past South. And nearly to the Hall of Philosophy. But even with his head start and natural speed, he still heard the whirr of Mole's golf cart, like a swarm of bees, chasing him.

To lose the cart, he made a diversionary move. He dashed up the steps to the Hall of Philosophy. He ran through the chapel, came out the other side by the Hall of Missions and turned right on Clark.

He slowed some to catch his breath. But then, seized by fear, he took off again hoping that the redbrick path—that had too many barriers to accommodate cars and bikes—couldn't accommodate golf carts either.

Unused to post-season Chautauqua, Jake expected to run into someone, anyone, on the way to Bestor Plaza. Or a cop summoned by his mom to rescue him.

But the redbrick path was empty. And church house after church house looked dark.

Jake kept up a pretty good pace. At each corner, Cookman, Peck, Foster, he glanced to see if anyone was there. When he reached the Amphitheater, he thought he heard the golf cart again.

He wasn't sure. But, not taking chances, he tried another detour, running through the empty theater, then out it the back and around the library.

Even Bestor Plaza was, amazingly, dark and quiet. As Jake passed the bookstore, post office and *Daily* offices, he thought he saw an approaching light. A bike light.

He feared it was wishful thinking. But, gradually, the frame, the wheels, the rider, took shape.

And Jake's wish evolved from, no longer wanting just a bike but wanting *a cop* on a bike.

As the bike neared, he realized the driver was a kid, maybe a college-aged boy. Blond. With a helmet.

Should he drag anyone else into his mess? Definitely not.

His plan, then, was to make eye contact and maybe, if possible, mouth the words, "Get Help."

Jake practiced as the bike drew near.

When they were inches away, the kid picked up his pace and, while yelling "Hey," zoomed past, maybe showing off.

And that was that.

Jake's only hope?

He hoped not.

While turning left at the Colonnade, Jake found himself looking for saviors behind every tree and flower box.

"Stop, k-k-k-id. I've g-g-ot you. Enough of this n-n-nonsense."

Mole, gun drawn, stepped in his path, from behind a maple tree by the Saint Elmo.

Jake, terrified, froze.

When Mole's gun exploded with a loud kaboom, Jake took off, running in a zigzag pattern like fleeing people do in movies.

He tried to ignore a sharp pain in his shoulder. Blood on his shirt. And two more shots.

Running for his life, he passed the darkroom and Sadie J's. He ran up an incline around Kellogg Hall. And up Ramble which he hoped was too steep for a golf cart.

What he wanted to hear most were cop sirens. But instead, he heard his own sobs and frantic breaths. And the sound of an engine straining, then chewing its way through gravel and grass heading for Jake's same destination: the cluster of fifty-two little dark-brown shingled practice shacks, including one named for the "I've Got Rhythm" composer, George Gershwin.

The shacks were dark inside and out. And surrounded by trees and brush.

The brightest light nearby came from ankle-high illuminated blocks leading to Lenna Hall, a new redwood concert hall, next to the shacks.

Their light didn't carry. Nor did light from a few street lamps, a nearby Pepsi machine and the rim of a phone booth.

At the first practice shack, Jake jiggled the door knob. Locked. The second shack was locked, too. And the third and the fourth.

How do musicians get into these things? Didn't anyone forget to lock up?

Pausing, Jake looked for a central spot with keys. Or a good place to hide.

He didn't see either.

A shabbier-looking shack, two away, with a buckled door and peeling paint, did catch his eye.

It looked like the flimsy structure one of the Three Little Pigs might have built. But when Jake reached it, its door, too, of course, was locked. And wasn't flimsy. Jake couldn't force the knob. Or the door that he tried ramming with his one good shoulder.

When he heard footsteps crunching the gravel, again he wished they were cops' steps.

But, doubting they were, he kept going. He tried two more shacks. In vain. They were locked, too.

When Jake noticed a partly open window on the very next shack, he jimmied the window open wider and squeezed inside.

Now what?

With the footsteps crunching louder, Jake couldn't risk attracting attention by closing the window.

So he just tried to curl himself up as small as he could in a musty corner, behind a baby grand piano in the practice shack.

The footsteps, meanwhile, were unhurried. They started. Stopped. Started and stopped. Occasionally, Jake noticed a stripe of light.

Inspecting his shoulder, he confirmed that he'd been shot. He pressed a hand to the wound to slow the bleeding, then stifled a cry of pain.

"It's only a m-m-m-atter of t-time, kid. It's just m-m-me and you."

Jake hoped Mole was wrong.

But he only heard one set of footsteps nearing.

When they were one shack away, Jake tried to make himself even smaller.

A light flashed nearby, then inside Jake's shack. It rested on a water bottle someone left on a ledge by the door. It moved to the piano. The piano stool. Then to Jake crouched in the corner.

"T-t-t-time's up, k-kid."

Jake closed his eyes, bracing for the worst.

Then came a deafeningly loud gunshot.

"Got 'em," a woman yelled. "I think I got him. Oh, my God."

Jake, ears ringing, made himself crawl, shaking and crying, to the door.

When he opened it, Lieutenant Wilson was right there.

He scooped Jake up and carried him to a waiting ambulance. Past Mole's bloody corpse. And past Mimi, Jake's mom, who knelt, weeping, in a daze, gun dangling from one hand.

Chapter Sixty-Five

"Hey, did you see the headlines in the special edition of *The Daily*?" Mack asked Mimi two days later as they sat side by side on a worn wooden dock at Heinz Beach.

"Chautauquans Solve Murders."

"So they're calling me and Jake Chautauquans?"

"Yes, they are. Usually takes a few generations to earn the title. But you're honoraries after one season."

"Pretty cool."

The lake, to Mimi, was as beautiful as she could remember it. Turquoise blue with dark ripples rushing south toward Jamestown.

There were few boats out. She and Mack had the beach to themselves, dragging their feet in the water, enjoying the peace.

"You okay?" Mack asked.

"I guess. It's hard to accept that I killed a man but—"

"You ABSOLUTELY had to. No choice."

"I guess."

"No guessing. It's true. It was him or your son."

Reaching into his gym bag, Mack said, "I've got a few things here you might enjoy. The hospital forwarded them to the sheriff's department. And the department gave them to me to give to you."

As Mack withdrew a stack of envelopes, he read some of their return addresses aloud.

"Betsy Gates, Buffalo. Violet Greenwood, Erie. Wentworth, your boss at *The Daily*, who's back in Maryland. And a few I didn't recognize."

As Mack made a pile, he kept browsing addresses.

"You've got a big fan club," he said. "I'm looking for my favorite."

After removing a few more envelopes, he waved a white one triumphantly.

"From the lawyer," he said. "Justin Winters and the Ryan twins."

"Together?" Mimi asked.

"Exactly. The grapevine says that when their mom wasn't there to take the boys home when they were released from jail the second time, Winters stepped in to claim them. Apparently, they're staying with him and his wife for a while. And, from what I hear, Winters may even apply for guardian status."

"Wow."

"Okay," Mack said, "Now, it's time to give it up."

"Right here?" Mimi smiled. "On the beach?"

Mack chuckled.

"Get your mind out of the gutter, lady. Or, at least, for now. Maybe later, we can revisit this matter and . . ."

Mimi smiled wider.

"What I meant," Mack said, "was how did you figure things out? What led you to Mole? Just the fact that he'd taken the first Mrs. Hansen to the hospital?"

"Not just that. There was also an old photo Doc had from the nineteen-forties showing that Mole and Margaret Hansen were sweethearts. And the fact that Brad Hansen was killed on Margaret's birthday. And that Doc was killed probably after asking Mole about the photo, for a caption for *The Daily*."

Now Mack was the one smiling.

"It reminded me of a case I remembered from *The New York Post*," Mimi continued. "The story of a murderer avenging a love lost something like fifty years before. The man snapped and killed his ex-lover's husband. He'd been carrying the torch silently and bitterly all his life."

"Was that it?"

"A few other odds and ends. If Brad's poison came in a pill, Mole was a likely source. His utility-shed shelves look like a drugstore. When the hiding spot was in the garden that also pointed to Mole. Do you know how he got into my apartment to leave the pills?"

"Remember he was the one who changed your locks?"

Mimi nodded.

"He must have kept an extra key," Mack said. I wouldn't be surprised if he was the one who picked the locks, too. Pretty impressive sleuth work."

"I've really gotta thank you for summoning Lieutenant Wilson. And thank him for getting to Chautauqua with the EMTs fast enough to save Jake."

"What's the latest on the boy?"

"Great news today," Mimi said. "The big specialist doctor from Buffalo examined him and predicted Jake's shoulder will heal a hundred percent. He said he'll get out maybe Friday or Saturday."

"Excellent. And speaking of Lieutenant Wilson, he wanted me to pass a message on to you."

"What?"

"He said I should tell you that he was right."

"*He* was right?"

"Twisted love was the motive. And he said that's what he predicted from the get-go."

"Right motive, wrong killer," Mimi huffed. "Lieutenant Wilson *wasn't* even close to right. He thought the killer was Francine."

Mack laughed.

"I think he just enjoys getting a rise out of you."

Mimi shook her head.

"Want to know how you can thank me?" Mack said, moving closer and taking her hand.

Mimi, sorely tempted, just smiled.

"You're not gonna make me wait fifty years, are you?" he asked.

"When it comes down to it," she said, "I'm as square as any Chautauquan. So I probably really do belong here. You know you tempt me very much. But I've got some high-and-mighty voices in my head to answer to. I know myself. I couldn't be happy with a married man."

Mimi, unable to look at Mack, stared at the churning lake.

"How about one whose wife has left him?" Mack asked.

"Is that true?"

As soon as Mimi looked into Mack's face, she knew it was.

He nodded.

"How could that be?"

"Not everyone is as big a fan of mine as you are."

"Hey, no need to get cocky now."

"Believe me, I'm not."

"Did she take Kevin?"

"Yes, back to her mom's in Sherman. I see him most weekends and we're trying to have dinner together Wednesday nights. Maybe he can stay over then, too."

Mack struggled to keep his voice even.

"When did she leave?"

"A month ago."

"A month ago? Hey, why didn't you say anything? I've seen you a bunch of times since then. And even asked about her. And even today, you never . . ."

"It doesn't make a lot of sense," Mack said. "But I haven't told anyone. I had this crazy idea that somehow if I didn't say it aloud, it never happened. Or maybe I thought she'd come back. And then it would be awkward to say she'd left. So I just . . ."

"Your family doesn't even know?"

"No."

Mimi squeezed Mack's hand.

"You could have told me. Really."

"You had enough on your plate. I didn't want to add to your problems."

"And now you do?"

After sweeping Mimi into a deep long kiss, he smiled adorably.

"If you'll let me?"

Acknowledgments

I HAVE LOTS OF PEOPLE to thank for their support through the writing and rewriting of this novel and other writing follies over the years.

On Chautauqua history, special thanks go to: the great Alfreda Locke Irwin, journalist, archivist and author of Three Taps of the Gavel; the patient Chautauqua Library staff; and the 2011 PBS special "An American Narrative."

On other topics, thanks go to: carpet expert Irving Nusbaum; Chautauqua Symphony Orchestra violinist Lenelle Morse; Chautauqua and Old First Night Run experts David Zinman and Bud Horne; Yiddish mavens Pearl and Howard Fishman; former Chautauquan Daily sports editor Mark Altschuler; Chautauqua Buildings and Grounds staffers; and the Chautauqua County police and Sheriff's Department.

Because of the passage of time, I can't remember everyone who helped in 1997. But I'm sure, I should thank my usual readers including: Ruth Heide, Mary Crotty and Pearl Livingstone; Catherine, Andy, Jeff, Irene and Pia Pines; Dirk Allen and Leslie Cimino.

This time around, I'm particularly grateful for thoughtful suggestions from Maggie and Pearl Livingstone, Catherine Maiorisi and Jon Lehman.

Extra thanks to Paul Riney (for the cover), Maggie Livingstone (for her computer wizardry) and my inner circle, Dave, Josh and Liz Livingstone (for everything else).

20162130R00243

Made in the USA
Charleston, SC
01 July 2013